P9-CKS-535

Praise for Jessica Clare

"Clare has a knack for creating chemistry between the most unlikely of characters and clearly revels in defying expectations in her stories." —RT Book Reviews

"Great storytelling . . . delightful reading . . . It's fun and oh so hot." —*Kirkus Reviews*

"[Clare is] a romance writing prodigy." —Heroes & Heartbreakers

"Blazing hot." —*USA Today*

Titles by Jessica Clare

ALL I WANT FOR CHRISTMAS IS A COWBOY

Roughneck Billionaires

DIRTY MONEY
DIRTY SCOUNDREL
DIRTY BASTARD

The Billionaire Boys Club

STRANDED WITH A BILLIONAIRE
BEAUTY AND THE BILLIONAIRE
THE WRONG BILLIONAIRE'S BED
ONCE UPON A BILLIONAIRE
ROMANCING THE BILLIONAIRE
ONE NIGHT WITH A BILLIONAIRE
HIS ROYAL PRINCESS
BEAUTY AND THE BILLIONAIRE: THE WEDDING

Billionaires and Bridesmaids

THE BILLIONAIRE AND THE VIRGIN
THE TAMING OF THE BILLIONAIRE
THE BILLIONAIRE TAKES A BRIDE
THE BILLIONAIRE'S FAVORITE MISTAKE
BILLIONAIRE ON THE LOOSE

The Bluebonnet Novels

THE GIRL'S GUIDE TO (MAN) HUNTING
THE CARE AND FEEDING OF AN ALPHA MALE
THE EXPERT'S GUIDE TO DRIVING A MAN WILD
THE VIRGIN'S GUIDE TO MISBEHAVING
THE BILLIONAIRE OF BLUEBONNET

All I Want for *Christmas* Is a Cowboy

JESSICA CLARE

JOVE
New York

A JOVE BOOK
Published by Berkley
An imprint of Penguin Random House LLC
375 Hudson Street, New York, New York 10014

Copyright © 2018 by Jessica Clare
Excerpt from *Dirty Money* copyright © 2017 by Jessica Clare
Penguin Random House supports copyright. Copyright fuels creativity, encourages
diverse voices, promotes free speech, and creates a vibrant culture. Thank you for buying
an authorized edition of this book and for complying with copyright laws by not
reproducing, scanning, or distributing any part of it in any form without permission.
You are supporting writers and allowing Penguin Random House to continue to
publish books for every reader.

A JOVE BOOK and BERKLEY are registered trademarks and the B colophon
is a trademark of Penguin Random House LLC.

ISBN: 9781984802187

First Edition: November 2018

Printed in the United States of America
1   3   5   7   9   10   8   6   4   2

Cover art: cowboy and dog by NaturePL; snowy trees by Jeff Schultz/
Alaska Stock—Design Pics
Cover design by Sarah Oberrender

This is a work of fiction. Names, characters, places, and incidents either are the product
of the author's imagination or are used fictitiously, and any resemblance to actual persons,
living or dead, business establishments, events, or locales is entirely coincidental.

If you purchased this book without a cover, you should be aware that this book is stolen
property. It was reported as "unsold and destroyed" to the publisher, and neither the author
nor the publisher has received any payment for this "stripped book."

CHAPTER ONE

E li Pickett wasn't a big fan of holidays.

It wasn't that he had something against Christmas in particular. As holidays went, it was a perfectly nice one. The songs were catchy. The decorations were festive, if gaudy. The food was all right. What he liked least about holidays was that no one worked.

Having grown up in foster care and now making a living as a rancher, he found the concept foreign to him. Cattle didn't care about holidays or spending time with family. They wanted to be fed. They wanted their hay freshened. They wanted to go out to pasture even when it was deep with snow outside. Holidays didn't account for ranch animals.

As he sat down in the main room of the lodge, oiling his boots, he watched the others get ready to leave, rushing back and forth to pack last-minute items. Maria, the housekeeper and cook, had three entire suitcases full of presents for her grandbabies and fussed over how to get a box of cookies into her purse.

Eli watched with amusement as she packed and repacked things. "You know you're only going for two weeks, right?"

"No lip from you, mijo," she told him, pulling things out of her oversized purse and trying to squeeze the box into it. "I feel bad enough that you're going to be staying here by yourself over Christmas."

He shrugged. Things had been different around the ranch since the new owners bought it. The cattle herds had been downsized from thousands to four hundred. The Texas oil tycoon who'd bought the land had plans to build a ski lodge on some of the rolling hills. The ranch itself was used for a tax break, thus the downsizing. Eli had kept his job, but the ranch itself had gone from a dozen employees to five. It was just him, Maria, Old Clyde, Jordy, and Dustin. Once upon a time, he'd have spent the holidays here with a few other ranch hands who opted to care for the animals over Christmas instead of going home.

Now it was just him. But he had a job, and he loved this ranch, and that was all that was important. "It'll be fine. I don't mind being on my own."

She clucked at him, shaking her head before pulling out even more stuff from her purse and trying to push the cookie box in there. "I don't like it. Young man like you should go home for Christmas. Spend the holidays with family. You could come with me. My older daughter Alma makes a lovely spread and you know she's single now." Maria gave him a knowing glance. "She's very pretty. I showed you pictures, remember?"

Yikes. He remembered. Maria's daughter *was* pretty, but he was also sure that she wasn't right for him. For one, she lived in Los Angeles, which might as well be hell as far as he was concerned. And for two, he doubted she'd want to come live on the ranch in Wyoming with him, and he had no intention of leaving. "'Preciate the thought," he told Maria. "But someone's got to feed the animals, remember?"

She rolled her eyes. "Old Clyde should stay. He's not a young man who needs to think about family. He can do it."

"I heard that," Old Clyde bellowed from the next room over.

Eli just shook his head and paid attention to his boot. Maria'd been trying to get Old Clyde to trade places with Eli for the last month now, but Clyde was visiting his daughter in Tucson. Eli didn't have anyone to visit. Truth was, he was ready for the others to go. It'd give him a few weeks of quiet to settle his head, not have to worry over people prying about family that he didn't have. They'd return in January, ready to work again, and then things would get back to normal.

By the fire, Frannie whined and thumped her tail, looking over at him hopefully.

"This boot ain't for you," he told her, grinning. The dog responded to his tone, getting more excited by the moment. She got up and waddled over to him, her pregnant sides sticking out from the white fluff of her thick coat. Eli put the boot aside and rubbed Frannie's face. Two weeks of just him and the dogs, which were the best company a man could ask for. No, he didn't need more than that.

"She better not have her puppies before I get back," Maria told Eli. "I want to be here."

"I'll tell her to keep 'em in until you return," he vowed, grinning. Like that would happen. Already Frannie looked ready to burst, and she wasn't a small dog. Great Pyrenees were devoted herders and perfect on a ranch, but they were also destructive chewers when they were bored. And since Frannie was being kept close to the ranch house due to how pregnant she was, a lot of boots were getting destroyed.

He knew how she felt. Well, not the pregnant part. The stir-crazy part. If he had to leave this place for two weeks, he'd probably start chewing on boots, too.

Maria just shook her head at him. "You and those dogs." She turned her head and yelled over her shoulder. "Jordy! Dustin! We've got to go! Ándele!" She turned back to Eli and gave him another motherly look. "Are you sure you don't want one of us to stay with you over the holiday? That big storm's rolling in—"

"No," he told her for the hundredth time already. "Ain't calving season for another two months. No one's going to be dropping. We drove in all the cows and moved 'em to the pastures close to the barn so I can cake 'em easy—load them up on protein and extra food—when it's cold. The storm will be fine. Me and the dogs will handle it like we always do."

She just shook her head at Eli, exasperated. He was pretty sure she was more disappointed that he wasn't into Christmas and family like she was, but that just wasn't his thing. "I'll bring you back some fruitcake," she compromised.

"You sure don't have to do that," he joked.

A moment later, Dustin, Jordy, and Old Clyde came stomping down the stairs of the farmhouse. At their heels were the other ranch dogs, Jim and Bandit. All herding dogs, they worked twice as hard as most of the ranch hands did. Definitely harder than Jordy, Eli thought with amusement. Jordy was still new and tended to hinder more than help, but in time he'd be a good cowboy.

"Let's go," Maria told them, slinging her bag over her shoulder, gray ponytail bouncing. "If they shut down the airport and I have to spend the holiday with you idiotas, I'm not going to be happy." She moved to Eli's side and gave him a motherly kiss on the cheek, then patted his face. "You call if you get too lonely, mijo. Mama Maria's always a phone call away."

"Will do," he promised her, though he was thirty-two and didn't much need a mama. Maria just cared. Weren't no harm in that.

"Try to have yourself a good holiday," she told Eli.

He nodded. Maria was never going to realize that some people just didn't care about Christmas. It was just another day to him. Another day of ranch work and cattle tending, except without the extra hands around to make working in the upcoming winter storm easier.

It'd be quiet. Peaceful.

He'd enjoy the next two weeks for what they were and not worry about the rest.

CHAPTER TWO

Cassandra Horn sang along—loudly and badly—to Bing Crosby in her rental car. The more enthusiastic the Christmas song, she hoped, the more holiday-ish she'd feel. So far it wasn't working, but she wasn't going to give up hope. It was early yet, after all. She had a week before Christmas to get herself into the holiday spirit. Surely between now and then she could muster some sort of enthusiasm.

Theoretically.

The wind whistled against the windows and threatened to push her car off the icy roads. Biting back a nervous scream, Cass clenched the steering wheel tighter and turned down the music. She needed to concentrate. Driving in Wyoming in the mountains was a heck of a lot different than driving in the city. Oh, who was she kidding? She lived in Manhattan. She didn't drive. She took a taxi or an Uber anywhere she wanted to go.

But there weren't a ton of Uber drivers heading into the

mountains in this part of the country, so she'd rented a car and headed out on her own. She'd driven herself everywhere back in her college days, after all. This was just like one of those road trips, just a solo one. No big deal.

Of course, she didn't quite remember having blizzard conditions back in college, either, but she was pretty sure she could handle it. Reasonably sure. It was either that or turn around and go back to the airport, since she didn't have the money for a hotel.

So yeah, blizzard it was, because she was *not* going home for the full two weeks she had off. No way, no how.

She needed a break from work. No, she amended. She needed a break from her boss, not the work itself. Cass loved what she did. Or she used to. Being a personal assistant to a successful fashion model had been exciting and fun. She got to hang out with a famous friend all day. Well, sort of friend. They'd been chatty since college, but after Cass took the job, Rose made it clear that they were employee and employer. Cass didn't mind, most of the time, and she understood that Rose was under a lot of pressure. Rose Gramercy's career had skyrocketed in the last couple of years and so Cass did everything from grocery shopping to Starbucks runs to handling Rose's calendar to even lunching with Rose's people when Rose was too busy to meet anyone. She worked weird hours and that was all right. It wasn't as if she had a boyfriend or family to go home to. She had a small, pretty apartment in Rose's building so she could be nearby, but a lot of the time, she just slept over at Rose's place in case Rose needed her.

That was BKW, though. Before Ken Wallis, when everything became miserable.

To think that once upon a time, Cass had been excited to meet Ken Wallis. He'd starred in some of her favorite movies—the remake of *Titanic*; the romantic and lush *Nutcracker Prince*; and her personal go-to when she was feeling lonely, *The Eyes of the Queen*. When she'd found out that Rose was dating him, she was beyond ecstatic. And at first, Ken was nice. He was friendly, he was charming, and he was approachable. Cass had happily grabbed coffees for him when she got them for Rose. She'd pick up his dry cleaning when his assistant was unavailable, and she truly didn't mind that he tended to sleep over at Rose's place a lot, even if it meant Cass would have to head home to her own quiet place.

It was great for a while. Then things started to get weird.

Rose went to Milan for a friend's wedding without Cass. Ken was still in Manhattan on a shoot. He'd asked Cass to pick up a few items for him at a local bodega, and since she'd been doing that sort of thing for him for a while, she didn't think anything of it. She showed up at his apartment with the cigarettes and beer only to find that he answered the door naked.

It was clear that he'd expected her to come in. And it was clear that he had more than assisting on his mind.

She'd managed to stammer out an excuse that day and had turned and run. Ever since then, working for Rose had become less about working and more about avoiding the boyfriend. Ken was everywhere. He showed up when Rose was on set and made sure to harass Cass. He showed up when Rose was out of town. He texted her. God, did he text her. Every day, her phone was blowing up with messages from him that she was always careful to answer neutrally and in a way that would never make it look like she was betraying Rose. Even just responding was stressful.

She'd tried talking to Rose about it, but it was clear that Rose didn't think Cass was pretty enough to get Ken's attention. He's just being friendly, Rose would say with a laugh. Don't worry. You're not his type.

It seemed that his type was "unavailable," though, because the more Cass told him no, the more Ken hit on her. It got so bad that she was on the verge of a nervous breakdown. Her interesting job had turned into an absolute nightmare, and she couldn't even say anything to Rose. Ken was too good of an actor and Rose was in love.

Cass was just the employee.

She shuddered and clutched the steering wheel harder.

That was one reason why when Rose said she was going to the Riviera for the holidays, Cass decided that she was going to go on a trip as well. She was not about to stay in NYC alone, because she didn't trust Ken not to show up at her apartment. It was to the point that she wanted to go to the police. But who'd believe her? *Yes, I'm the average-looking assistant to Rose Gramercy, and her movie-star boyfriend is hitting on me.* She'd hinted about it to a few people, but they just laughed in her face. In photos, Ken was utterly devoted to Rose, and their romance was one that sold tabloids like crazy. No one believed Cass, and so she stopped mentioning it.

So . . . a cabin by herself for Christmas, it was. She was originally going to stay with her family, but her parents were overseas having a second honeymoon somewhere in Europe, and her favorite cousin was staying with her husband's family in Idaho and there was no room for one more last-minute straggler. She'd decided to rent a car and head up to the family's old cabin in the mountains in Wyoming. Of course, she hadn't been here in ten years, but it'd be a nice place to hang out for a while, unwind, and figure out what the heck she was going to do. The trunk of her car was full of paperback books and snacks, her email was cleaned out, and her voicemail was changed to an out of office.

She was ready for a vacation.

Cass hadn't counted on the weather, though. She should have guessed that Wyoming in December would be cold and snowy. She hadn't exactly considered that "cold and snowy" could quickly turn to whiteout conditions in the space of an hour, which was how long ago she'd left the airport. And as she let the car gently crawl around one icy curve of road after another, she worried that she was being stupid. Maybe she should turn around. Fly back to New York—because two weeks of hotel fees would break her meager wallet—and just pretend not to be home. Maybe that'd be smarter than trying to get this automatic sedan up a snowy mountain road.

Her phone buzzed with an incoming text.

One hand tight on the steering wheel, she picked up her phone and glanced at the screen.

Ken.

The car swerved slightly and she dropped the phone onto the passenger seat, holding tight to the steering wheel. Her heart pounded with alarm and she looked for a place to pull over. When she couldn't find one, she slowed the car to a halt and put on her blinkers. It was stupid, of course, but the road was empty thanks to the weather, and she was only going to stop for a moment.

Cass quickly checked the phone, terrified of what she'd read. It was like a train wreck—she knew she shouldn't look, but she couldn't help it.

KEN: You abandoned me for the holidays? Naughty Cass! Where are you?

Cass bit her lip, trying to figure out the best way to respond. She couldn't be rude to him. Rose would get upset
with her and Ken would just spin it to make her seem unreasonable. She thought for a moment, anxiety spiking, and
then quickly texted an answer.

CASS: Cabin in the mountains for Xmas. Have a
good holiday!!!

The response came back immediately.

KEN: The set shut down for the week. Got room for
one more up there?

He attached a smiley face, as if that would make everything seem sweet, innocent. In reality, her skin crawled. He
wasn't going to visit Rose for the holidays? He was going
to try to hook up with Cass? Ugh. She didn't know what
to do.

CASS: No, sorry. Family event! Go see your family!

And she stuck a smiley face on there, too.

KEN: Your family's back from Europe?

Crap. How did he know about that?

KEN: I'm thinking someone's playing hard to get.
Tell me where you're at and I'll get a flight out there.
You shouldn't be alone for Christmas . . . and we
need to talk.

No smiley face that time. Cass's stomach clenched miserably. Talk about what? Talk about "them" even though there was no "them"? Talk about how he'd been discreetly harassing her? Talk about Rose? She knew it was bait to get her to continue the conversation—Ken was great at that sort of thing—but she forced herself to ignore it. She couldn't keep her car idling in the middle of a mountain pass, no matter that no one else was coming up the road. The wind and the snow were getting worse with every moment, and she'd be stupid to stay here longer than necessary.

CASS: Gotta go! TTYL.

She tossed the phone back in the passenger seat and turned off her blinkers, then started the car again. The tires spun on the ice, and for a heart-pounding moment, she worried she was going to be stuck out here in the middle of nowhere. The mountains rose high around her, and she didn't remember much about this area, just that the roads sometimes closed in the winter due to bad storms . . . and crap! Why hadn't she thought of that sooner? She'd been too rattled, too distracted by the enticing thought of getting away from Ken and his sleaziness.

Cass thought about turning around. Play it safe, go back down to town and forget all about her Christmas vacation. But she was close to the cabin. Had to be. Even driving as slowly and ultra-carefully as she was, it couldn't be more than another fifteen, twenty minutes away. Town was at least an hour out, and it seemed silly to turn back when she was so close. She leaned forward over the steering wheel and gazed out at the skies, the wipers working furiously against the windshield. Snow was still flurrying down and showed no sign of stopping. Well, she had plenty of food and an entire case of ramen noodles in the trunk. She would be perfectly fine snowed in for a couple of weeks.

And if her return home got delayed, it wouldn't be the worst thing. In fact, it might not be a bad idea at all. With that thought running through her head, Cass put the car into drive and headed up the road a bit farther. Visibility was no more than a few feet before everything turned into a whiteout blur, but no one else was coming or going, and she could go slow. No problem at all.

She even turned the Christmas music on again.

Just as she rounded another snowy curve, her phone rang again.

"Shoot," she whispered under her breath and turned off the radio once more. She didn't answer, though. She stared ahead at the blizzard and glared out the windshield as her ringtone sang happily out in the car. When it stopped, she let out a breath and waited for her voicemail chime to come on. She could answer voicemail later. Much later.

Instead, her phone just rang again.

And again.

And again.

As the car crawled forward and the snow poured down, Cass gritted her teeth and endured refrain after refrain of Beethoven's Fifth as someone desperately tried to call her. She leaned over and grabbed the phone, sliding it into her lap. The storm was too fierce for her to look at the screen right now, and up ahead, the road would fork, one route leading to her family cabin, the other to the big ranch that extended all through the mountains and into the valley. She couldn't miss that turn, because she was pretty sure that there was no way to turn around her car at this point, thanks to all the snow. Plus, going downhill in this seemed like a scary proposition. She had to pay attention.

But the car kept going, her phone kept ringing, and that fork in the road was nowhere to be seen. Her nerves fraying by the moment, Cass's imagination started to get the better of her. What if it was her parents, calling because something was wrong? Someone calling to warn her about the weather? What if it was Rose and there was a problem in the Riviera and she was needed? It was her job to remain on call at all times, no matter the hour. Rose wouldn't call her while she was on vacation, because she'd promised to give Cass real time off. Every time the phone rang, though, she worried a little more.

Then, it happened. One ring, then a hang up. Two rings, then a hang up.

If it rang again, that was the SOS. When she'd first started working with Rose, they'd established a code to let the other know that there was something super urgent that had to be discussed. Out of habit, she grabbed the phone and fumbled it up to her ear, gaze glued to the disappearing road. Was the storm getting even worse? How did people even see in this sort of weather?

"Hello?"

"You are an expert at playing hard to get." Ken's silky voice rolled across her ear.

Horrified, Cass dropped the phone.

There was no emergency. It was just Ken, not taking "no" for an answer.

The phone slid between her feet and landed against her shoe, resting lightly on the gas. She tried to kick it aside, but it got wedged against the gas, and then she spent a moment trying to nudge it away from the pedal. Oh please. She didn't need this right now. *Come on, come on*, she silently pleaded with the phone, jammed against the side of the gas. Frustrated, she kicked it—

And accidentally floored the gas pedal. The car surged ahead, just in time to smash into the big tree that split the road in two. She heard the awful crunch of metal before her head banged against the steering wheel.

The world faded.

CHAPTER THREE

He was missing a cow. Damn it all.

Eli rode his horse through the clustered herd again. His mount didn't like the blizzard weather but knew better than to balk at him. Nearby, flouncing through the snow, Bandit and Jim raced back and forth at the edges of the herd, and Eli pressed a clicker, counting cattle head. They couldn't go far, because this pasture wasn't more than ten acres or so, and he'd put out feed and hay for 'em to keep them comfortable through the worst of the blizzard. When the other ranch hands got back, they'd drive the cattle back out farther, but for now, he should have all four hundred right here near the barn.

But he kept getting three hundred ninety-nine.

If it was calving season, he'd assume a cow had split off to drop her calf somewhere. But that was two months away, so there was no reason for a cow to wander away from the herd unless something was wrong. Heck, this was just what he needed. He'd been thinking all day about what he was going to do to fill his time now that the others were gone. Not that it would be a problem—the opposite, in fact. There was so much to do around the ranch that he was having to mentally prioritize what items to tackle first. It was a good thing, because then he wouldn't notice just how quiet it was late at night, knowing he was the only one on the entire mountain.

Well, that wasn't entirely true. Doc Parsons was probably up at the Swinging C Ranch on the other side of the mountain, but that was a little too far for visiting.

Eli whistled at the dogs and then began to ride his prancing horse around the edges of the fence, looking for answers. There was one particular cow that liked to run off, and he looked for the familiar white blaze on her nose in the herd of black cattle. When he didn't see it, he circled back and looked again, and then cursed. Just as he suspected.

Houdini. Damned cow.

There was one in every herd that didn't play nice with others. One that always tried to go her own way or was more trouble than she was generally worth. That was Houdini. If there was a fence, she'd escape it. If there was a blizzard, she'd find a way to make them chase her down. The cow had a wandering soul, and he'd threatened to sell her off many times, but fact was, she always gave birth to fat, healthy calves, and that counted for a lot. So they kept her around.

On days like today, though, he regretted it. Now he'd have to go out into the blizzard and hunt her down. With a bit-back curse, Eli led his horse closer to the fences. Sure enough, one had been leaned on until it was knocked over. Most of the herd was smart enough to stay near the hay. Not Houdini. Either she was the dumbest cow they had, or the cleverest. Either way, she was gone and he was gonna have to go after her.

Eli repaired the fence, cursing the entire time, and then got back on his horse. "Jim, Bandit, come on. Let's go find ourselves a cow."

To think he'd been looking forward to a quiet night by the fire. So much for that.

The good thing about tracking a cow in the snow was that it left a nice, easy trail to follow. Houdini had left a set of footprints that was plain to see, though he was lucky he'd found it when he did. Much longer and the falling snow would have covered it up. He gigged the horse forward, noticing that they were heading out toward the mountain road. That was all right. No one would be coming up the pass during this storm. Likely the roads themselves would be closed off at the base of the mountain if things got bad enough. That was a good thing, considering no one'd be able to see a runaway cow in this blinding white.

Nearby, the dogs began to bark. First Bandit, then Jim. They raced ahead of the horse, disappearing into the storm. Good. That meant they'd found the cow. Thank goodness, because he was about done with this, mentally and physically. It was getting colder by the moment, and while he was used to terrible weather, that didn't mean he enjoyed it. It was hard on the dogs, hard on the horses, hard on him.

Maybe it was sappy of him, but he also wanted to get back and check on Frannie, see if she'd had her pups yet. All of the ranch dogs were hard workers and well trained, but he had a special bond with that one in particular.

The dogs' barking grew louder, and he heard the angry low of a cow. Finally. With his gloves, he grabbed his rope lasso and began to give it length even as he drove the horse forward with his knees. As he got closer, he saw that the

pregnant cow had stopped in the shelter of a nearby tree
and was cornered by Jim and Bandit. She'd be easy to rope,
now that she was done with running. He managed to loop
her and tie her back to the saddle within minutes, all the
fight gone out of her. "That's right, Houdini," he encouraged her. "You and me both'll go back to the barn and we'll
have a nice dinner and forget all about adventurin' for a few
days."

The cow just bleated a protest and jerked against the
rope, but when the dogs nipped at her heels, she turned
obediently toward the ranch.

Eli pulled his hat down and scanned the area. Sure
enough, the cow had gone to the main road. There wasn't
much of one up the mountain, and what was there was more
of a winding, twisting gravel path that tourists ripped around
a lot faster than was sane during the summer, and no one
came up during the winter.

Which, he supposed, was why he looked twice when he
thought he saw a hint of beige amid the whiteout conditions. Wasn't a lot that was beige out here in December.
Things were either white, white snow, yellow snow, brown
mud, and the occasional black cow. Beige didn't happen.
He peered harder but the wind picked up, whipping an icy
blast against his face. He tipped his hat low and closed his
eyes, waiting for the frost to melt away from his lashes, and
when he looked up again, that beige was still there. There
was just a hint of it between gusts of snow, but it was still
there.

Well, now he had to check it out.

He dismounted, tied his horse to the tree, checked the
rope on the cow, and then began to wade through the foot-
deep snow toward that spot of color. The dogs began to

bark again, dashing off in that direction, and his skin prickled with alarm. This was not good.

A few steps more, and he saw a bumper.

Definitely not good.

"Jim! Bandit! Over here," he called as the dogs' barks
grew more shrill with excitement. He put a glove on his hat
as the wind picked up, threatening to rip it from his head,
and leaned into the gusting breeze as he approached the car.
It was half buried in the snow, which meant that it had been
here for a while. At least an hour, if the way the storm was
filling up his footprints was any indication. He circled the
car slowly. It was off, the front end crumpled against a big
tree at the split in the road. Someone hadn't been paying
attention, it seemed, and had gone straight when they should
have gone left. Right would have taken them straight to
Price Ranch, and Eli sure wasn't expecting visitors. Left it
was. Likely the owner of the car had gotten out and headed
in that direction, but when Eli looked at the ground, he
didn't see footprints.

His gut clenched as he ran his glove over the windshield
and saw that it was cracked. There was a dark spot inside.
Blood, probably. Maybe the person inside this car didn't get
out after all. If it was a dead body, it was likely going to
have to stay for weeks, until a tow truck or the ambulance
could make its way up the mountain. This place was near
impassable after a blizzard. Eli swallowed hard and pressed
his face against the glass, trying to see inside. With the
shattered spiderweb of cracks, it was hard to tell. He
grabbed the door handle and pulled, expecting it to be iced
over. Instead, it fell open easily—a sign the interior was
warm—and he saw the woman sprawled inside.

Dark brown hair spilled over the steering wheel. Her

figure was slight, and she was wearing a black sweater over jeans. Her purse had erupted all over the passenger seat, and in the back of the car, he saw a few Christmas decorations and what looked like boxes of food.

What kind of fool drove up here in a sedan during a blizzard? Now she was dead. With an angry growl, he pushed her body backward so he could get a good look at her face.

Even as he tipped her back, she groaned.

Still alive.

Shocked, Eli stared down at the woman. She was in her late twenties, maybe about his age. Her face was covered in blood and there was a massive bruise right smack-dab on the center of her forehead where she'd hit it against the windshield—or the steering wheel. Or both. He didn't know.

All he knew was that he couldn't leave her out here. She'd die for sure.

Eli knelt beside the car and gently shook her shoulder. "Ma'am?"

Her head lolled and she didn't respond.

After a few gentle attempts to rouse her, it was obvious that he'd have to take her back to the ranch with him. Just like a wounded calf, she'd be safer someplace sheltered and warm. "We're gonna get you to safety, ma'am," he told her politely, even though he was pretty sure she couldn't hear a word he said. Talking to her made him feel a little better, though, and less like she was going to up and die on him.

He dug through the back seat of the sedan and found a bag of clothing, but everything he pulled out was not nearly warm enough for a Wyoming blizzard. He didn't have time to dither, though. He had to get himself and the dogs back to the ranch, and get his horse and cow out of this mess. And his woman, he added to the mental list. Well, not his woman. Whatever. He was just flustered at finding a pretty brunette near dead.

He was supposed to be alone for the holiday, damn it. Now he had a problem. A pretty brunette problem, but still a problem. Eli pushed a couple of her thin little sweaters over her head and tugged them down over her body, hoping she didn't have bruised ribs or anything. It still didn't seem warm enough, so he grabbed the Christmas tree skirt in the back seat and wrapped it around her, then eased her out of the car.

"Sorry about the cold," he murmured to her as he cradled her against his chest. "But I can't leave you here, and I can't call you a car. Ain't nobody heading in this direction for the next while, so it's just you and me. Hang tight and I'll get you somewhere safe."

She didn't answer. The dogs barked, but the girl against his chest was limp and lifeless.

Eli just hoped he wasn't too late.

CHAPTER FOUR

It wasn't easy getting an unconscious woman, a pregnant cow, two dogs, and a horse through a blizzard, but somehow he managed to get them all back to the ranch without losing anyone. He cradled the unconscious woman on the saddle in front of him against his chest. She didn't stir, which worried Eli. There wasn't anyone around that could make the pass through the mountains in this weather. They'd have to wait until it cleared, and if her injuries were bad enough, it might be too late.

Luckily, his horse was well trained. She knew the way home even with minimal guidance, and Eli was grateful to see the sloped roof of the large barn come into sight. He hurried his horse over to the pasture, left Houdini with the rest of the herd, stabled the horse in the barn, and then carried the woman inside the house, the dogs nipping at his heels. Normally, he'd unsaddle the horse and rub her down before tending to things in the house but this couldn't wait.

The horse would be all right for a little bit and the girl in his arms might not be.

First things first.

Eli kicked open the door and Jim and Bandit rushed inside, even as Frannie danced around his legs. "Back up, girl," he told the dog, and she moved away, watching him closely, her tail wagging with excitement. She probably thought this was a new fun game.

It was cold inside the house, since he didn't like leaving a blazing fire going when he was the only one at the ranch. He gently laid the woman down on the couch and then moved to the wood-burning stove, desperate to get some heat going. After a few logs were put in, he closed the stove door and then peeled off one of his gloves, rubbing his face.

Most days he liked being alone. Today? The weight of his responsibilities dragged him down. There was so much to see to and everyone needed attention right away. Frannie whined at him, her tail flicking against his leg.

Eli peered over his hand at her. "Do me a favor and don't have your puppies today, all right? Man can't take much more than this."

Excited that he was talking to her, Frannie sat on her hindquarters and wiggled, an enormous white mountain of fluffy fur. Just the sight of her made him feel a little better, and he rubbed her head and then got back to his feet.

One thing at a time.

He'd take care of the woman first. Make sure she was out of danger. Then, the cowboy in him would kick in. He couldn't neglect the ranch. There were too many animals waiting to be fed. He'd check the herd one last time. Feed 'em their cake pellets and put out more hay. Since the weather was getting colder by the hour, the cattle needed to eat more to keep their systems warm. Luckily, they'd moved the herd closer to the ranch itself and it wouldn't be difficult to put out more feed, just time consuming. Then he could check on the animals in the barn . . . and then on his unconscious patient.

But he had to make sure she was well enough to be left alone first.

Moving to the sofa, Eli sat down on the edge and stared down at the woman. He thought he knew a bit about doctorin'. He'd pulled more calves from pregnant cows than he'd thought possible. He could give an animal medication without blinking an eye. He'd stitched his own gashes and wrapped twisted ankles so he could go back to work. He'd set bones and popped a shoulder back into the socket before. He kinda had to be self-sufficient this far up in the mountains, because if he stopped working every time he got hurt, he'd never get anything done.

He'd never done this sort of thing for a woman, though, and never a stranger.

Gently, he unwrapped the Christmas tree skirt from her body and then felt her arms and ribs for protruding bones. When nothing seemed out of order, he pulled up the clothing and looked at the skin underneath. Bruised, but nothing looked swollen or bloated, which would be a real bad sign. She was breathing regularly and sounded okay. He heaved a sigh of relief and ran a hand over his mouth again. So far, so good.

Frannie moved to the edge of the couch and began to lick the woman's face. "Not now, Frannie girl," he murmured to the dog, though she probably had the right idea. He retrieved a towel from Maria's kitchen, wet it down, and then began to gently wipe the crusted blood from the woman's face.

There was an enormous gash on her forehead, and the

dark bruise right smack between her eyes seemed to be getting darker. Her face was swollen, but he thought that underneath it all, she was probably really pretty. Young and pretty, and driving alone in the mountains close to Christmas. *Some guy out there really screwed up and let his woman get away*, Eli thought to himself. He finished cleaning her face and then tapped her cheek to try to wake her. "Miss?"

She moaned but didn't wake up.

He didn't know if that was a good thing or a bad thing. What should he do? Frannie laid her head on his knee and gave him a soulful look, as if she wished she had the answers. "Me too, girl. Me too." He patted her absently and then an idea hit him.

Phone. Doc Parsons was still at the Swinging C over the holidays. Maybe he'd know what to do with an unconscious woman. He got to his feet and raced across the house, looking for the cordless phone. Eli found it, and then spent several minutes searching for Maria's note card of important phone numbers. Of course, it was on the fridge. With an angry snarl, he grabbed it and dialed the Swinging C Ranch.

After four rings, Doc answered. "I'll be damned. This Eli? Using a phone?" He sounded amused. "Hasn't been but a few days since the others left. You brand yourself out of boredom?"

"Ain't got no time for chitchat, Doc. I got an emergency over here," Eli warned him. Damn Doc of all people. He was smart and knew a lot about medicine and animals, but he was also the jokiest man, and Eli didn't much like joking around when a perfectly good, straightforward conversation would do. "I pulled a woman out of a car on the pass. She's unconscious. Hit her head, I think."

Doc's tone changed. "Broken bones?"

"Not that I could see."

"Ribs?"

Eli could feel himself blushing. "She's got some. I guess. I didn't really check too close." He didn't want to strip her down in case she woke up and saw a strange man standing over her with his hands under her sweater. "Doc, what do I do?"

"Well," Doc mused, in that slow, jokey way of his. "Normally I'd say don't move her in case you make her injuries worse, but I guess that horse has already left the barn."

He was tempted to throw the phone down, but gritted his teeth. "I couldn't leave her in the car. There's a blizzard outside."

"I noticed. Spent all day caking the cattle up here. Hungry little buggers. You'd think they'd never been fed before. She local?"

Eli rubbed his forehead, trying to follow Doc's line of thought. "I guess? No, wait. She wasn't wearing a very big sweater. Must be a tourist."

"Maybe Santa left her for you to find." He chuckled.

He grit his teeth in frustration. "Be serious, man. I've got an injured woman over here."

"Right. Sorry." Doc cleared his throat. "Well, I'd say I'd come over and take a look at her, but I can't go anywhere in this weather without turning into an icicle myself. One of the cows is aborting and I need to make sure it's clean or else we're gonna lose her, too. I can't do much on your end, either. You did good, Eli. Just be patient and she'll wake up. Keep her warm, do a quick check for broken bones and internal bleeding, and hope for the best."

Hope for the best? "What kinda medical advice is that?"

"You need more? Okay. Walk over to her."

Eli raced back to the woman's side. "I'm there. What do you want me to do?"

"Look at her. Has she lost control of her bladder?"

What? "No . . ."

"She defecate on herself?"

"No." He squinted at the air, scowling.

"Congratulations, she ain't dead. Now, you wait for her to wake up and ask her how she feels, and then call me back."

He gritted his teeth. Sometimes Doc was no help at all. "How do I wake her up? I tried shaking her."

"Well, don't do that. Don't slap her, either. If she's unconscious because of medical reasons, that ain't gonna help."

"She's got these awful bruises all over her face, Doc," Eli said in a low voice. "She looks terrible."

"Now, now, it ain't her fault she ain't a looker," Doc told him, amused.

"That wasn't what I meant—"

"If she's not vomiting or seizing up, that's a good sign. Might not be more than just a knock on the head. Just wait for her to wake up normally. That's about all you can do. Lay her on her side, don't put a pillow under her head, and listen to her breathing. Make sure there's no gurgling or choking, and make sure her lips don't turn blue. And then you wait. Feel free to call me no matter what time, day or night, once she wakes up."

Finally, he was getting somewhere. "Okay, I can do that."

"No Christmas carols or music, or television, because if she's got a concussion, it might set off a seizure."

That shouldn't be too hard for him. He didn't have any sort of Christmas crap anyhow. "Fine."

"Try not to leave her alone. Keep her resting. That's it."

It didn't feel like enough, and yet Eli's brain felt overloaded anyhow. "All right. Thanks, Doc."

"Call me back if she gets worse," the other man said cheerfully, as if they were dealing with no more than a sick calf. But looking at the unconscious woman on the couch, Eli felt like he was the one in danger of throwing up. He could handle just about anything the ranch threw at him . . . but he didn't know what to do with an injured woman.

Hell.

She shifted, moaning slightly as her head moved on the pillow he'd jammed under her head.

Pillow! Aw, crap. Eli raced over to her and carefully dragged the woman onto the floor. He took the pillow away, even though it felt cruel, and turned her carefully on her side. As he did, her dark hair spilled out over the worn rug and she looked . . . downright pretty.

Well, if it wasn't for the nasty bruising and the fact that she had dried blood along her ear and jaw. But he didn't need to be thinking about how pretty she was. He needed to be worried about what to do with her if she didn't wake up. He thought for a minute, and then wrapped one of Maria's quilts around her, then patted her gently as if that solved everything.

Don't leave her alone, Doc had said, but Eli had chores that had to be tended to. He hesitated, watching the unconscious woman sleep, but he didn't know what to do. He could sit here and stare at her, but there were a million other farm chores that wouldn't wait for her to wake up. But he couldn't leave her, not if she needed help.

As if sensing his thoughts, Frannie moved next to the woman and curled up beside her, pregnant belly sticking out. Her tail thumped and she licked the woman's forehead, then looked up at him with her dark eyes. It was like she was telling him that she had it under control. That she'd watch over her.

He rubbed her muzzle. "You're the best girl, Frannie. You come and get me if she's sick, all right?"

Frannie's tail thumped against the floor, and that was that.

CHAPTER FIVE

Cass's head was surrounded by fur. Not just a little fur, but a choking amount of white fur that looked pretty but smelled terrible. In fact, it smelled like . . . dog? Which was weird, because she didn't have a dog. She didn't have any pets. This had to be a mistake.

She pushed the fur aside and something smacked across her forehead. The dog's tail thumped against her with excitement, but it hurt so much she nearly blacked out again. Oh, jeez. Pain rolled through her head and she carefully lifted a hand to her throbbing skull. It felt swollen and hot, and it hurt.

What had happened? Where was she?

And why was there a dog?

When the pain faded from "overwhelming" to "dull roar," she squeezed her eyes open again. The ceiling overhead slowly came into focus, and she saw she was staring up at naked wooden beams. Huh. That didn't seem familiar. Neither did the dog licking her forehead.

In fact, none of this seemed all that familiar. Cass slowly sat up, wincing as everything ached and throbbed in response. Ooh, that was going to hurt in the morning. She should have known better . . .

Better than to what? Her brain was foggy. She pressed a hand to her forehead and tried to think. Nothing was forming. She needed coffee and some aspirin, maybe, to shake the fog from her brain. Cass looked around the room, frowning to herself as she did. None of this looked like her sort of thing. For one, it looked very . . . rustic. The walls of the house were bare wood, like the ceiling, and a metal star hung off one wall, next to several pictures of horses. There was a deer head over the fireplace, along with a rifle, and the mantel had a Navajo vase on one end and a cow skull on the other. A cast-iron stove was on the opposite side of the room and it was the source of all the heat in the area. As for Cass, she was wrapped in a faded Navajo quilt. The couch itself was brown and red, and there was a rocking chair in one corner and a TV set that looked as if it predated the Internet. It was all very bold and Western and strange.

This . . . didn't seem like her. Cass glanced down at her black sweater and jeans. That looked familiar, at least.

The dog at her side thumped its tail again and gave her an eager look, getting to its feet and running around in excited circles.

"Do you need to go outside?" Cass asked, curious. That's what dogs wanted when they got excited, right?

At the word "outside," the dog got even more excited, letting out a high-pitched yip.

"Okay, we can do that," Cass told her, and worked on getting to her feet. Her clothes felt slightly damp and the room was chilly despite the heat given off by the stove blazing in the corner. She didn't have her shoes on, though she didn't recall leaving them somewhere. This was odd, too. If her head would just stop throbbing, she'd be able to concentrate for a moment and clear her thoughts. As it was, she was having a hard time focusing.

The dog yipped again.

"Right. Outside." She managed to pull herself to her feet, and a wave of pain crashed over her, knocking her backward onto the couch and making her pant. Oh god, everything hurt. Her head hurt, her face hurt, and her chest hurt, too. Her knee throbbed like it had been twisted, but her chest was the worst—it felt like one big bruise and she wanted to cry with the pain. Was this a heart attack? Was this how she was going to die?

Cass put a hand to her chest, alarmed, and then realized that the simple act of touching her chest caused another shock wave of pain. She tugged down the collar of her shirt and saw a hint of what looked like an enormous bruise covering her from her breastbone on down. Judging from the feel of things, it probably covered her all the way down to her navel.

Well, good grief. Where did that come from?

She pressed a hand to her forehead, trying to think, and that hurt, too. Okay, bruise on the forehead and the chest? What had happened to her? Was this why she couldn't think straight? Cass ran her fingers lightly over her brow and felt a cut there, too. She was definitely banged up.

She just didn't remember what had happened to do all the banging.

Cass got to her feet again, bracing herself, and this time the pain wasn't as excruciating. Now upright, she staggered toward a hall and found a kitchen, and a mudroom. There was a door outside in the mudroom, and it had a window. The window itself showed nothing but dark and chill, and when she stepped into the mudroom, it was freezing, her feet painfully cold. "Are you sure you want to go outside in that?" she asked the dog.

The big fluffy white dog whined at her.

"All right." She touched the doorknob—ice cold—and fumbled with it, trying to figure out how to open the door. A moment later, it opened and snow poured inside. She gasped, stepping backward, but the dog didn't seem like it was going to go outside anymore.

Well, she didn't blame it. After a moment, Cass shut the door again, rubbing her arms and staggering back into the warmer kitchen. "We need coffee," she told it. Coffee might help her brain clear up. She moved into the kitchen—again, with a rustic Western theme and pine cabinets, and cold Saltillo tile that made her toes curl when she stepped on it—and looked for her coffeepot. She couldn't find it. Well, no, she took it back—she found a coffeepot with a plug and a percolator, and she had no idea how to use it. Wasn't there a Keurig somewhere around here?

But she couldn't find one. That didn't make sense.

She'd make tea, then. Cass frowned at the cabinet, looking for tea bags. She didn't see any, but a huge bag of sugar stared right at her. That seemed odd, given that she took her coffee . . .

She paused and waited for her brain to fill in the blank. It didn't.

A note of panic crept into her mind. She forced herself to calm down. It was just coffee. Maybe she didn't have a "way" she took it. There had to be other things she remembered, and not just this big blank. Like . . . the dog's name. She stared down at the big white fluffy beast. It was fat and huge, almost up to her waist. It had dark eyes and wagged its tail so fetchingly she felt a surge of affection for it. And its name was . . .

Cass had no idea.

She swallowed hard and touched the sore spot on her brow. Perhaps these things were connected. Okay, she wouldn't panic yet. She knew her name was Cass, and her last name was . . .

Was . . .

Her brain didn't fill in the blank. There wasn't anything when she tried to access that memory. She didn't know who she was. She tried thinking of other things. Where she lived. Where her job was. *What* her job was. How old she was.

Anything. Everything.

She had nothing.

Cass squeezed her eyes shut and tried to picture her face. Surely she'd remember her face. When nothing came to mind, a sob caught in her throat and she hobbled forward, passing through the kitchen and down another hall. There had to be a bathroom around here. A bedroom. Someplace with a mirror—

There! She caught sight of a bathroom with beaten copper sinks and a rope-edged decorative mirror. Breathing hard, she flicked the light on and stared at her reflection, clutching the sink for balance.

Her face didn't look familiar. Oh, it kind of did, in that weird "have I met you somewhere before?" feeling, but other than that, it was like looking at the face of a stranger. She had brown hair and blue eyes, and a hellish-looking bruise on her forehead. Her nose was huge, and when she touched it, it felt squishy and painful. Swollen, then. Her brows were dark and it was hard to tell if she was attractive or not because there were massive bruises under her eyes and she looked awful.

Just awful.

Hot tears threatened to seep out, and she dashed them away. She wouldn't cry over a stupid ugly reflection. Not when there were bigger problems like *who the heck she was*. Her heart hurt . . . but that could have been the bruising. "Right," she whispered to herself. "Bigger problems than a big schnoz, Cass. It's not like you have someone to impress—"

And then she paused, because did she? Maybe she did and she didn't remember, and wouldn't that just be awful?

Maybe . . . maybe her cell phone would have the answers. Excited at the thought, she made her way back out of the bathroom and limped back to the living area. It was huge, but she didn't see a purse or any place she'd have plugged in a cell phone. Maybe she kept it by the bed? She explored the lower floor of the enormous house, looking for bedrooms, but all the doors she found were locked. If there was a key, she had no idea where she might have left it.

Down a long hallway, she found a small, cramped room that was stacked high with paperwork, shelves full of clutter, and a dusty computer with a CRT monitor that took up most of the rickety desk it was perched on. She sat down on the folding metal chair in front of the computer and tapped the keyboard to unlock the screen.

A box popped up on the screen.

Password.

Crap.

She thought for a moment, and then pushed the keyboard away. She had no idea. She had no idea about anything. She didn't know where her damn purse was, where her phone was, or anything. She didn't even have a pair of shoes. She didn't know the date.

Feeling hopeless, she gazed around the small, messy office looking for a calendar. There was one on the wall . . . for the entire year.

Of 2008.

A helpless, horrible little laugh bubbled up in her throat. Okay, she was pretty sure that was the least helpful calendar of all time. She knew it wasn't 2008, because that was when . . . was when . . .

Well, it didn't matter. She didn't know what the date was, but her brain knew a few things. She had her name. She knew it wasn't 2008. Maybe if she worked at it, she'd remember other things.

There was a mug shaped like a boot with some ballpoint pens sticking out of it, so she grabbed one and a piece of paper and started to write.

CASS, she wrote at the top, and then added . . . ASSANDRA? with a question mark, because she wasn't entirely sure, but it felt right. Tapping the pen, no other names came to mind.

As she flicked the pen back and forth, she noticed it had writing on it. Her head throbbed, but she forced herself to read the tiny words.

PRICE RANCH.

Hmm. So this was a ranch. That explained the decor and the fact that it was a big house, big enough for multiple people to live in. Why was she living on a ranch? Cass chewed on her lip and then wrote PRICE next to CASSANDRA. That didn't look right.

So who were the Prices, then? How did she know them?

The dog's head went up, and the tail began to wag furiously. Before Cass could ponder this, the fluffy white monster was off like a shot, barking. A moment later, she heard the sound of a door slam somewhere in the direction of the mudroom.

Someone was here!

Wobbly, Cass raced back toward the kitchen and the mudroom, even as two other dogs came racing up to her, tails wagging with excitement. These weren't the white, fluffy monsters like the other one but smaller with patchy coats and excited, wriggling bodies. They were thrilled to see her, at least. A low voice murmured something and her heart skipped a beat at that. A man.

Her man, maybe?

She touched her ring finger but there was nothing there. Of course, that didn't mean anything. Maybe when she'd smacked into whatever she'd smacked into, she'd lost her ring, too. Cass rubbed her finger as she headed into the kitchen, moving slowly so everything didn't hurt.

When she entered, the breath sucked out of her lungs.

Standing in the doorway of the kitchen, fresh from the outside, was a cowboy. Not just any cowboy, but a cowboy that looked like a cross between the Marlboro Man and something out of a woman's secret fantasy. He was busy knocking snow off a tan hat, and his legs were encased in dark jeans. A red flannel shirt covered a strong upper body, and he had a belt buckle that shone like a star. His face was tanned and handsome in its solemn severity, but the most noticeable thing was the silvery gray of his eyes, and they reminded her of the ice, too. Crisp and clear and bright. Match those perfect, handsome features with those broad shoulders and the cowboy hat?

He was a fantasy come to life.

Oh goodness, this was her man? God, why didn't she remember this?

The cowboy stared at her expectantly, and Cass supposed she needed to point out that she'd lost her memory. Instead, what came out was "Are you my husband?"

CHAPTER SIX

Was he her husband? Eli stared at the woman in surprise.

He hadn't expected to see her up, though he supposed that was good. Meant she wasn't so injured that she'd need a hospital after all. Still, she looked a hell of a lot more fragile upright than she did unconscious. Now he could see the slim lines of her body, the delicate build of her figure, and just how bad the bruising on her face was. She was pale, the cut on her forehead and the bruise there looking like intruders on her face. Didn't even matter that her nose was red and swollen.

She was a beauty.

Dark blue eyes the color of sky in summer looked up at him, and her full mouth was pink and eye-catching. He'd never seen anything so lovely—and helpless—as the woman before him with her dark, tousled curls tumbling over her thin black sweater that wasn't winter-appropriate and wouldn't last five minutes for someone that worked outdoors. It did outline her breasts quite magnificently, though, but he tried not to look at that. Wasn't right.

Eli cleared his throat. "Ma'am?"

"Are you my husband?" she asked again, and her voice was small and timid with worry.

"Well, uh, no. No I'm not." Eli took off his hat and set it down on the kitchen counter. His hair was sweaty and he raked a hand through it, feeling mighty uncomfortable at her confusion. Why would she think he was her husband? That didn't make sense.

The woman looked around, her eyes full of confusion. "Then this isn't our house?"

"Nope. This here's Price Ranch." He just stood there, because he didn't know what to say. Was this an act? Did she really lose her memory? Did she truly think he was her husband? Man, Jordy and Maria and the others would have a field day if they knew that. They'd laugh and tease him forever, because Eli was the one that never dated, never went into town to get a drink and meet women. He was all business.

Husband indeed.

"Oh." One hand headed to her brow and then fluttered away, as if she remembered that it was injured. "I'm not a Price, then?"

"No, you aren't. I found your car on the road. You crashed into a tree. Who are you?"

She bit her lip. "I was hoping you could tell me."

"You can't remember anything?" His voice was a little more harsh and impatient than he wanted it to be. But if this wasn't just his luck. Not only was he stuck with a pretty stranger, but she didn't know who she was? It felt like a trick, almost.

Except he'd seen the blood all over her face. Even now,

he could see the bruises coloring up. She was gonna have two black eyes, and her nose would probably be purple for a while.

"I remember my name is Cass," she told him in a faint voice. "But that's about all I remember."

Before he could comment on that, she sagged against the counter, and his instincts kicked in. Eli quickly moved to her side and slid an arm around her waist. "You need to sit down. I've got you."

She clung to his arm, her fingers cold through his sleeve. "I'm sorry. I'm sorry. I guess I'm a bit more tired than I thought. I'm really sorry—"

"Quit apologizin'," he told her as he tucked her body against him and more or less hauled her into the living room. "Ain't like you tried to run your car into a tree on purpose, did you?" The couch was still covered with the blankets he'd left with her, and he guided her toward it. Frannie had made herself a nest at the far end of the sofa and he snapped his fingers and pointed at the floor. The dog immediately raced to where he pointed, bouncing around like the other two. To them, this was a fun game. They loved company.

In that, Eli differed very much from the dogs.

"I hate feeling weak," the woman protested. Cass, he reminded himself. Her name was Cass. It was pretty enough. Kinda delicate, like her.

"I suppose anyone'd feel weak if they got their head smashed into a windshield like you did," he told her gruffly as he helped her sit down on the end of the sofa. He didn't like how she collapsed against it as if she had no strength at all. "Not your fault I'm stuck with you through this blizzard."

Jordy would laugh at him, all right. Dustin would probably try to stake his claim, deciding that the woman was better for him than Eli. Not that Eli wanted her, of course. Didn't matter that she had the prettiest eyes or that she fit under his arm like she was made for him. She wasn't from around here, which meant she wouldn't be staying. Eli had learned that girls like her were just heartbreak waiting to happen, so he didn't want anything to do with them.

"What?" Her eyes went wide, the bright blue of them searching his face.

Damn it. Now he'd gone and said too much. Eli pursed his lips, wonderin' if it was too late to take back those words. Guess so, judging from her reaction. Best to bluff through it. "Which part threw you?"

Her mouth worked silently as she gazed up at him. Damn it, did she have to have such gorgeous eyes? He was having a hard time concentrating with her looking up at him like that. It made it hard to think. "You're . . . stuck with me?" She gasped, trying to get up from the couch.

He put a hand on her shoulder, pushing her back down. "Stay there. Frannie, come here." He pointed at the woman's lap, and the big dog immediately moved forward, climbing over her thighs and settling herself in. "Good girl. Don't be trying to get up. You had a hard knock on your head and you need to rest. Frannie'll pin you down if she has to. Hope you ain't allergic."

"Not me," she said, and then frowned. "Someone is."

"Who?" Her man? Why did that thought bother him so much? Just because she was pretty and vulnerable didn't mean she was there to hit on. That wouldn't be right.

"I don't know." She bit her lip. "Is that why you're stuck with me?"

Man, she sure was fixated on those words. "Well, you can't exactly drive your car down the mountain, seeing as half of it's all over the road."

She winced. "I don't know how I did that. Normally I'm such a careful driver. I think." She fluttered her hand toward her brow again. "It feels like something that I'd be. Careful."

"Mmm."

"I might be wrong." She looked woebegone. "I don't remember anything."

"Anything at all?"

Again, she shook her head.

Well, damn. "You hit your head," he told her unnecessarily. "I'm sure you just need to rest and your memory'll come back to you soon enough."

"Okay," Cass said, voice quavery. "And you and I, we're not . . . ?"

"No." Maybe his voice was a little too firm, too emphatic, because she blushed, and then he could feel his own cheeks heating. "I don't know you."

"I see." She glanced around and her hand slid onto Frannie's back, petting her. Frannie licked her arm, tail wagging, and a little smile crossed the woman's face. "This isn't my dog, right? I seem to recall something about . . . about animals. But I don't think she's mine."

"She's mine," he told her, a little gruff. "Her name's Francesca. Frannie. The others are Jim and Bandit."

"Hi, Frannie," Cass said in the sweetest voice, and Frannie wiggled with excitement. "Your owner sure likes to feed you, because you're crushing my legs."

He had to chuckle at that. "If you promise to stay down, I'll get her off you."

"I promise. I'm not sure where I'd go even if I was up." She tried to smile, but he could tell it was difficult for her, and he felt guilty. Maria would know what to do in all this. She was the one that was good with people. Eli, well, Eli was good with cattle. And hard work. Not pretty women. Not wounded, fragile women. Certainly not strangers.

"Well, if she bothers you, let me know," he added, patting a nearby cushion so the dog would hop off Cass's lap.

"Oh, she's not a bother. I love dogs." She frowned to herself immediately. "I think. I guess that's not a big deal. Everyone loves dogs, don't they?" Her hand went to her brow and she rubbed the edges of her bruise again. "I feel like I'm supposed to be somewhere."

"Well, there wasn't anyone in the car with you. So if you're meeting a boyfriend or a husband, he's just gonna have to wait for the storm to clear up." Now he sounded really damned surly, and he wasn't sure why. Maybe because Cass deserved better? If she had a man and he made her drive that car up the mountains, he was an idiot and she definitely deserved better.

"Maybe," she said, but she didn't sound convinced. "So the storm's that bad?"

"Couple feet of snow in a few hours. The pass here's gonna fill up overnight and then the roads won't be passable until we get a good melt. You're gonna be here a while."

"Oh. I guess I'm lucky you found me. Thank you." Her voice was small and full of wonder. Or confusion. Was hard to tell. "Say, what's today?"

"Nineteenth of December."

Cass's eyes flicked with recognition. "It's almost Christmas. Maybe that's what I feel like I'm missing." She glanced around. "Do you not celebrate?"

"Not much."

Her expression turned to one of sympathy. "Is it because you're here by yourself at Christmas?"

He scowled. "You make it sound like that's a bad thing."

She shrank back. "Of course it's not. I just thought . . ." She shook her head. "Never mind. It's not important."

No, it wasn't. The fact that he wasn't a big fan of Christmas wasn't anyone's business. "You need anything?" When she shook her head, he grunted. "You can stay in my room tonight and I'll sleep on the couch. We'll figure the rest out in the morning." There were other rooms in the house, of course, but they belonged to other people and he didn't feel right about sleeping in someone else's bed when they weren't there. The couch was fine.

"All right," she said softly, and then he felt like an ass for making her uncomfortable. Then he wanted to smack himself. This was his home. Why should he be the one that was uncomfortable? She was intruding on his peace and quiet. He was gonna have enough to do over the next couple of weeks taking care of the cattle by himself and running the ranch alone. He didn't have time for a woman, much less a pretty, clueless one sitting around and asking him why he wasn't celebrating Christmas.

If he wasn't overly friendly, that was just too damn bad for her.

CHAPTER SEVEN

Her savior was kind of a jerk.

Handsome and rugged, but definitely a jerk.

Cass was silent as she followed him into his bedroom, where she'd be sleeping for the night. He didn't say much, just pointed at the bed, then at her, and then left, Frannie wagging her tail and following at his heels. The other dogs, Bandit and Jim, just kind of stared at her for a moment, and then they left, too. She closed the door behind him and then leaned against it.

Her head hurt.

Her chest hurt.

Her heart hurt, and it wasn't even injured.

Her brain felt like mush.

She couldn't remember squat. This guy didn't like her, and she was stuck with him until the snow melted and the pass through the mountains was clear. Too bad she didn't know what mountains, what pass, or even what she was doing here. And he didn't give her any answers.

Heck, he didn't even give her his name.

Cass sighed heavily and pushed off from the door. If he wasn't going to give her answers, she was just going to have to get them on her own. She moved around the room, leaning heavily on the furniture for support because her knees still felt weak and shaky. The room itself was fairly sparse. There was a queen-sized bed in the center of the room with natural, rustic wood for the frame. A dark blue quilt covered the bed and there was only one pillow. On the nightstand, there was a picture of a tiny white ball of fluff that must have been Frannie as a puppy. There were no pictures of family or friends, no clutter, no nothing that would mark this place as someone's home. There was no television set, no Xbox or DVDs. It might have been a hotel room for all of its personality, and that struck her as odd. For a moment, she'd thought that maybe her savior had reacted weirdly to her question about him being her husband because he already had a wife or girlfriend somewhere, but surely he'd have pictures of her? And if she didn't live here, wouldn't he have a laptop so he could Skype with her? Something?

She gazed down at the bed with the one pillow. At the single dresser across the room that was devoid of everything atop it but a spare cowboy hat. Maybe he was just a boring guy. And because she couldn't help herself, she casually sat down on the edge of the bed and pulled out the drawer of the nightstand. She was nosy. So what.

Inside, there was a bit more personality to him at least. There was a wallet with a credit card and a driver's license. She stared at the picture. It was him, looking dead-eyed into the camera and annoyed that someone was taking his picture. Still handsome, though, even if impatience was stamped across his stern features. Her eyes blurred as she tried to read the tiny writing on the license.

Elijah Pickett. He even sounded like a cowboy. His birthdate was on there. January 31. She counted back the years to figure out his age. Thirty-two. All right. Elijah was four years older than her.

Oh.

Pleasure blossomed through her at the realization of her own age. She was twenty-eight, then. The knowledge had come to her without even thinking about it. Maybe if she pricked at her mind with other small things, the memories would fill in. Encouraged, she slipped his license back into his wallet and replaced it carefully. There was a comb in here, a wood-handled knife with a symbol engraved on it, a gaudy belt buckle with a big E on it that didn't seem like him at all. There was a leather-covered Bible and a copy of *The Call of the Wild* that had a page dog-eared about halfway through it. Underneath that there was a magazine, and she absently picked it up. No family photos, no condoms, no nothing by the bedside.

Cass couldn't decide if that was charmingly straitlaced or worrisome.

The magazine looked like some sort of ranching periodical. She absently flipped through it, thinking about her age and hoping that something else would stir loose, when she paused on a picture of a cowboy atop a horse. It was Elijah, holding a lasso of rope above his head while a calf fled in front of him. It was an action shot but there was a look of such concentration and determination on his face that she shivered.

He was handsome. Really, really handsome. The photo had captured his strength and ruggedness perfectly. Was the article about him? She skimmed it. Some stuff about Price Ranch and the number of cattle they drove, and how the herds they used to run were a fraction of what they were ten years ago and . . .

And reading made her head hurt. Like, really bad. The words swam and she rubbed her eyes. Maybe she'd read it tomorrow. After all, what was she trying to find out about Mr. Elijah Pickett? If he was married? She could look at his ring finger in the morning, though she suspected it'd be empty. Everything about this room spoke of a guy who didn't have a woman in his life.

Or anyone, really.

She supposed that made her sad, that one lonely picture of his dog on his nightstand. And she thought about the fact that it was almost Christmas and Elijah was here alone, with no decorations or anything to celebrate. It seemed wrong. Christmas was a time for family and love . . . wasn't it? She tried to think about her own family, but nothing popped up.

Cass couldn't shake the feeling that someone was waiting on her, somewhere. But who? And where? She rubbed her bare ring finger. A husband? She didn't think so. Boyfriend seemed unlikely, too. A kid? An ex? Was someone sitting out there, watching the road and waiting for her to arrive? Gosh, she hoped her memory returned soon, because she hated the thought of worrying people.

Maybe she'd ask Elijah about it in the morning. Maybe he knew everyone on this mountain and would know who she was visiting. Heck, he could take her back to her car and let her get her things, at least. Perhaps when she had her stuff or saw the car itself, that'd jog something loose. Encouraged, she began to gingerly undress for bed.

* * *

It was clear that this woman—this Cass—was not a rancher.

Eli frowned up at the clock on the wall that read nine in the morning. He'd already caked the cows and spread hay for them, did a head count, and made sure they had water. He'd been up since five and hard at work. His guest hadn't even stirred.

He wasn't sure if he should be concerned or not. Just because he didn't sleep late didn't mean that she was sick. Still . . . he'd work in the barn for a bit, then come inside to grab a drink of water, and listen outside her door. It was quiet.

Too quiet, maybe.

Should he go inside? Eli hesitated outside the door. He didn't want to barge in if she was sleeping. But if she wasn't . . .

The phone rang, and Eli headed over to the kitchen and picked it up. "Yeah?"

"Good morning," Doc Parsons said cheerily. "I thought I'd check on our patient. How is our girl feeling?"

Eli frowned into the phone. "Don't know. She hasn't woke up yet."

"Hasn't woke up? Did you watch her last night to make sure she was all right?"

"Well . . . no."

Doc made a noise of distress on the other end of the line. "How did she seem?"

How did she seem? "She doesn't have her memory, but other than that, I guess she seems all right."

"No memory?"

"Nope. Unless she's faking." Though he couldn't think of a reason why she'd fake her memory loss. And she'd seemed downright distressed over the whole thing.

"You tell me—does she look like she hit her head hard enough for something like that?"

Eli thought about the bruises and the gash on her brow. "Yeah. I think so."

"Were her pupils a normal size? One wasn't larger than the other?"

"I didn't check."

"Check today. It's possible she has a concussion. If that's the case, I'm going to need you to watch her while she sleeps."

Watch her while she slept? Was the man serious? "Doc, I've got a ranch to run here. I can't sit around and watch some stranger sleep all day long."

"If she sleeps all day long, that's a bad sign," Doc told him. "Look, we got a ton of snow overnight, or I'd suggest you bring her over here so I can watch over her. As it is, you'll just have to do the heavy lifting on this one. Watch her closely, keep her away from screens and reading, or anything else that could tax her brain. We don't know for sure if she has a concussion or not, but if she is having trouble with memories, let's not do anything to make it worse. Oh, and no strenuous activity."

He didn't know what to say. Didn't sound like she could do anything but sit on the couch. "All right."

"Just keep her calm and relaxed." Doc chuckled as if that was funny, and Eli felt a surge of irritation.

Keep her calm and relaxed, and watch her every damn minute of the day. He wasn't asking for too much at all, was he? "So what am I supposed to do with her?"

"Be hospitable," Doc said cheerfully. "Call me if you need anything else. I know you're impatient, but treat her as good as you would one of your sick calves. I'm going to have some tea and then cake my cows again before we get another round of snow. Weather forecast is looking kind of bleak."

He cursed. If that was true, and looking at the skies, it most likely was, Eli needed to cake his, too, but apparently he also had to babysit. "Thanks, Doc." He hung the phone up and paced toward his bedroom. Time to wake up Sleeping Beauty.

Eli knocked on her door—his door, really—and waited impatiently for her to open up. He wasn't prepared for the sight of her. She'd changed out of her clothing sometime during the night and now wore one of his shirts, the buttons loose around her neck and revealing a hint of creamy cleavage—and her bruises. Her dark hair was tousled and spilled around her shoulders like a cloud, and both of her eyes were deeply shadowed with bruises. She was a mixture of sexy and broken all at once, and he didn't know how he felt about that.

He kept staring at his shirt, though.

"Good morning," she said softly, and then bit her lip. "I don't suppose you have aspirin?"

Jerking his gaze away from the glimpse of thigh under the hem of his shirt, he realized that her eyes were slitted, as if the light pained her. Heck. Here he was wondering if she was wearing anything under his shirt and she was in pain. He was an idiot. *Just treat her like one of your sick calves*, Doc had said. If she was in his care, he'd have fired himself for how he was treating her. Just went to show that he was way better with animals than with people. "I do. Follow me."

Mouth dry, he turned on his heel and marched back toward the kitchen, his thoughts whirling. He hadn't told her to change into his shirt, but it made sense that she did. Of course she should. She was hurt and needed to be comfortable. The problem was his own reaction to the sight of her like that, because it reminded him just how long it had been since he'd had any sort of relationship with a woman. Years, really.

Not that he wanted one with this one. She was pretty, but too fragile and helpless for his taste. 'Sides, it wouldn't be right.

But he couldn't pretend that he wasn't affected by the sight of her vivid blue eyes as she gave him a pained look and clutched at her head. Her steps weaved a bit as she moved forward, and he stopped to put an arm around her waist. He could feel the material of the shirt bunch up against his arm, but he stared straight ahead, because he wasn't gonna look. Gawking at an injured woman's thighs seemed like a straight shot to hell.

"I can walk," she protested.

"No you can't." He ignored her attempts to break free and guided her down the hall to the kitchen, keeping his gaze straight ahead. "Last thing we need is you crashing into something else and breaking your head open. Again." He helped her toward the table at the far end of the kitchen and hauled a chair out for her. "Sit."

She did, and he noticed that she thumped into the seat rather wearily.

With his charge deposited, Eli found some aspirin, poured her a cup of coffee, and then sat down across from her. "The coffee's a bit old but it's still hot."

With trembling fingers, she took the aspirin from him, then washed them down with a sip of coffee . . . and nearly choked. "How old is this coffee? Five years?" She coughed into her hand.

He couldn't help but grin at that. "More like five hours. I like mine strong."

"Five hours?" She took another tentative sip of the coffee and grimaced. "You must get up early."

"Yep."

"I'm sorry I slept so late." She sounded ashamed, and he felt like a real ass for thinking the same thing not so long ago. "I feel like I'm being the rudest guest and I never thanked you for saving me, Elijah."

Something fierce rippled through him at the sound of his name on her lips. "No one calls me Elijah."

"Oh." She bit her lip and looked so uncertain that he felt like a jerk all over again.

"Eli," he told her, and was rewarded with a smile that made him want to smile back at her.

"My nickname's Cass. At least, I think it is." She gave a tiny shrug. "I'm not the best authority on those things at the moment."

She was trying to make a joke out of it? That was cute, and he appreciated a sense of humor. "I'll take your word for it. How are you feeling this morning?"

Her fingers cupped the coffee mug and she stared down at it. "Like I got smacked in the face with a big immovable object?"

"Because you did?" He gestured that she should lean in. "Let me look at your eyes. Doc told me I should make sure your pupils are the same size."

Cass blinked at him in surprise. "Someone else is here?"

"No, he's on a ranch on the other side of the mountain, but I called him when I found you. He's a vet." At her smothered laugh, he couldn't help but grin, too. "I know. But that was who I knew was available, so I called him."

"As soon as my head stops hurting and it stops snowing,

I'll be out of your way, I promise." She obediently leaned forward so he could gaze into her eyes.

Lost in the bright blue of them, Eli blinked and had to take a moment to focus on what she was saying. "Your eyes look all right," he told her gruffly. "And I'm not sure where you think you're going."

She blinked, her long lashes drawing his attention back to her eyes. Damn it, why did he find her so pretty? She was nothing but trouble he didn't need. "Oh, well, I figured once it stopped snowing I'd be on my way."

"Two things," Eli drawled, leaning back and crossing his arms over his chest. "One. That snow ain't going anywhere for weeks, most likely. There's several feet on the ground and we're due to get another round later today. Mountain's not going to be drivable for a while."

"Oh," she whispered, and she sounded so woebegone he felt like an ass. "What's the second thing?"

"You got any idea of where you're going?"

She chewed on her lip. "I'm sure something will come to me."

"That's kinda what I thought. Look, neither of us are happy about this, but it is what it is." He hated that she flinched. He was just trying to be honest, damn it. "You're stuck here until you get better and until the roads clear. Might as well get used to it. Until then, Doc tells me that you're not allowed TV or computer screens or reading."

"I'm not?" Cass blinked at him.

"Nope. No strenuous activity, either."

"So . . . I'm supposed to what, sit on the couch and twiddle my thumbs?"

"You can pet Frannie."

"Oh, well," she replied tartly. "That should burn a whole five minutes. Thank god."

A laugh erupted out of him. "It ain't ideal, I know, but you don't want to mess your head up worse than it already is."

"No, I guess not." She ran a long finger around the rim of the mug, and he noticed that her nails were short and natural. "I don't suppose you got my purse and my cell phone from my car, did you?"

He hadn't even thought about it. He'd been so rattled at the sight of her, covered in blood, that he hadn't thought about anything else. "I didn't. If you need it, I can try to go back in a few days once the worst of the snow passes."

"A few days?" she echoed.

"Not safe to take the horses out in this weather. They're not fans of it, either."

"Oh. Of course." Cass toyed with the mug. "Well, I guess I'll just . . . sit around here. Are you going to keep me company?" She gave him such a hopeful look that he felt longing stir in his body.

Damn it. Not appropriate. "No." And he jumped to his feet and reached for his hat on the counter. "I've got work to do. No time to sit around jawing."

CHAPTER EIGHT

That hadn't gone well.

Cass finished sipping the terrible, terrible coffee, wondering what she was supposed to do with herself. She couldn't read, couldn't watch TV, couldn't do anything, really. She looked over at Frannie, but the dog was asleep by the woodstove. Napping wasn't a bad idea.

She needed to eat something first, though. Getting to her feet, Cass rummaged through the tidy kitchen. It was clear that although Eli was here by himself, someone had thought of him. Plastic bags of Christmas fudge had been left out, tied with green and red ribbons, and there were a few plastic containers labeled *For Christmas Dinner*. That was sweet. A wife, maybe? She really needed to check his finger. Cass toyed with the collar of the shirt she'd borrowed. It probably made him feel weird to see her dressed like this. All right, she would change, then, after she ate.

She found some bread and jam and made herself a couple of pieces of toast, and then found that her eyes were heavy. A quick nap, then. When she got up, she'd make a list of things to ask Elijah—no, Eli—that she could do around the place. Maybe there was something she could help out with so he'd stop looking at her with such frustration in his eyes.

When she woke up, she dressed in her jeans again and her shoes, but she kept his shirt on. Hers had blood all over it, and she decided that the first thing she'd do was laundry. Searching through the rooms of the cozy ranch house felt a bit like more snooping, but she told herself that Eli wouldn't want to be bothered. A quick glance outside had shown her that it was snowing harder than ever, and she could just barely make out a distant figure on a tractor of some kind, spreading hay in one of the nearby snowy fields. He was busy. She'd just be self-sufficient and stay out of his way, then.

The washing machine was old, and maybe she wasn't much of a homemaker, but it felt like solving a puzzle to try to turn the darn thing on. Eventually she got it started and added a cup of powder to the machine, then sat on top of the washer and waited for it to finish. As it worked, she swung her legs and noticed that the laundry room doubled as storage, because she saw some boxes labeled *Christmas*.

Would it be all right to decorate? she wondered. Or would Eli hate the thought? She made a mental note to ask him. And then because she kept thinking of even more things to ask him, she hunted for a pen and paper and began to write things down to ask about.

1. *What kind of car was she driving when he found her?*
2. *Did he know where she was going?*

3. *Who else lives here?*
4. *Can she decorate for Christmas?*
5. *Is he married?*

She blushed at the last one and then scratched it out. It shouldn't matter if Eli was married or not. He was just a nice man who was helping a stranger out. That was all.

And surely a guy as good-looking as he was would already be taken. She couldn't help but think about the strong arm he slung around her waist, helping her to the kitchen. It made her feel dainty, cherished. Not that it mattered, she told herself. He was just being nice. She remembered the fudge in the kitchen, tied up with thoughtful little bows. Definitely taken. She thought of the Christmas ornaments and such, carefully put away. He wasn't celebrating because his family wasn't here. She felt sorry for him.

That was why he was so cranky.

Resolved, she wrote a new number five down.

5. *Can she help out with any chores?*

Her head was hurting after just writing those few things down, and her eyes felt itchy and tired. He'd said the doctor told her not to read, so maybe writing was included in that. Well, she had to do something. She drummed her pen on the paper and thought about those little bags of fudge. Those were tasty, of course, but not much of a meal. She imagined he'd be hungry after working all day.

Well, she could cook, couldn't she? Cheered, she headed to the kitchen and began to pick through the cabinets. She could make him a nice lunch to say thank you, and in the meantime, she'd stay busy. Pancakes and bacon, she decided after looking through the ingredients in the kitchen. The bacon felt . . . forbidden, which was weird. Maybe she was on a no-bacon diet before all this? Either way, he was a guy and he'd probably eat enough for both of them.

With that decided, Cass found a frying pan, began to heat it up, and got to work, humming to herself.

Lunch today, and maybe she'd make some Christmas cookies later tonight. Who knew? She had all the time in the world to cook. Glancing over at Frannie, who was wagging her tail hopefully, Cass beamed. "Lunch is on me today, girl. You and your dad are gonna have yourselves a nice feast."

Normally, Eli would stay out until the sun set and eat enough dinner to make up for the fact that he hadn't stopped for lunch. But with the vulnerable woman back at the house, he didn't feel right staying out all day. So he finished putting down a round of cake for the cows, broke the ice on the water one more time, and then headed in for a quick lunch and to check on his "guest."

The smell of . . . something . . . hit him the moment he went inside. He wasn't exactly sure what it was. Something akin to burned bacon and glue. That was damned odd. He pulled off his hat and overcoat and hung them in the mudroom, then stuck his head into the kitchen to see what was going on.

The kitchen was hazy with old smoke, and Cass stood near the stove, sighing as she poked at a few bits of charred bacon. Frannie was at her feet, wagging her tail eagerly, waiting for scraps. As he watched, she picked up a blackened bit and handed it to the dog, who snatched it up. "We won't tell your dad about that one."

"Tell me about what?" he asked, stepping forward.

She gasped, turning around so quickly that she hit the handle of the frying pan and it went skidding across the stove. He snatched up a potholder and grabbed the handle, stopping the thing before it could slop grease everywhere. "Oh. You're back. Is it lunchtime already?" She looked over at the clock and then rubbed her eyes. "I lost track of time."

"And that's why you burned the bacon?" he guessed. "You walked away?"

"Uh, actually I didn't." Her cheeks turned pink, which made her bruises stand out more. "I guess I'm not a very good cook."

Eli looked around at the mess on the countertops. Maria considered the kitchen "hers" and kept everything as neat and tidy as possible, with nothing left out. She'd have a stroke if she saw what Cass had done to her kitchen in the space of a few hours. Cabinet doors hung open, their ingredients scattered all over the countertops. A fine coating of flour covered everything as far as the eye could see—even Cass. Several plates had what looked like a breakfast of some kind on them. He supposed she'd tried to make pancakes, but the sad little creations on the plates didn't much look like that to his eyes. They looked more like melted biscuits. She'd used a heck of a lot of flour, too, and that would make Maria throw a fit as well, since the food supply had to be accounted for.

But Cass looked so sad standing in front of her cooking failures that Eli didn't have the heart to chastise her. He patted her shoulder. "I'm sure it's all perfectly fine."

"You say that," she muttered, "but you haven't tried one of my pancakes."

"I'm sure they're fine—"

"Frannie won't eat them."

He paused. "Uh . . ."

"Yeah." She picked one up and knocked it against the counter, and the thing splintered and crumbled like it was made of brick mortar instead of flour. "I'm no pancake expert but I'm pretty sure they're not supposed to do this."

Eli did his best not to laugh. "No, ma'am."

Cass gave such a sad sigh it took everything in him not to laugh all over again. "Do you have pigs on this farm? Maybe they can eat these."

"No pigs," he told her. "We're a cattle ranch."

"Drat."

He took the hard pancake out of her hand. The only place it was going to go was the garbage. Pretty bad if the dogs wouldn't even eat it. Even now Bandit and Jim were giving him hopeful looks that had a lot more to do with the bacon than the pancakes, he suspected. "If you're hungry, I can whip you up some proper pancakes."

She sighed unhappily and gazed at the pancake in his hands. "That defeats the purpose of me making you lunch."

Eli stared down at her in surprise. It was probably a bad time to realize that she didn't come higher than his shoulder, or that her tousled brown hair had even more curl in it than he thought. Or that she was the perfect size to fit under his arm if she were his. It wasn't right for him to think about stuff like that. She was injured and afraid.

But she'd tried to make him lunch. Him. As if she wasn't the one that was hurting and didn't have her memory. He felt a rush of warmth for her. Even if she was a stranger, she had a good heart. "You didn't have to do that," he told her.

"I wanted to. You've done so much for me and I don't have any way to repay you." Cass's bright blue eyes looked up at him. "Unless you can think of some other way I can thank you."

He felt his cheeks grow hot. It was clear from the way she was looking up at him that she didn't realize what she said. He sure wasn't going to point it out to her. Wouldn't be right. "No need to pay me back," he said gruffly. "Just doing what anyone would do in that situation."

"Most people wouldn't give me their room or not mind that I borrowed their clothes." She fingered the collar of her shirt—his shirt. "You've been very kind."

And that made him feel like an ass, because his thoughts hadn't been kind. Hell, they'd been downright resentful most of the time. She was another problem he didn't want. He had enough on his plate with the others being gone during the holidays, and with the blizzard dumping several feet of snow on the mountain, it meant that he'd have to feed the cattle twice as much just to keep them warm. It was all extra work, and he didn't have spare time as it was.

But it wasn't her fault, either. It wasn't like she'd asked to crash her car into a tree and end up with no memories. She certainly hadn't asked to be stuck up here with him through the holidays. Somewhere out there, someone was missing a daughter, or a girlfriend, and worried sick about her. "I'd have done it for anyone," he said, and that was that.

"Well, I appreciate it," Cass told him. "And the good news is that I think I've figured out the pancake batter, so I'm happy to make another batch for you."

He grunted. She looked so hopeful he didn't have the heart to tell her no. She held the bowl out to him for his approval, beaming, and he had to admit, it did look an awful lot like batter. But just in case . . . "How many eggs did you put in?"

Cass blinked her pretty blue eyes at him. "Eggs?"

"Yeah, eggs."

Her gaze went wide. "Oh. Maybe that's what I'm missing."

He was in for it now. "Maybe so."

"I'll add them to the batter and get it going," she told him, excited. Then she paused. "You think two is enough?"

"Two's fine for starters." Well, if the other pancakes didn't have eggs, maybe he could feed them to Maria's chickens.

"Wonderful. You go wash up." She gave his arm a little pat.

That small touch felt like rocket fuel through his body. How long had it been since a young, pretty woman had touched him? How long since someone had been thoughtful enough to make him lunch? Maria had, of course, but it was Maria's job to look after the ranch hands. No one ever did things for him just because.

It was humbling, and it was appreciated, and he was going to eat every damn disgusting pancake she put on his plate. So Eli went and washed his hands and then returned to the kitchen, sitting at the table. As he did, he saw her list.

1. *What kind of car was she driving when he found her?*
2. *Did he know where she was going?*
3. *Who else lives here?*
4. *Can she decorate for Christmas?*
5. *Can she help out with any chores?*

Next to number five, she'd scratched out *Is he married?* He looked over at her in surprise, but she wasn't facing his direction, concentrating on beating eggs into the pancake batter. "I'm not married," he blurted out.

"What?" Cass turned around, a big yellow bowl clutched in her hands. She was getting batter all over his shirt, he noticed, but it was kind of cute.

He tapped a finger on her list. "You wondered if I was married. I'm not."

Her face turned bright red. "Oh. Uh. That was just me being nosy. I'm sorry. I crossed it out." Her voice held a hint of panic. "It's none of my business."

Seeing her get all flustered like that felt . . . good. He didn't know why, because it shouldn't matter. But it did matter to him for some crazy reason. "Never been married," he admitted. "Most women aren't big fans of the ranch life. Too much work and not enough reward."

"Oh." She leaned over the batter, stirring it slowly. "Is that how you feel, too? That there's not enough reward?"

"I think it's in some people's blood," Eli admitted, though saying how he felt wasn't something he was comfortable doing. Not many people asked cowboys why they did what they did. You either were a cowboy or you weren't. No analyzing to it. "I came out here one summer because I needed a job, and never went back."

"You're lucky you found your calling," Cass told him. "Some people never do."

"You find yours?"

"I have no idea," she said with a chuckle.

He felt stupid. Of course she didn't know. She'd lost her memories. "How's your head doing?"

"It feels like it was split open and someone stuffed what was left of my brain back in there." She smiled over her shoulder as she poured batter onto a hot skillet. "But it's better than it was earlier, so I'm hopeful that something will jog loose at some point."

"I'll get you some more aspirin," he told her, and then they fell into an easy silence while she cooked. It was interesting, how nice it was to just be in the same room with her and not feel like he had to make conversation. He was prone to silences on the best of days, and around strangers, he wasn't much of a talker. But she wasn't demanding, and that was good.

He did keep thinking about that note she'd written down, though. She'd wondered if he was married. Heck, he wondered if she was married, too.

Eventually, two of the pancakes were ready and she gave him both and a few pieces of cold, too-crispy bacon, and then sat across from him with a hopeful expression.

Swallowing hard, Eli wondered if it was too late to escape back to the barn. All three dogs were watching him with interest, just waiting for their chance at scraps. He decided to avoid the bacon and go straight for a pancake. It cut all right, and he put a piece into his mouth. Rubbery, chewy, and tasted like eggs and salt. "S'good. Thank you."

The smile that lit up her face took his breath away. Didn't matter that her nose was swollen and both of her eyes were shadowed in huge bruises.

She was beautiful.

He forced himself to eat bite after bite, watching her as she got up and returned to the stove to cook more of the pancakes. She slipped the dogs a few more bites of bacon, and he probably should have told her not to, but he didn't have the heart. It was clear she loved the dogs almost as much as he did, and it was nice to see. Besides, the dogs worked hard. They could have a little bacon now and then. He methodically ate as she flipped more pancakes, thinking about what he needed to get done that day. There were saddles to be repaired, and he had to muck out the horse stables and spread fresh hay, and repair the spooler that spread the hay for the cattle. Usually it didn't matter that there were a million small chores that mounted on the ranch every day, because he had help. When the other hands were gone, it didn't matter if he was the only one here because he'd just buckle down and get everything done.

But having Cass here threw a wrench into things. He was torn between wanting to take care of her and keep her company, and the things he needed to get done around the ranch. It felt wrong to leave her alone for long periods of time, knowing that she had a head injury . . . but the cattle couldn't wait for her head to heal. They needed tending every day, along with all the other animals on the ranch.

She was fine, he told himself, chewing through another rubbery bite of pancake. She'd understand that he needed to work. That he couldn't stop the entire ranch just to tend to her. She hadn't even asked that, so he had no idea why the thought was in his head.

Cass sat down across from him with her own stack of pancakes, took one bite, and then gave him a horrified look. "You are such a liar. These are terrible!"

"Yeah, they are. But you worked hard on 'em," he told her, and ate another bite, just because.

CHAPTER NINE

After lunch, he checked her head and her pupils again, just to make sure that everything looked okay. Her face was more swollen today than yesterday, but she seemed more alert, so he took that as a good sign. He was putting his coat back on to go out to the herd again when the phone rang.

Cass gave it a worried look and then turned to him. "Should I answer that?"

"Nah, I'll get it." It was probably Doc again. No one else would be calling the ranch because they knew he was the only one here. He moved to the phone and picked it up. "Hello?"

"Feliz Navidad, mijo!" Maria called out cheerfully to him. In the background, he could hear music playing and the sound of one of her children chattering up a storm. "Well, almost. Close enough. How are you holding up? I heard the storm was pretty bad. Did you see the fudge I left for you?"

"I did, and yes, and fine."

She laughed, then clucked her tongue at him through the phone. "So talkative. How are you holding up by yourself? Are you lonely?"

There was a knowing note in her voice that made him scowl. Doc had gotten to her. He was a good vet, but damn if the man wasn't a terrible gossip. "Doc called you, I take it."

"He did," she gushed, as if she couldn't keep the news to herself. "He told me that you rescued a pretty woman and pulled her from her car and now she's sleeping in your bed and she doesn't remember who she is. What does she look like? Do you like her? Is she young? Pretty? You have to tell me the details, mijo."

He pinched the bridge of his nose. Of course Doc would make it sound like a hookup. His imagination was probably running away with him over on the other side of the mountain, from all the "excitement" of the mystery woman. "It's fine." He watched as Cass left the kitchen, heading down the hall toward the laundry room. He lowered his voice so she wouldn't hear him talking about her. "Her name's Cass and she hurt her head. When the pass clears, she'll be on her way. Nothing to any of it."

Maria made a noise of disbelief. "Nothing to it! You are the loneliest cowboy I have ever met and now you're stuck with a woman for the next few weeks? I can't decide if you're going to kick her off the mountain or marry her. This is you we're talking about, after all. You haven't told me if she's pretty yet."

"Yeah," he said after a moment's thought. Cass had lovely dark hair; big, soulful eyes; and a happy smile. He hadn't paid too much attention to her figure but what he'd felt through his shirt when he put his arm around her waist felt . . . mighty nice. "But that doesn't matter. She's just staying until she feels better—"

"Oooh, mijo!" Maria's voice was getting a squealy note of excitement in it. "You need a girlfriend! Maybe she'll want to stick around after the snow's gone, date herself a nice handsome cowboy—"

"You're reading too much into this, Maria," he warned her. It was gonna be bad enough when they returned and would give him crap about being up here alone with Cass. He didn't need it over the phone, too. He didn't blame Maria, though. She treated everyone at the ranch like they were her children, even Old Clyde. To distract her, he changed topics. "How are your girls?"

Maria made an exclamation in her throat. "Ay, pobrecita. My youngest is pregnant again. With twins this time. She has been puking all day long. I've been cooking all kinds of things for her to eat but she's still too skinny." She tsked again. "It's a good thing her mama's here to fatten her up. Now, did you eat the fudge I left out for you?"

He chuckled. "I haven't yet, but I will."

"I made treats for your little Francesca, too."

"That's because you're the best," he told her, and he could hear her pleased laugh through the phone.

"It's important to feed the babies when they're in the belly," she told him, and then began to talk about how her son was working until the day before Christmas so she was watching his children and how her daughters were helping them make a gingerbread house, but he wasn't really listening. Cass had wandered back in, holding a sweater in her hands, and had a fierce frown on her face. At least, he thought it was a sweater. She picked a dryer sheet off of it and then held it out to him in disbelief.

It was the black sweater she'd worn when he'd pulled her out of the car, except now it was the size of a doll's sweater. Uh-oh. He was guessing that "laundry" was probably on the list of skills that Cass wasn't great at. He did his best not to laugh, but a chuckle still came out.

Cass bit her lip and snort-giggled, too, shaking her head at the sweater. She bent down to Jim's side and held it up to him, as if it might fit the heeler instead of her. And that made him laugh all over again.

"Uh-oh, sounds like I'm interrupting," Maria told him, her tone all gleefulness. "I'll let you go, mijo. I just wanted to check on you. If there's anything you need or if you have questions, you call me, all right? I'm not there, but I know where everything is, including the condoms."

He felt his face go bright red. The words choked out of him. "Uh . . ."

"Main bathroom, under the sink, behind the extra rolls of toilet paper. I'm not saying, I'm just saying. Now, I have to go. I think my poor mija's going to throw up again. Merry Christmas, and I'll call you soon!"

"You too," he said blankly, still a little shocked by the turn that the conversation took. "I, uh, I've got to cake the cows. Talk soon." His ears felt like they were burning as he hung up the phone. Did Maria and Doc really think he was going to sleep with Cass just because they were trapped up here together?

Damn, he really wasn't going to hear the end of it when the others returned.

Cass gave him a curious look as she stood up. "Everything okay?"

"That was just Maria, the housekeeper. She runs things around here and wanted to check on me. Doc told her you were here."

Her eyes widened. "I hope I'm not going to get you in trouble."

"Not at all. Anyone that's driven these roads knows what they're like in winter." He nodded at the sweater. "Problem with the dryer?"

She grimaced and held it up to her body, and he mentally congratulated himself on changing the subject so easily. "I think I should have read the tag. It says 'dry clean only.' I hope you don't mind if I wear your shirt for a little longer. Unless I can wear something of Maria's? Or we can get my bag from the car?"

He shook his head at her. "Like I said earlier, it's still too hard on the horses in this weather. We'll go in a few days when the sun comes out and things start to melt. Until then, you're welcome to wear my stuff."

"I'm sorry to be such a bother." She chewed on her lip. "Do you really feed the cows cake?"

"What?"

"You said you have to cake the cows. Like . . . birthday cake?"

A laugh snorted out of him. "Not exactly. We call it cake but it's more like feed pellets. They're these big chunks of hard food that have additional protein and vitamins, since they eat hay most of the time. In the cold you have to feed the cattle more. Digesting helps keep them warm."

"I didn't know that," she admitted, and sounded impressed. "I had this mental image of you feeding cows slices of cake and I figured that couldn't be right."

"Nope. But that's why I've got to go out and feed them so much during this weather. Normally they range out in the further fields, but since it's just me, we've got to keep them all close nearby so I can make sure they're fed."

"And you also have to babysit me. I'm sorry I'm such a

bother." Cass wrapped her arms around her torso and gave him a worried look. "Can I help out? I'd like to."

He shook his head. The call with Maria—and now this— just reminded him that work on the ranch didn't stop, even when the schedule was a bit thrown off. "No. Doc said you need to take it easy. He'd kill me if he found out I was putting you to work on the ranch."

"He doesn't have to know," she told him brightly. "Please. I won't be in the way."

Eli shook his head again. "Sorry. I'll be back later. Just take a nap or something."

She sighed heavily, and he tried not to let that affect him. He couldn't entertain her and keep on everything that needed to be done at the ranch. The sooner she came to realize that, the better.

CHAPTER TEN

Having a head injury was incredibly boring, Cass decided.

She napped. Again. Of course she did. There was nothing to do but nap. Oh sure, she cleaned up the kitchen and flipped through recipe books to see what she could make. She washed the shirt she borrowed. She made Eli's bed. And she napped again. Every so often, she'd go to the windows and look outside at the endless white snow. There were cattle up on the hill, and she'd see Eli on horseback, riding around them, or driving a tractor-looking thing that dragged hay behind it. She'd see the other dogs racing around with him, while she and Frannie sat inside and were bored to death. The dog seemed equally miserable, hovering near the doorway and whining whenever she'd see Eli in the window.

Me too, girl, she thought absently. Not that she wanted to be out in the snow. She just wanted to be doing something.

She couldn't read, so the cookbooks didn't stay out for long. Couldn't watch TV. She just mostly stared out at the snow coating the trees and wondered why Eli wasn't decorating for Christmas.

Maybe she could do that for him. Maybe she could make this place as welcoming and Christmassy as she wanted, as a way of saying thank you to him for saving her.

Then maybe, with something to do, she wouldn't be here slowly dying of inactivity. *Here lies Cass*, she thought dramatically. *The endless boredom did what the snow couldn't.* She turned to Frannie and told her, "Feel free to say something at any time."

Frannie didn't, of course.

The sun went down, and Cass heated up some of the chili she found in the fridge, and left it warm for when Eli returned. He'd been gone all day, and while she understood it, it didn't make it easier for her. What did she normally do when she was bored? she wondered. Crossword puzzles? Phone games? Facebook? Sewing?

She doubted it was something with her hands. Her cooking skills hadn't seemed up to par, so it was probably more like Facebook. Still, even as she gazed out the now-dark window onto the moonlit snow, it seemed like a frivolous way to spend time. Eli was out there killing himself from sunup to sundown and she wanted to help.

If she had something to do, maybe she wouldn't worry so much about the gaps in her memory. All she could think about right now was if someone else was out there wondering if she was okay. If they were worried sick.

If she had a boyfriend and he looked anything like Eli. What if she was dating someone that was awful and, when she got her memory back, she compared him to Eli? How could anyone possibly measure up after she'd been rescued by the world's most handsome cowboy?

As if he could hear her thoughts, Eli came in from the mudroom, and she blushed, getting to her feet. "Hi," she told him breathlessly, running her fingers through her hair. Then she stopped herself, because lord, this wasn't a date. He was coming home after a long day of work. He didn't have time for her.

But he nodded politely and rubbed the back of one hand across his brow. His cowboy hat was gone and she could see that his hair was sweaty despite the deep blanket of snow outside. "I need to shower before I'm fit company."

"Is there anything I can do to help?" she blurted out.

He paused, and she could have sworn he turned as red as she was.

"I mean, like, around the house. Or, um, with the cows. Not in the shower. I'm sure you can do that just fine." Ugh, why wouldn't her face shut up?

"You don't need to do anything but rest," he reassured her, and then disappeared into his room. Her room. The room they were sharing . . . one at a time anyhow. He'd be getting naked and stepping into the shower right about now and she wondered if he was that tanned all over and—

Stop it, she chided herself. *He rescued you just to be nice! It's clear you're nothing but a bother.*

Maybe she was obsessing over Eli because she didn't have anything else to do. That had to be it.

All right. She officially needed to keep herself busy or she was going to go stir-crazy. She thought about doing more cooking, but she'd wasted so much food earlier with her botched pancakes that she worried about ruining more. She paced through the house, looking for ideas. There was a rag rug by the front door, and she wondered if she knew how to make one of those. Probably not, she decided as she gazed down at it. It looked rather crafty, and it didn't seem like it'd be something she was good at. She moved around the living room, putting another log into the woodstove, before pausing by the laundry room again.

Not because she wanted to do laundry—she could, of course, if there was more laundry to do—but because all those boxes of Christmas ornaments were there.

Decorating was something she could do that wouldn't tax her physically, and wouldn't be a strain on her brain. It'd be fun, and after all, it was almost Christmas. They could use a bit of Christmas spirit around here. It was strange to see no decorations and the endless sea of snow outside. It didn't make sense. She had the white Christmas part. Now she needed the rest of it.

A tree.

Garlands.

Wreaths. Ornaments. Snowman cookies. Christmas carols. Holly.

Mistletoe, her traitor brain whispered, and she mentally steered away from that thought. Eggnog, if she could find a recipe for eggnog.

Well, maybe not eggnog. But surely they could still celebrate Christmas a little.

Eli emerged from his room a few minutes later, his wet hair newly slicked back and combed. He wore a plain white T-shirt over jeans, and droplets of water sprinkled his shoulders as he padded into the kitchen. "You hungry?"

She stared at his behind as he walked past. Just dressed like that, he looked good enough to eat.

Good lord, what was wrong with her? Had the knock on the head set her libido on fire? Did she have a savior complex? Or was it because Eli was just that handsome? She studied his backside, trying to be unbiased about it. As butts went, it was a nice one. Small and taut and with just enough of a muscular bubble to fill out his jeans—

"Cass?"

"Hm?" She blinked and got to her feet.

"Hungry?" He turned and glanced over at her.

"I already ate. There's chili warming on the stove. I hope that's okay."

"Totally fine." He shoveled a huge amount into a bowl and then loped over to the table, sitting down.

She sat across from him and folded her hands. "Can I help you on the ranch?"

"No," he said between mouthfuls.

"Then can I decorate for Christmas?"

Eli paused midbite and gazed at her for a long moment. She mentally panicked, wondering if she'd touched a nerve. Was there a reason why he didn't celebrate Christmas? Something about the holiday he didn't like? Or was it against his religion?

"Why?" he finally asked.

Why? Why did anyone want to celebrate the season? "Because we're here and it's Christmas? Because it'll give me something to do? Because you won't let me go outside to help you with the farm?"

"Ranch," he said between bites. "It's a ranch, not a farm. And if you want to put some holiday crap up around this place, I won't stop you."

Well, that was a win . . . theoretically. She smiled brightly at him. "Thank you. So where do we get a tree?"

He swallowed and looked up from his bowl. "Tree?"

"Christmas tree? You don't know what a Christmas tree is?"

"I know what a tree is." He scowled at her. "Just seems like a lot of hassle. Can't you just decorate the tables or something?" He waved his spoon at the kitchen.

"No. That's not how it works."

He looked at her like she'd just grown a second head. Maybe he just expected her to cave to whatever he said, since she was his guest. But she was also bored and cranky, and her head hurt. If she was going to be here until the snow melted—which looked like a while, if the windows were any sort of indication—she needed something to do, damn it.

And decorating for Christmas without a tree was . . . silly.

"Did you just say no?"

"I *did* just say no." She gave a little grin, because he looked so incredulous. Was he never contradicted, this hard-edged, handsome cowboy? If so, it just made her want to push back against what he said all the more. Just for fun. Just to alleviate her boredom.

Just because it pricked at him, and she was curious about him.

Eli took another slow bite of his chili, as if thinking—or trying to figure her out. He swallowed and she started to grow impatient as he took another mouthful. Was he going to ignore her, then? That might be worse than having nothing to do at all. Nothing to do *and* no conversation seemed like hell.

But eventually he looked up from his bowl and met her eyes. "If you want to help out, you can get eggs from the chickens every morning and feed them."

Cass wasn't sure if she was excited or disappointed in his answer. It was something to do, at least, but it also didn't sound like something that would take much time. And he didn't answer her about the decorating. "So no tree?"

He leaned back and sighed. "If you're determined to re-decorate the place just to take it all back down again in a couple weeks, fine. I'll take you out when your head's better and we'll get you a tree, all right?"

She'd won! Well, not that it was a contest, but she felt like she'd won some sort of prize. Excitement bubbled through her and she bit her lip. Without realizing what she was do-ing, she reached across the table to squeeze his hand with excitement.

That small touch made everything in the world stop for a moment. Skin-on-skin contact was . . . different than just co-existing in the same space together. It changed things, be-cause even though she pulled away immediately, she couldn't stop thinking about how warm his hand was under hers, or how rough with calluses it was. How firm and strong.

And how just that small touch made her entire body prickle with awareness of him.

It was clear that he was caught off guard, too. He grew still and just stared at her with those intense gray eyes of his.

"When your head's better," he repeated, and then got up and took his bowl to the sink, and the moment was gone.

CHAPTER ELEVEN

E li lay on the couch the next morning, his hand under his head, staring up at the ceiling in the quiet moments before dawn. There was no rooster crow yet, so it wasn't quite time to get up and start the day. Didn't mean he could sleep, though. He was too busy with his head full of clutter, and most of that clutter was centered on the woman down the hall, sleeping in his bed. In his shirt.

It was hard not to have thoughts about her. Hard not to think about her soft skin brushing against his.

Everything was hard, and in completely inappropriate ways.

She was a guest, though. Injured. Helpless. Couldn't remember much about herself. He had no business thinking those kinds of things about her. Thinking about if her breasts had pink tips or if the skin in the valley between them was as soft as the rest of her . . .

Completely inappropriate. But Eli's mind kept straying back to it no matter what he did.

He needed to get over it. She wasn't a woman for him to moon after. She needed to feel safe and secure here, and if he flung himself at her, she'd be terrified. Also, he didn't want her to think she had to "repay" him for her rescue. The thought made him sick. He had to be very careful with this situation. He tried to put himself in her shoes and vowed that, whatever happened, he wasn't going to do anything to make her feel uncomfortable.

No matter how pretty he might think she was, especially when she moved. Yesterday, he'd found himself fascinated by the simple act of her tucking her dark hair behind one ear. Funny how such a small thing could set his imagination on fire like that.

He'd never been like this around women before. He'd seen plenty of pretty ones and had gone out on dates with several, but there was something about Cass that drew him. She was lovely, sure. But she was also strong and determined despite her vulnerability and the odd situation she was in. He'd expected her to cry and mope about her problems and her injuries, and instead she was restless and bored and trying to help out. She didn't like being idle, and that was something he admired.

Sure, she was terrible in everything she tried to help with, but the attempts counted for a lot in his book.

Of course, her big blue eyes and vulnerability didn't help things. But he told himself that the appeal wasn't that she was vulnerable—it was that she was strong and determined despite it. He'd give her something to do, and then he'd do his best to keep his distance from her so he didn't make her nervous.

A woman alone on a mountain with a strange man would be anxious no matter what he did, so he had to play this delicately and, above all, treat her with respect.

Respect, he reminded his aching cock, and adjusted himself surreptitiously under the blankets. Lying on the sofa in the living room was definitely not an appropriate place to get hard at the thought of the woman sleeping in his bed. He doubted there was an appropriate place, but it sure wasn't here, not when she could walk out at any moment.

As if she could sense his thoughts, he heard the door to his room open and footsteps on the creaking floorboards in the hall. Was she sleepwalking? Hurt? Eli sat up on the couch, concerned. "Cass?"

A jaw-breaking yawn met his ears a moment before she emerged from the shadows, rubbing her eyes. She wore one of his shirts again, this time knotted at the waist, and her legs were clad in jeans. "I'm up," she mumbled at him, even though she looked as if she could use a cup of coffee or six. "Don't go without me."

"Go where?" The only place she looked like she needed to go was back to bed.

She blinked at him. "To feed the chickens and get a Christmas tree, of course." Then she padded into the kitchen, flicking on lights. He could hear the smack of the coffeepot as she set it on the burner.

Slowly, he got out of bed—well, the couch, really—and rubbed the sore spots on his back, because the damned thing was too short for him and made his body crick up something fierce. He pulled on a pair of jeans over his boxers—because he hadn't expected her to emerge from bed for hours yet, and so there'd been no need to sleep fully dressed—and then wandered into the kitchen.

"How come you're up so early?" he asked as he walked in, noticing that she'd pulled her long, curly hair into two tails that sat atop her shoulders like puffballs. It was damned adorable, and he forced himself to stop looking at it, because that way lay madness. "Thought you'd be asleep for hours yet."

"Hours?" she asked, tossing scoops of coffee grounds into the percolator. "Really?"

"At least until noon," he teased. "You know what you're doing with that coffee pot?"

"Nope," she said. "But I figure if I throw in enough grounds it'll make something caffeinated." She gave a little chuckle that made him glad he'd put his jeans on, so she couldn't see how just that soft, throaty sound affected him. "I wanted to wake up early. We've got a lot to do."

"We do, huh?"

"Yup. You have just acquired the world's best chicken wrangler," she told him with a lofty tone, and then added, "after a little on-the-job training, of course."

"Chicken wrangling? Sounds dangerous." Damn, but she was fun to tease.

"Highly," Cass assured him with a nod. "Lots of pecking for the inexperienced."

Well, she wasn't wrong there. "Sounds like you've got a full day ahead of you."

She cast him a flirty look over her shoulder. "After all the chickens have been wrangled into giving up their goodies, it's tree time."

She wasn't going to let him forget about that tree, was she? "That today?" he drawled. "Thought we'd wait until your head was better. Ribs, too."

"I'm totally fine," she quickly said and patted her side. "What do you want for breakfast?"

Nice try, he thought to himself. She was speedy to change the subject, that was for sure. "I'll be the judge of whether or not you're fine. Let me see your face."

Cass turned toward him with an exasperated expression,

but did as she was told. She turned her face up toward his, and for a moment, he was caught in her deep blue gaze and saw nothing but those big eyes, and his pulse raced just a little more than it should have. It was nothing, he reminded himself. She was just vulnerable and his brain was trying to squeeze her into a damsel-in-distress role. Still, he didn't have to touch her face as he examined her, but he did. Just because he could. He cupped a hand under her chin and stared down at her features. The bruises on her forehead were mighty hideous, but the swelling had gone down, and they were turning greenish and purple, a sign that things were healing. Same for her nose—it was now half the size it was yesterday and her eyes had the shadowy discolorations, but they were fading, too. In another day or two, she'd look normal again.

In another day or two, she'd be so damn pretty he wouldn't know what to do with himself. Because right now, despite her swollen features and bruises, she was far too tempting. When she was free of all of those? She'd be a heartbreaker.

Part of him hoped that snow melted soon so he could send her on her way. Of course, the other part of him didn't want that at all. He wanted her to stay forever. But that never happened. Women didn't much care for the ranch life, and he'd seen the other cowboys get their hearts broken a dozen times over when their girlfriends wanted them to leave their jobs to "settle down," or they just up and left the guy for some city fool with a fat wallet and a gray suit. He'd learned his lesson long ago, and Cass would be no different, despite her soulful eyes and cheery attitude.

"Face seems to be okay," he said after a moment.

An impish smile curved her mouth. "Well if that isn't damning a girl with faint praise."

His ears grew hot. "You know what I meant."

"I do. I was just teasing. But as you can see, everything's healing up all right, except for the big hole in my memory." She grimaced and stepped back, just enough to leave his grasp.

"Mm. No changes on that front?"

"None. I don't even remember my last name." Cass chewed on her lip and stared at the coffeepot. "This thing starts to percolate soon, right?"

"Soon as you turn on the burner, yeah."

"I knew that." She quickly switched it on and gave him a sideways look. "I'm fine, Eli. Don't worry about me."

"Ribs," was all he said.

"Huh?"

He flicked a finger at her, indicating she should approach. "Let me see your ribs and I'll tell you if you're fine or not."

A bright splash of color appeared on her cheeks and she put a hand to her waist. "You don't have to look."

"I'm the only person on this side of the damned mountain, Cass. If it looks bad, I need to find a way to get you over to Doc Parsons. Now lift your shirt up."

"You're a jerk," she muttered to him, but she did as she was told. Cass undid the knot at her waist and then hiked up her shirt to just under her breasts, displaying a pale stomach mottled with bruises.

He got down on his knees to get a better glimpse, aware that this was an uncomfortably intimate moment for both of them. She seemed restless and shifty, which he supposed wasn't a bad thing. After all, if she was that twitchy, her ribs probably weren't broken or she'd be in agony. Eli put a hand on her side—the uninjured one—to make her stand still, and at that small touch, she froze in place. Good. "I'm just looking," he murmured so she wouldn't feel alarmed.

"I know," she whispered.

Seemed she felt as rattled as he did. He was close enough to breathe on her skin, to kiss the small freckle near her navel that he wasn't supposed to be paying attention to. He was supposed to be looking at her waist, but all he saw was soft, soft skin that was begging to be kissed. Damn it. He clenched his jaw to clear his mind and tried to focus. Skimming his fingers over the worst of the bruises, he was glad when she didn't even suck in a breath in pain. Her ribs looked lined up nice and proper, though it was hard to tell. "Any of this hurt when you move?"

"No. It's fine, really."

"No pains when you breathe?" He was not going to look up, not where the shirt rested just under the swells of her breasts. He would not.

"Nope."

"How's the bruising on your upper chest?"

The shirt immediately came down with a yank, and Eli stared at the checkered pattern of it instead of her skin. "I'm not showing you my boobs!" Her voice was indignant and more than slightly nervous.

"That wasn't what I asked." Now he was the one who blushed. "I just wanted to know if the bruising was okay there, and if the swelling had gone down. You hit the steering wheel and airbag pretty hard."

"It's all fine. Can we just have breakfast now?"

Eli got to his feet again. "That we can."

They ate a breakfast of oatmeal, and then Eli cooked more in a pan, which obviously mystified Cass, especially when he said it was for the chickens. He pulled it off the heat to cool, and then it was a process to show Cass how to bundle up for the weather. He doubted she'd be familiar with the idea of bundling up if she wasn't from around here, but the truth was that it was bitterly cold outside, below zero and so frigid that his breath felt like it froze in his lungs . . . and he was used to it. The snow and overcast sky made it worse. He thought again about telling her no, that she should stay indoors where it was warm and safe, and glanced over at her. She was practically dancing in place with enthusiasm at getting to feed the chickens, of all things.

He didn't have the heart to take that from her.

So he took her in the mudroom and showed her how to bundle up. To put on two pairs of wool socks and then a heavy pair of borrowed boots to protect her feet from the snow that she'd have to trudge through. Since he doubted she was wearing warm flannels under those rather tight jeans of hers, he made her put on Old Clyde's bright orange insulated jumper that they always teased him for wearing. After that came a thick overcoat, a scarf, a hat with flaps, and gloves. She meekly submitted to all of the dressing, and when they were done, she clapped her gloved hands like a child about to go sledding. "Can we go now?"

"Give me five," he told her, and then bundled up himself. By the time he was dressed, she was at the window to the mudroom, staring outside at the early dawn snow. She looked excited.

Excited to do ranch chores. Either she really, truly was bored or she'd hit her head harder than he thought. He pulled on his gloves and gave her another stern look. "You sure you're feeling up to this?"

"I'm sure." She pressed her gloved hands together and beamed at him. "I'm going to be so much help, wait and see."

Somehow he doubted that. Still, if she wanted to help, he'd take an extra pair of hands. "If you start to feel weak or slow, you tell me. All right? The last thing I need is you passing out."

She just smiled at him. "You're so stern and protective. That's cute."

Eli grunted at her, though he could feel his ears getting hot again under his cowboy hat. He'd see how she handled the chickens and judge how much help she'd be beyond that. Even if she wanted to help him—and he needed the help just to keep on top of things—he had nightmares of her walking behind one of the cattle and getting kicked.

Chickens were safe. He'd let her do them. Nothing else. Not until she showed she could handle it. She might be eager, but it didn't make her a rancher at heart. Hell, he wasn't even sure if she was a cook at heart. He had to constantly step in and retrieve the food before she burned it, because she didn't seem to pay much attention to what was on the stove burners.

But when she looked up at him with those big, expressive eyes, he couldn't say no to her.

Chickens it was. "Grab that oatmeal and let's go."

CHAPTER TWELVE

Not only were chickens assholes, they were also a lot of work.

Cass was surprised at just how much went into caring for a bunch of (literally) stinking chickens. It was so bitterly cold outside that she was shocked that her fingers didn't turn to Popsicles, and it turned out she was going to have to go outside multiple times to tend to the chickens. Cass had thought that feeding the chickens would mean laying down some seed for a handful of well-fed birds, picking up a few eggs, and then heading back into the house, smug at how much she'd contributed.

Ha.

Ha ha.

The chicken run had to be prepped before the birds could even go inside out of the cold. Because there was snow on the ground, Eli shoveled the worst of it out of the chicken run, and then they had to lay down hay so the chickens' feet wouldn't freeze. Not only were there at least twenty chickens, but they were all stupid. The moment she entered the henhouse with Eli, the birds poured out the front as if it wasn't a jillion degrees below zero outside. Eli fed them inside the henhouse, and then they all climbed back inside. The hay stank of chicken poop, and Eli told her that it had to be changed every other week, and he'd spare her that for now. As it was, feeding the chickens was going to be enough for her. They got warm oatmeal in the morning, he told her, feed pellets after lunch, and then cracked corn before dusk to keep their digestion going so they'd stay warm through the bitter night. It also seemed that chickens didn't lay much in the winter, so she had to check the henhouse for stray eggs, and then add more hay if needed. She had to give them warm water because it would freeze over otherwise. She had to check their feet and combs to make sure they didn't have frostbite, and if they did, she'd somehow have to wrestle them down so she could tend to it with a salve. She had to be on the lookout for signs of foxes or predators somehow getting into the coop, and if so, she'd have to stuff the hole and alert him immediately so the birds could be saved. A hole could appear overnight, so she had to be vigilant—all the while doing her best not to step on the birds that wandered underfoot, clucking and flapping their wings as if they didn't have a care in the world other than when dinner would be served.

It was a lot to do for a bunch of stinky birds that only laid one egg overnight. Not one each. One total.

Of course, she didn't share these complaints with Eli. She'd begged him to give her something to do and he had, so she was going to do it, damn it. So she brought warm water from the barn—not too hot, because the chickens wouldn't drink it hot—and slopped it into the water trough. She spread oatmeal in the food trough while they pecked at her hands in their eagerness to get their food. She spread hay. She listened as Eli showed her where the rest of the feed was and the times to get it.

She let the chickens out in the run, but only for a short time because it was too cold for them, despite the fact that the run was along the barn and sheltered from the worst of the wind. So she supervised the chickens even though she didn't have to, standing out in the cold while Eli began his work in the barn. Frannie stood at her side, wagging her tail and looking completely unconcerned by the bitter chill even as Cass hopped in place and wished the chickens would go back inside. If they wandered back in, she could justify shutting them back into the coop. Maybe she was doing this chicken thing all wrong, but it was important that she get this right.

She didn't want to let Eli down.

She wandered to the front of the barn, where Eli was giving horses fresh water and feed. He'd told her earlier that after the barn was tended, he'd have to give the cattle out in the pasture their first round of food, then let the horses out for a while so he could muck out the stalls and add fresh hay and sawdust. Then he'd have to let them back in and feed the cattle again, and then he listed an even longer litany of chores that stacked up and had to be done, to the point that her eyes were glazing over.

"How do you get anything done around here?" she called out to him, tucking her hands under her arms. If he was half as cold as she was, he ignored it. Jim and Bandit wandered up and down the long alley of the barn, wagging their tails, while Frannie stayed parked at Cass's side, as if she was a puppy that needed watching.

"You do what you can," he told her with a slight shrug of his shoulders, reaching up to pat a horse's white muzzle before moving down to the next stall. "There's always more to be done. Certain things have to happen—like feeding and tending to the animals—and other things you just get to when you can."

"I guess this is why you don't get time off for the holidays."

"Nope," he drawled, dumping feed into a horse's trough. She watched as the horse's head immediately dipped to start eating, and he gave it a rub and then moved down to the next stall. "The animals don't care if it's Christmas or not. All they care about is their hungry bellies."

"Well, I'm not going to tell you how to do your job," she teased, bending down to rub Frannie's fluffy head. "But this beggar should probably be fed a little less. She looks like a big furry sausage."

He gave her the most incredulous look that she wondered for a moment if she'd said something wrong. Then a slow grin spread over his face, and it did something a little crazy to her insides. "You do realize she's pregnant, right?"

Cass blinked. "She is?"

"That's why she's sticking with you in the house and not going out in the field with me. She's gonna give birth any day now."

"Oh my goodness, Frannie!" Cass sweetened her voice as she rubbed the dog's ears. "What a good girl you are!"

Frannie just thumped that white tail, excited.

Eli didn't say anything, but she could have sworn he was pleased with her affection toward the dog. He ran hot water for a time, filling up buckets, and then moved back out to the stalls while she petted Frannie and checked on the dumb chickens that pecked at the hay in the run and puffed up their feathers against the cold. Jim and Bandit saw the attention Frannie was getting, and then Cass was surrounded by all three dogs, doing her best to equally pet the needy, adorable heads.

After a time, Eli spoke, glancing over at her as he took his empty bucket back to the sink. "Thought you said you hated animals."

"No, I said I couldn't have them. Someone's allergic." She thought for a moment, but no one's face swam to mind. "It's not me . . . but someone."

"Sister? Brother?"

Cass shook her head. "I don't think I have those."

"Me either."

"No? Is that why you don't mind being up here alone for Christmas when everyone else is with family? What about your parents? Are they alive?"

Instead of answering, he nodded at the chicken run. "You should go ahead and put them back inside. If they won't come in, give 'em a handful of feed to lead them back. You can let them out again when it's lunchtime."

"All right." Cass got to her feet, wondering at the abrupt change of subject. Perhaps she'd prodded a bit too much. Gotten too friendly, when it was clear she was just another ranch chore to be looked after. To Eli, she was another cow, another chicken, another horse—heck, another dog— to feed.

The thought was a depressing one.

The chickens were put back into the warm coop after a brief bout of freedom, and then Eli told her that he needed to feed the cattle and she should head inside. They'd get the tree later.

Cass wondered if they were going to get a tree at all, and she felt a little guilty for even asking about it. Today was the first day she'd seen how much Eli did around the ranch, and it was intimidating to realize that he never stopped moving, and that there were always more chores to be done.

Since she didn't want to be underfoot, she went inside with Frannie, who hung out near her legs, watching her and making Cass feel even more helpless because the dog was so attentive. She rubbed the furry white head as she stared out the window, watching Eli as he worked. He was a distant dark speck in the pastures, moving among the cattle and then taking a tractor-looking contraption out and bringing bale after bale of hay into the field. It began to snow again, big fat flakes that drifted onto the already thickly blanketed snow on the ground. With every flake that fell, she knew it was going to be that much longer for her to go back home.

Wherever home was.

For now, it was this ranch, and so she needed to not be a burden. Cass found an absolute crap-ton of eggs in the ranch's large walk-in freezer in the basement, which explained why the chickens weren't laying in winter, she supposed. They laid like fiends during the summer months. She moved some of the eggs to the fridge and then made egg salad sandwiches. For some reason, she knew how to make egg salad, so she guessed she wasn't totally vegan. She made extra sandwiches and put them in the fridge, propped up a note on the table to let Eli know, then bundled up and went out to give the chickens round two of their food.

By the time that was done, she was tired and her head throbbed. There was an old stereo with a CD player, and she found a bunch of classical music and a copy of *The Nutcracker,* so she put it on. Time to Christmas this place up. But by the time she pulled out a few neatly organized boxes of Christmas decorations and moved them into the living room, Eli's pillow and blanket on the sofa were too much to resist.

"Just a quick nap," she told Frannie with a yawn. "Recharge my energy and then go out and feed the chickens. Again."

Frannie just wagged her tail.

"Right. Sounds good to me, too." She patted the sofa, because if she squeezed up against the back of the couch, there'd be room for her and the dog both, and cuddle-company sounded nice. The dog hesitated long enough to make Cass wonder if Frannie wasn't allowed on the sofa, but then she jumped up and lay down next to her, and it was so nice and snuggly that she didn't care. Pregnant mamas needed naps, too. Cass sighed and closed her eyes, resting her head against the pillow.

She'd just rest for a minute. That was all. The "Dance of the Sugar Plum Fairy" swirled around her, and Frannie laid her head against Cass's arm, and she dozed off.

A crash woke her up.

Cass jerked awake even as Frannie scrambled off the couch. She rubbed her eyes, squinting at the large window in the living room. It was nearly dark outside, the snow a purplish blanket on the ground. Oh no. She'd slept for longer than she thought. "The chickens," she murmured aloud to herself, flinging the blankets aside and sliding her legs over the side of the couch. It was dark inside, and she hadn't fed the woodstove, so it was also cold.

"They're fed," came a gruff voice from the far end of the room. Eli. "Go back to sleep. I knew it was too much for you to do. That's my fault. I shoulda made you just nap all day."

"It wasn't," she exclaimed, a sinking sensation in her stomach. She'd messed up. She'd fallen asleep and he'd counted on her and she'd failed him. "I promise it won't happen again, Eli. I didn't mean to sleep so long." She stumbled over the blankets and moved across the room, flicking on the light switch. Cass turned around. "I'm so sorry. I—"

She stopped.

In the opposite corner of the room, the cowboy had dragged in a massive Christmas tree. It was clear he'd just cut it down, as it was dripping snow and water all over the floors, and pine needles were everywhere. It didn't matter. He'd gone out and gotten her a tree. She felt suspiciously like weeping. "I slept through getting the tree? I'm so mad. I wanted to help."

Eli's mouth crooked up on one side. He let the tree thump to the floor, and it made another horrific crashing sound. She wondered if there was ice on the dang thing. Probably. "You were tired, so I let you sleep. Figured I could go out and get you a tree." He gestured at it with one glove. "This one okay or do you need something bigger?"

Bigger? Cass was pretty sure if you stood this one up on end, it'd be at least a foot or two taller than her, and the branches were fat and thick. "I don't think bigger would fit inside this house."

"Sure it could." He turned around. "Give me an hour and I can have a larger one back—"

"No," Cass blurted, moving forward to stop him. "No. I love this one. Don't go get another."

He paused, tilting back the brim of his hat as if suspicious of her answer and needing a closer look. "You sure?"

"I'm sure. It's wonderful. I'm just surprised you brought it back." She pressed her hands over her rapidly beating heart. "I thought you'd skip it since I didn't go."

"Even I could tell you were tired." His voice was soft, soothing. "It's been days since you had a brutal accident, Cass. You need to rest. If that means you take a lot of naps, then you take a lot of naps. I'd rather you do that than push yourself too hard and get hurt again." He pulled off his hat, and his hair was sweaty and rumpled underneath it. "Let me strip down and I'll help you set it up."

"Strip down?" she squeaked, surprised. "You're going to get naked?"

"Get naked? What? No." His eyes went wide and she could have sworn a hint of a blush crossed his tanned face. "No, I meant get out of these extra layers. The cattle are all fed for the night."

"Oh." Now she was blushing, too. Of course that was what he meant. There was no such thing as naked Christmas-tree trimming. At least, she didn't think so. "Wait—I should feed the chickens one last time—"

"All done. No more chores for today. All you have to do is relax." He winked at her, the movement so natural and easy that she felt like hugging him. Why was he so wonderful?

"I wanted to help," she told him, feeling silly and useless. "I really did."

"I know." Eli's smile was so warm and genuine that she felt her body heat up in response. "But just having company for the long winter nights is enough right now. Don't worry about it."

"I'm not worried," Cass protested, moving closer to him. She told herself it was because she wanted to look at the tree, but the truth was, it was impossible to look away from his magnetic gaze. Was he sweaty? Yes. Was he tired? Yes. Was he still utterly gorgeous? Oh yes. If he was hers, she wouldn't care about a bit of sweat or dirt. She'd curl her hands in that jacket of his and pull him against her for a long, swoon-worthy kiss that would make her toes curl. He had a nice mouth for kisses, she determined after studying him for a moment. Firm but with full enough lips that it'd be a pleasure to taste him.

He stared down at her for a long moment, and she realized she was gazing at his mouth. She also realized she was standing so close to him that it wouldn't take much for them to kiss. He would just need to lean down a little, and she could wrap her arms around his neck . . .

The room felt charged with electricity, and she gazed up at him, holding her breath. The look in Eli's eyes was soft as he regarded her, and for a time, it felt as if he was going to touch her. That he'd take the first step and put a hand around her waist and pull her against him. That he'd kiss her. The air practically crackled with attraction, and she knew she wasn't imagining it.

Eli wanted to kiss her. His gaze flicked to her mouth and his lips parted.

Yes, she thought. *Now. Do it. Kiss me.* It seemed so natural. Hadn't they been fighting attraction for what felt like days? She'd thought her world was upended when she lost her memories, but having Eli here with her, at her side, made her feel . . . anchored. Safe. Like it wasn't a problem. Like the Cass she was right now wasn't lacking. She was just . . . perfect.

So she waited, her face upturned, her eyes dreamy. Waited for him to make the first move. His lips were so close to hers, and her skin tingled with the moment.

He leaned in. "I should go change," he murmured, and then headed to the kitchen, leaving her alone in the living room. "Be back in a flash so we can put that tree up."

Oh.

"Okay," she said, and was proud that her voice didn't wobble. All right, maybe they weren't feeling a shared attraction. Maybe she was the only one that had felt it. That stung a little. But she'd thought for sure that there was loneliness in his eyes, and she'd understood that.

She'd thought maybe they wouldn't have to be lonely anymore because they could have something together. But maybe that was just wishful thinking.

CHAPTER THIRTEEN

Cass was quiet as Eli fitted the trunk of the tree into a base and set the entire thing upright in a corner of the living room, far away from the woodstove. She had him turn the thing this way and that, trying to get the fullest part of the tree visible. She directed him with words and gestures, of course, but the openness she'd had earlier was gone.

He supposed that was his fault. He hadn't meant to practically kiss her. It had just happened. He'd returned to the house, tired and a little irritated that the chickens hadn't been fed one last time. It was dark and cold, and the snow was pouring down again. But the moment he'd gotten inside the ranch house, the way he'd felt changed. She'd looked so pretty and soft sleeping on the couch under his blankets that it had made his body react with fierce hunger. With need and longing. She was so innocent and lovely as she slept, and he could have woken her up with a kiss like they did in the fairy tales.

Instead, he'd gone outside to feed the chickens and scrubbed his overheated face in a handful of snow.

He'd almost broken his own word. Eli had vowed to never make Cass feel unsafe while she was stuck up here with him. Of course, the moment she woke up, what did he do? Loom over her and practically kiss her because she was so damned sweet that he couldn't resist.

He'd ruined whatever they'd had going. That energy between them. That easy camaraderie that sometimes morphed into something else, something deeper, better. That budding something. Now she stood awkwardly with her arms crossed over her chest, and he didn't know what to say. They both just stared at the tree in the corner of the room.

"Thank you," she said after a moment. "I know it doesn't seem like I'm grateful, but I am."

"Didn't say that. You've got a lot going on, that's all." His tone was flat. He was disappointed in himself. If she didn't smile anymore because she didn't feel comfortable around him . . . he'd never stop blaming himself. She needed safety right now more than she needed a cowboy slobbering all over her. "Least you got your tree," he added lamely.

"*We* have a tree," she corrected. "And tomorrow, I'm going to decorate it."

Eli glanced over at her and her eyes were shining with happiness just staring at that stupid tree. Like it meant something to her. Like it represented more than just a holiday where people handed out cheap garbage gifts and pretended like they meant something. Like it was more than just commercialized nonsense. He didn't say that, of course. He didn't want to see the light go out of her eyes. So all he said was, "It's nice."

Cass smiled at him, and she was so lovely that his heart

near broke in his chest. He wanted to smile back at her, but he didn't trust himself.

After a moment, her smile faltered and she gestured at the kitchen. "I made egg salad sandwiches. If you're hungry."

He nodded. "Thank you. That's kind of you." Inwardly, he was thinking back to her last attempt at cooking. Egg salad sandwiches sounded like something that could go very, very wrong. He'd eat every damn bite, though, if it would make her happy.

"I made enough for both of us," she told him, and brushed past to move into the kitchen. Her arm grazed against his and Eli could have sworn that it sent a shock wave through his body. "Wash up and then we'll eat. I'll put on some coffee."

Coffee with egg salad for dinner? "Just water for me, thanks. And I'll be right back." He headed to the mudroom, stripped off his layers, and then went to the guest bathroom of the ranch house—since his was attached to his room, and to get there he'd have to go through his bedroom, which was currently hers, and that would have felt like a violation of her privacy. He splashed off the worst of his grime and soaped his face and hands, then dried off with a red towel. When he pulled it away from his face, he saw a Santa figure staring back at him. Damn. Even here he couldn't get away from Christmas. She was mighty determined to make the house festive, wasn't she?

Instead of being annoyed by it, he was starting to think it was . . . cute. Sweetly idealistic. That was the kind of person Cass was, he figured. Seeing the best in people and situations. Trying to smile through life. Not like him, where everything had made him bitter early, and now all he wanted to do was put his head down and plow through each day.

He quickly changed into a plain white shirt and pulled

it down over his head even as he came into the kitchen. "I appreciate you making food, but you don't have to—" Eli paused when he saw her blank expression. She had a plate full of sandwiches in her hand, but her gaze was locked onto him. Specifically, on his abdomen . . . which she might have just seen. "Everything all right?"

"Oh my, yes," she breathed, and then jerked her attention back to his face, a guilty look on her features. "I mean no. I mean . . . what was the question?" Flustered, she moved to the table, now set with two big glasses of water, and placed the sandwiches between the plates. "Here, let's sit and eat."

Eli watched as she slammed into her seat, avoiding looking in his direction. He rubbed his stomach. He didn't have tattoos or any piercings under there, so all she'd have seen was his stomach, and he wasn't out of shape or anything. She was acting like she'd seen his dick, which was pretty odd. He couldn't figure out what she was thinking.

Sitting down, he took one of the sandwiches and ate a careful bite. Not bad. He ate an entire sandwich and picked up another before noticing she was only nibbling on hers and feeding bites to Frannie under the table. If it was one of the other ranch hands, he'd have reached over and smacked the sandwich out of his hand for ruining the dog—because a dog given scraps begs forever. But with Cass, he couldn't get mad. She had a soft heart for his Frannie, and he loved that.

So all he said was, "Might want to share with Jim and Bandit, too."

Cass gave him a shy smile and took another one of the sandwiches and pulled it apart. The waiting dogs thumped their tails eagerly, and she laughed with delight when they gently took the food from her fingers. "They're such good dogs. I love them."

"You sure you don't have pets?"

"I'm sure." The look on her face grew sad. She glanced over at him. "It's been days, Eli. When do you think I'm going to get my memory back?"

"Dunno. You want to look it up on the Internet? There's a computer in the back. If we can get a satellite signal, you should be able to use the web. I'll give you the password."

For some reason, she seemed strangely reluctant at the thought, as if getting online bothered her.

"What is it?"

"I don't know." She rubbed her arms briskly, as if she was cold. "It kind of feels like if I use the computer, I'm . . . exposed? It's hard to say. It's just a weird feeling. I can't explain it. I just don't want to. Does that make sense?"

"To me it does. I'm not a big fan of it myself." At her faint smile, he added, "I'll call Doc Parsons in the morning and ask him, if you're worried."

"It's all right. Let's give it a few more days. Maybe I'm panicking." She propped one elbow up on the table and studied him as he methodically ate another sandwich. "Since I'm a big blank, will you tell me about you?"

His mouth went dry. She wanted to know about him? "Ain't much to tell."

"Nothing at all?" Cass looked so very disappointed. "I don't have anything I remember about me. I can't believe we're both big blanks."

"I find it hard to believe you've got nothing under there," he said, trying to ease her fears. "I bet there's plenty. You just have to bring it to the surface."

"Like what?"

Well, damn. Now he was on the spot. What did all those magazines that Maria was constantly flipping through say? "Uh, favorite color? Do you have one?"

She blinked for a moment, her lashes fluttering as she considered his question. "I . . . think I like red. You?"

"I like red," he agreed, mostly because she liked it. "And you like dogs. That's two things."

"Wow, two whole things," Cass teased, leaning back in her chair. "Why would a girl ever think to worry?"

"All right, then." He gestured at the sandwiches. "Favorite food?"

Her brow furrowed in the most adorable way. "Cashew butter." Then she giggled at his revolted look of disgust. "What? I love cashew butter."

"How the heck do you butter a cashew?"

"No, silly." Her smile grew wider and wider, and the bigger it got, the more his heart felt like it was expanding. Funny how the two were connected. "Cashew butter is like peanut butter, but made with cashews instead. It's yummy."

"You mean to tell me that you could pick any food in the world as your favorite, and you pick a fake peanut butter?"

Cass's giggles grew louder. "It's not fake!" She mock swatted him, reaching across the table. "It's delicious!"

"Then why wouldn't you eat regular peanut butter? Don't tell me you eat a cashew and jelly sandwich?"

"I don't, because a lot of breads aren't vegan." Her brows furrowed again. "But I haven't been eating vegan since I got here. I . . . I don't think I like being vegan."

"Then don't be vegan. My favorite food's a steak." He gave her a nod. "Nice big juicy one seared in butter. Lots of fat."

She wrinkled her nose, but her expression was thoughtful. "I think I'm vegan because of the same reason I don't have a dog. What that reason is, I don't know, though. I just feel like they're connected." Frannie put a paw on Cass's leg, and the woman leaned down and gave the dog a smile and a scratch behind the ears. "I wonder why I'm doing those things if I don't like them?"

"Dunno."

Her expression grew sad. "I wish I could remember. It's bothering me so much that I have these enormous gaps. It's like I have pieces still there, but the parts that connect everything are missing." She touched her forehead as if she could encourage it to process, to remember. "I wish I could shake them loose, so I could finally get who I am. It's so hard not knowing who you are."

It made him feel oddly guilty. But he understood what she meant about not knowing who she was, and that made it worse. "Maybe this memory loss is a good thing. Maybe it'll show you all the things you need to change in your life."

She gave him a weak smile. "Easy to say when you have all of your memories."

"I'd be fine with losing some of them," Eli told her in a dry voice. Just thinking about his past made him want to volunteer for something along those lines. He'd be fine with losing memories of everything before coming to the ranch.

She fed Frannie another crust of her sandwich and gave him a soft look. "Since I don't have anything to share, why don't you tell me about you? I think if you keep talking, it'll help loosen something up in my head."

He immediately shook his head. "Nah."

Cass's eyes widened. "What do you mean, nah? You can't do that. You share, I share."

"Then you share," he countered.

"Fine, ask me something," she retorted.

"Are you married?" He hated that the words came out of his mouth so quickly. He shouldn't have asked, shouldn't have said anything . . . but now there was nothing to be done about it. It hung out there, between them.

He expected her to tease him. To get all flirty about why he was asking, when it should be obvious why he was asking. But all she did was rub her ring finger thoughtfully. "I don't think I am. It feels wrong. Not wrong, I guess. Like the idea doesn't fit. And I think I'd see something here." She rubbed the base of her ring finger again. "When I was in high school, my grandmother gave me a ring one year for Christmas and I thought it was just the prettiest ring ever. I wore it and wore it, and I even slept with it on. After a while, my finger had a tan line and this little indention where I wore the ring. I don't have anything like that, so I can't imagine that I am. I think I'd feel it if I was married. That there'd be more people I've got holes in my memory about, and it doesn't feel like that."

"But someone's vegan," he reminded her.

"Not a romantic someone." Cass looked thoughtful. "Funny how I can remember that ring from years ago, but I can't remember my own stupid last name."

"You hit your head," he told her gently. She seemed so disappointed in herself and that bothered him. "These things take time."

She nodded, and then reached across the table and took his left hand in hers. "I don't see a ring indentation on your finger, either. No tan line. You said you weren't married. Divorced?"

He wished she'd rub his finger like she'd done hers. He imagined her light fingertips grazing over his skin, and his entire body wanted to shudder in response. "Neither."

"Really? You a ladies' man, then?"

"Not really," he said, wondering absently if he should pull his hand from her grip. It felt good there. Felt right. But he didn't want to make her uncomfortable, so he just remained very, very still. "Never dated much, either."

"Now, that I find hard to believe." Cass's smile showed a hint of dimple on her cheek. "You're a great guy, Eli."

He snorted. Didn't know what else to do.

"It's true. You're kind, thoughtful . . . employed." She gave his hand a squeeze and then released it, and he immediately felt the lack. "You're good with animals, and you rescue damsels in distress. All of this is a great dating résumé."

Good with animals. He laughed, just because it was the most absurd thing to think of telling a girl when you want to date her. But he loved that Cass could make him laugh and smile, even when he didn't much feel like it. "I'll keep that in mind for the future. You know of a lot of women that want a résumé from a guy before they date him?"

"Only the smart ones, I imagine," she told him impishly.

They grinned at each other for a moment and then the silence grew awkward. She fed another crust to the dogs, spoiling them rotten, but he didn't say anything about it. He finished his sandwich, glanced at the clock, and then took a swig of water. Anything to avoid the intense gaze of those gorgeous blue eyes that were so sad and sweet at once. If he could, he'd give her back her memory right away, even if it meant she left in the morning. He just hated to see her hurting.

Of course, she couldn't leave in the morning. The snow through the pass was easily ten feet deep at this point. They needed sun and warm weather for a few days before the roads would become passable again. She was stuck here with him. All the more reason to keep things easy and casual and not push her. So he got to his feet, taking his plate to the sink. "Once you're finished, why don't you show me what ornaments you want pulled into the living room? Maria's got boxes and boxes of them."

"I'm finished," she said eagerly, and followed him. The dogs trailed after her, wagging their tails with excitement in the hopes of more scraps, he reckoned. Or maybe they just liked her.

He knew how that felt.

For the next while, she directed him and he retrieved items for her. He found the boxes in the laundry room, neatly ordered and packed carefully. It didn't seem like enough stuff to him, so he checked the attic, and sure enough, there were boxes of wreaths and garlands and the ugliest damn lights. There was a gigantic papier-mâché reindeer and blankets in Christmas colors that were carefully wrapped against dust and mice, and he even saw a fake tree, which he did not point out to Cass. She loved the real one so much that he'd have gotten her ten of them if she wanted.

Then, when everything was down in the living room and the place was filled with boxes, they sat on the sofa on opposite ends and drank a hot chocolate. Frannie immediately curled up against Cass's side, the traitor. Her snowy white head pillowed on Cass's thigh and he watched as Cass's delicate fingers stroked her head.

First time he was ever jealous of his damn dog.

She sipped her cocoa, stroking Frannie's head, and glanced over at him. "We've made a mess of the living room."

Eli gazed out at the boxes strewn over the floor. It was a lot. Enough to fill a store, he imagined. "I knew Maria had a lot of Christmas stuff. I just didn't realize how much. She's a big fan." He rubbed his chin. "A big fan or a Santa addict."

Cass giggled. "Strange addiction. Where is she, by the way? Maria? You've mentioned her several times."

"Home with her daughters for the holidays. They live out in California."

"And she's the housekeeper?" At his nod, she continued. "How many people live here?"

"Five—me, Maria, Old Clyde, Jordy, and Dustin."

"Which one's the owner? The Price of Price Ranch?"

He glanced over at her while drinking his cocoa. A lot of questions, but she seemed genuinely interested. "No one. The ranch is an investment for some rich guy. He's the Price. I think he wanted the land but he's not doing anything with it, so we ranch and raise cattle, and I imagine the years we don't make money, it's a tax write-off. Someone explained it to me once but I admit most of that's over my head." He shrugged. "I'm the one in the dirt, not the one with the wallet."

Cass sighed. "I don't blame you. It seems a lot simpler to be the cowboy rather than the rich guy. Nice, too. So how many cattle do you guys have? A thousand? Two?"

He choked on his drink at the thought. "More like four hundred and that's plenty. You need a lot more people to have a thousand head of cattle. We used to once upon a time, but when Price bought the place, he downsized. He might downsize again if we have a few bad years." Eli didn't like to think about that. "For now, though, he lets us run the place and as long as we make a profit, it's all good."

"And do you?"

"Most times, yeah. Sometimes the weather happens or the cattle get sick, and no matter how much you scramble, you're in the hole. But overall we do well."

Her smile was sweet. "You talk like this place is yours."

Did he? Eli grunted. "I know it's not. I think someday

I'd like to save up and buy my own ranch, maybe. I like it here, though. This is the only . . . ranch I've ever known." He'd almost said home. Damn it.

But she caught his hesitation. "This is the only place you've ranched at? Is that a word? Ranching? I guess it is? Anyhow, how long have you been here?"

"Ten years." Bandit stuck his head on Eli's knee, likely jealous of Frannie and the fact that she was on the couch and getting petted. He scratched the dog behind his ears so he wouldn't feel the lack. "Came here fresh out of the army just looking for something to do with myself. I didn't have any place to go and a buddy of mine had talked and talked about his family's ranch out west, so I hitchhiked out here from Texas. I asked around in several towns but no one wanted the help. Lot of ranches are family run." At her understanding nod, he continued. "I was just a stupid punk with a chip on his shoulder back then, so I imagine it was easy to turn me away. Only person that didn't was Old Clyde. I bought him a drink at the bar in town with my last few dollars and he told me he didn't have time for bullshit, and if I wanted to ranch, he'd spend a summer teaching me . . . but he wasn't going to pay me."

Her eyes widened. "So wait, you'd do all the work for free? That's a horrible trade."

Eli just smiled, picturing Old Clyde. The man was the epitome of a crusty range cowboy even back then. His jeans were stiff and weathered, his legs were bowed from spending so long in the saddle, and his face had more grooves than a vegetable patch. He was also a damn fine horseman and a lifetime cowboy.

"It was the best thing that could have ever happened to me. I hated it at first, but by the end of the summer, I asked to stay. By then, I'd shown I could work hard and wouldn't complain, so they kept me around. Paid me a salary this time, too." He winked at her. "Been here ever since. It's a good place for a man." Funny how he'd been so restless when he was younger, and found so much contentment here in the mountains among a bunch of smelly cattle. But it was home.

He might not have been born a cowboy, but it was in his blood now.

Cass looked fascinated. "You were in the army, you said? Did you hate it? Is that why you left?" She watched him closely.

She had a knack for picking up on the one thing he didn't want to talk about. "Sure are a lot of questions," he drawled, giving her a sideways look.

She blushed, and he had to admit, it was real pretty, despite the bruises and all. "I guess I'm trying to fill the holes in my memory with knowledge about you. If I'm being too pushy, let me know."

Now he felt guilty for shutting her down. "You're not. I'm just a cranky old cowboy."

That made her laugh. "Oh please. You are neither cranky nor old. I see no wrinkles or gray hair. Thirty-two, right?" At his nod, she rolled her eyes. "I'm twenty-eight, so if you think you're old, I guess I'm practically gray haired myself. Pretty soon my head will be as white as Frannie's and I'll look like a crone." And she rumpled the dog's fluffy white coat.

"Nah," he said softly. "You're beautiful."

Cass's lips parted. The room fell silent again and Eli cursed himself for saying that. Why was it that when he was around Cass, he couldn't guard his tongue? Why did he just blurt out things about how beautiful she was and crap like that? Next he'd be writing her love poems or some stupidity like that. Clenching his jaw at his own foolishness, he took another sip of cocoa and stared pointedly at the tree. "You remember your childhood?" he asked, since it'd change the subject, and he was desperate for that. "Or is that one of the blanks?"

She pursed those pink, fascinating lips of hers. He'd never been so taken with a woman's mouth before, but then again, he'd never met anyone that affected him quite like Cass. "I think most of it. It's pretty boring. Only child, loved by family but felt the need to leave the nest the moment she turned eighteen. Went to college, got her heart broken a few times, and then took a job . . ." She frowned, her brow furrowing. "That's the part where it gets fuzzy."

"S'all right," he told her. "Just making small talk. Don't let it bother you."

She looked frustrated that she couldn't remember. "It's one of those things where it feels like you have the answers on the tip of your tongue but it's not coming to you."

"I understand." And now he was going to be thinking about her tongue all night. "Don't push yourself too hard. It'll come back in time. Until then." He paused and gestured at the obscene amount of ornaments and boxes of decorations covering the floor. "You'll have your hands full."

Cass sipped her cocoa, looking thoughtful. "We have more than enough for the tree and the living room, but it seems a shame not to use everything. I wonder if the chicken coop can be decorated."

"Say what?"

She snort-giggled into her cup, and it was the most charming thing he'd ever heard. "I'm just kidding. You should see your face, though."

The laugh that rumbled out of him felt good. Real good.

CHAPTER FOURTEEN

The next day, Cass kept busy. She fed the chickens and it was sunny and only bitterly cold instead of Antarctic cold, so she let them out for a little while. Eli kept telling her that she didn't have to "walk" chickens like dogs, but she felt guilty at the thought of them all stuck in their coop all day long, so she let them out for a little bit and supervised. Once they were sufficiently "aired," Cass went back inside. Frannie barely looked up from her spot by the woodstove, thumping her tail to let Cass know she was excited to see her. Just . . . not all that excited. "Don't get up," she told the dog as she headed into the living room and surveyed her task for the day. All the boxes of Christmas decorations on the floors bothered her, so she vowed to get all the decorations up and out of the way as soon as possible.

Plus, she wanted to see what the boxes contained. In a way, opening each one and discovering the treasures inside was a lot like Christmas all on its own. It felt a bit like snooping, too, but she told herself that Eli wouldn't have gotten all the boxes out if it was a problem.

Just thinking about Eli made her feel all warm inside. She glanced out the large window in the living room and could see him out in the snow, a distant blur atop horseback. Later, he'd be a distant blur on a tractor, or the thing he called a "spooler," which unraveled all the hay for the cattle. He was a tireless worker, and she felt a little guilty she couldn't help out more.

She also couldn't stop thinking about what he'd said last night. *You're beautiful.* She'd gone to bed giddy over those two words, and this morning, she felt just as flustered and full of joy at the same time. Wasn't she too old to have a crush? She was, but did her mind care? Nooo. It made her want to giggle like a schoolgirl every time Eli looked in her direction. And who could blame her? Tall, dark, handsome, and cowboy. It was the stuff romantic movies were made out of.

Plus, he was nice. Attentive. Patient. And he looked at her like she was something special. She'd gone through a mental list of all of the ex-boyfriends she could remember, trying to think if anyone had ever looked at her like that. Unless she was missing several names (and that was a distinct possibility given her patchwork brain), it was a very short list, and none of them had ever made her feel as breathless with anticipation and hope as Eli did.

Cass told herself she was making too much of things. That he wasn't interested, and that was why he kept pulling away from her.

But he'd told her she was beautiful, and her face was wrecked with bruises. And he didn't seem like the type to lie, which also made her heart flutter all over again. She gave her cheek a little smack. "Get ahold of yourself, Cass. If it's meant to happen, it'll happen."

Of course, then she spent the afternoon daydreaming about him. About kisses and crawling into bed together. About what would happen if she—oops—ran into him while he was coming out of the shower. Would he carefully towel off those washboard abs she'd gotten a glimpse of? Invite her to lick them?

Or excuse himself and hurry away?

Her heart sank as she realized the most likely scenario was the third. That was so odd, because she felt like they had an attraction and a connection. Sometimes you just knew when someone else was attracted to you. It was like that sixth sense tingled with awareness, and she definitely felt that tingle around Eli. Heck, she felt all kinds of tingles around Eli.

But if he didn't want her, she couldn't force the issue. There had to be a reason he would hold back if he really was interested in her, and she was sure it was a good one. Above all, she was his guest. He'd saved her out of the kindness of his heart and gave her a roof, and she wouldn't repay that by flinging herself at him.

"No matter how flingable he is, Frannie," she murmured and sat down amid the sea of boxes, determined to get started.

Just unpacking everything took hours. At first, she was caught up in the wonder of what she was finding. Maria was obviously someone that dearly loved Christmas, because she had to have owned at least two of everything that was even remotely holiday-ish. Several lightweight boxes were full of wreaths of every make and shape imaginable. There were red ones, and green ones made of artificial pine. Blue and pink ones for some reason. One looked like a snowman. One was made entirely of mistletoe. She blushed and put that one aside, not entirely sure if she should put it up or not. Another was made of green and red ribbons, and there was a very large wreath that looked as if it had been made of repurposed gift bows. She carefully laid them out and then found boxes of garlands. And lights. Then there were boxes of Christmas skirts and tablecloths, placemats and napkins and napkin rings. There were snowman candle holders, Santa candles, stuffed reindeer, and three different kinds of nativities. There were throw rugs with reindeer hooves on them, stockings of all kinds, and gigantic bows to cover the doors. It was a mind-boggling amount of stuff, but there was no doubt that someone loved to celebrate Christmas. It must have killed her to not put up any decorations this year, and Cass vowed that she was going to decorate enough to make Eli feel like it was being celebrated after all.

Once she got past all of the room decor, she dug into more boxes and found tree trimmings. There were handfuls of tinsel carefully stored in Ziploc bags, clip-on birds, decorative candles, bells, and ornaments of every kind imaginable. Light strings of every color and shape—star, diamond, round, you name it—were available. They'd need ten trees to decorate with all of this stuff. Cass packed some of it back away. She liked the idea of a simple tree. It seemed wrong to be in such a rustic location and then cover it with store-bought plastic.

She picked out the simplest ornaments, glass balls in green and red, and then went hunting in the kitchen for popcorn. When she found it, she decided she'd make popcorn garlands instead of the heavily decorated ones that Maria preferred. She sorted through the items she selected, then boxed the rest of it carefully away and stacked the boxes in the corner of the room so Eli could put them up later.

Tree first, she determined, then the rest of the living area and kitchen afterward. That decided, Cass couldn't help but peek out the window, looking for Eli again. She knew he wasn't going to come in for lunch. He'd told her that he had to reinforce part of the fence at the far end of the pasture and it'd take some time, so he'd grabbed a protein bar, shoved it in his pocket, and then headed out the door. She didn't see him in the field, but there was hay spread among the snow, so she knew he was around. Just seeing that made her feel less isolated, and she went to the stereo, turned on the Christmas music, and hummed along as she decorated.

The day went by fast. So fast. It seemed like Cass returned from feeding the chickens, started decorating the tree, and then it was time to feed them again because it was dark. She hurried through the chores, proud that she'd gone through a whole day without having to collapse into sleep. That meant she was getting better, didn't it? That her brain was healing and she'd remember who she was anytime now. All she had to do was wait. She did mental exercises while she fed the chickens, and then came inside, unwrapping all her layers. It was dinnertime, so she washed up and made more egg salad sandwiches, and waited. When Eli didn't come in, she figured that he must have been busy, and put his sandwiches into the fridge, then went back to work on the tree. She turned the Christmas music off, though, because she wanted to hear when he came in.

Cass decorated and listened for the door to the mudroom. She hung the tree with green and red glass ornaments, and peppered it with a few of the clip-on candles and birds. The living room was pretty enough without a ton of lights, so she added a long string of plain white lights and wrapped them around the tree. The skirt she picked was a simple red and white that looked like Santa's hat, and she hung equally simple stockings on the mantel. Frannie immediately settled under the tree on the fuzzy skirt, and she looked so miserably pregnant that Cass didn't have the heart to shoo her away. It wasn't like there were going to be presents under there, anyhow.

Or were there?

She thought hard about that. Cass loved the idea of having a present for Eli. To have his face light up with surprise—and hopefully pleasure—at the realization that she'd thought about him and made him a little something. But what? She chewed on her lip and dug through the boxes again. She didn't have anything to give him, but maybe she could make him something? Christmas cookies were an obvious choice, and she could do those easily. Ditto popcorn balls. But that didn't seem like something worthy of wrapping up and putting under the tree.

Her hand skimmed over one of the boxes and she paused. It was clear that Maria was crafty in addition to being a Christmas-style hoarder, because one box had been full of craft items in various reds and greens. There were crystals, Popsicle sticks, pinecones, and lots of soft yarn.

Yarn. If she could find a needle, maybe she could crochet him something.

Wait, did she know how to crochet?

Cass picked up one of the skeins of yarn and fingered it. Oddly enough, she thought she might. If she didn't, she could always look up something on the Internet. YouTube videos had tutorials for everything nowadays.

The thought of going on the Internet made her stomach churn, though. It was one of those vague, nameless fears she couldn't put a finger on. One of the ones she suspected had a lot to do with her missing memories. Something out there bothered her, and she didn't want the outside world to find her and ruin her happiness here on the ranch. It was a strange thought, but she couldn't shake it. She didn't think she was a miserable person, but who knew? There was a large chunk of her memories that was missing right now. Maybe she was miserable.

Maybe that was why she was so fascinated with Eli. He presented a different set of circumstances. An escape.

Even as the thought crossed her mind, she discarded it. It wasn't that she wanted to hide out here because she wanted to be lazy. Lazy was boring. It made the time pass incredibly slow. It was something else.

What, then?

But her brain provided no answers. Frustrated, she pulled out skein after skein of yarn and eventually found a crochet hook. A smallish one, but still usable. As a test for her brain, she pulled the end of a red piece of yarn and tried to crochet it. The movement of the hook felt natural, and within moments, she had a nice, neat chain. Better than that, she knew how to keep going. She visualized a hat, something festively bright but not gaudy, because Eli wasn't gaudy. Earflaps to keep his ears warm. And a thin weave so he could wear it under his cowboy hat. She liked the idea, and she'd leave a few dollars for Maria to replace the yarn . . . once she got her purse back.

That unhappy, tense knot returned to her stomach. The thought of getting her purse back made her as uneasy as getting on the Internet did. But why? Was her brain deliberately blocking memories? Did something traumatic happen? She didn't know the answer to that.

And that bothered her most of all.

Disturbed, she went to her room and hid the yarn under the bed. She'd work on it during the day when Eli was out tending to the cattle. She checked the calendar—Christmas was in four days. She had time. A hat would be easy enough, she figured, and then tomorrow she'd bake up some special Christmas cookies just for him. That meant she'd have to find out tonight what was his favorite flavor or if he had allergies. It'd do no good to make peanut butter cookies if he was allergic.

After the yarn was stashed, she went back into the kitchen, humming. She'd found a deck of cards in one of the boxes—Christmas themed, of course—and had kept them out in the hopes that she could play a few rounds of something with Eli later. She knew poker and rummy, and she was pretty sure she could pick up anything else he threw at her. Heck, he could throw the cards on the ground in Fifty-Two Pickup style and she'd be thrilled as long as she got to spend time with him.

Man, she really did have it bad.

She checked out on the back porch, looking hopefully out into the snow for Eli, but there was no one. The light was on, showing glistening fresh snow with zero footprints. Oh dear. Sometime in the afternoon, it had snowed again. She wondered if she should get bundled up and go after him, but Cass worried that she'd just be in his way. He was working long hours, and a sandwich didn't seem like enough of a meal for someone who worked so hard.

Well, she was here with a nice big kitchen stocked full of food, wasn't she? Surely she could whip up something for him. That wouldn't be too hard. Encouraged at the thought of doing something to help, Cass smoothed the new snowman tablecloth on the table, and then hopped up to find a cookbook. She needed something she could make quickly. But what?

She decided on bacon and eggs again. She could make the bacon and then put on the eggs when he came in. What man didn't like bacon and eggs, after all? Cass tossed aside the recipe book and turned on the front burner on the oven, and then moved to the fridge, rummaging around looking for what she wanted. She'd seen a TV cooking show being filmed in person once, and they used sour cream with the eggs . . .

Cass paused, standing upright slowly. She'd seen a TV show in person? How did that happen? Did she know someone famous? She frowned, trying to concentrate. That feeling that the information was just out of reach returned, and she held still, as if her entire body could focus on the memory.

At least, she did until the scent of burning paper caught her nose. She sniffed and then turned around. The cookbook she'd tossed aside was on the stovetop, the burner scorching the paper. Ugh. With a spatula, she flipped the book onto the counter and then slapped it until the embers of the pages died out, leaving nothing but stink and charcoal-like ash. She lit a Christmas candle, but that didn't help much—now it smelled like ash and pinecones.

Well, shoot. She was already messing things up, wasn't she? Eli was going to laugh at her. He'd shake his head and say she wasn't paying attention, but she truly was. It wasn't her fault the book landed on the burner.

"Just bad luck," she muttered to herself as she pulled out an enormous package of bacon from the fridge and slapped it onto the counter.

The bacon was a new package, and of course, it was one of those "easy-open" packages that just wasn't. Cass wrestled with it for a few minutes, and even tried her teeth. All she got was a mouthful of plastic. Fine, then. She found a sharp knife on the counter and used it to poke a hole. Not a big one, because the package was too floppy, but it was a start. Encouraged, she put her hand on the wiggly, slidey package and jerked the knife through—

Just as Eli banged in from the mudroom.

Cass jumped. She sliced, and the plastic tore open. Unfortunately, her hand was at the end of the package and she managed to smack the blade of the knife right against her palm. It took her a moment to realize what she'd done, because the knife got stuck when it shouldn't have.

And then she saw the blood.

Really, she didn't know how she'd missed it, since it was now gushing everywhere. All over the counter, all over the frying pan, the bacon, her clothes . . . Swallowing hard, she grabbed a nearby towel and shoved it against her hand.

"Sorry I'm late," Eli said, and she heard him stomping his boots in the mudroom, shaking off the snow. "Seems like the entire damned fence has chosen this week to fall apart. I'd fix one section and check the next and it was coming apart at the seams, and . . . Cass? You in there?" He poked his head around the corner.

"Here," she said faintly. "Just, ah, making dinner." She was going to be sick. Hopefully not on the now-bloody counter, because that mess would be awful to clean up.

"You don't have to do that," he began as he entered the kitchen. "I was thinking that . . . what the hell?" Eli rushed to her side and grabbed the hand she'd swathed in the cute snowman kitchen towel she'd gotten out earlier. He stared at the blood soaking the fabric and then immediately raised her hand in the air, holding it in a tight grip. "What'd you do?"

"It was a showdown between me and a package of bacon," she said, her voice timid. "The bacon won."

Eli muttered a curse under his breath and tugged her along. "Come on. Let's get you in the bathroom and do something for this, because if you bleed out in the kitchen, I'm never going to forgive myself."

Because bleeding out in the bathroom was better? But she didn't protest, because in all the days she'd known Eli so far, she'd never seen him look that pale. She let him pull her along, and the cowboy headed into the bathroom, closed the toilet lid, and then put his hands on her shoulders, pushing her down lightly. "Sit and keep your hand elevated."

"It's elevated," she told him, determined not to whimper at how much it hurt. She wasn't going to cry. She wasn't.

With careful hands, Eli pulled the towel away from her wound and then began to wash it with the gentlest of touches. "It doesn't look too deep. Thank God." He shook his head as he delicately rubbed a wet washcloth over her palm, brushing it ever so slightly against the cut. "If we keep it sealed, it shouldn't require stitches, which is good. I've stitched up cows and horses, but if I had to stitch up a person, I'm not sure my stomach could handle it."

Cass couldn't help but chuckle at that. "So much for my image of a stoic cowboy."

"Stoic enough," he told her, "until you get hurt. Then I feel like I failed you."

"Because I'm a girl?"

"Because you're—" He paused and shook his head. "It ain't important. Just hold still." He dug around in one of the drawers and pulled out a tube of antiseptic.

She watched him, wondering what he was going to say. "Because I'm incompetent?" she asked, unable to let it go. "Because I'm not a cowgirl? Because what?"

Eli just glared at her. "It ain't important," he repeated.

"Well it is now, because I'm not going to be able to rest until I find out what you were going to say."

He scowled at her, his eyes narrowed. She wasn't afraid, oddly enough. She knew him well enough at this point that he was all bark and no bite. So she continued pressing him. "Because you're a . . . ?"

She watched as his nostrils flared with frustration. "Because you're my responsibility," he said after a moment, and she suspected that wasn't the real answer, but it was all he was going to give her.

"I see."

A tense moment passed between them. Neither spoke as Eli carefully dabbed more ointment on her hand, and then packed her wound with gauze and wrapped it. Now that all the blood was down to a trickle, it seemed like a lot of packing for a small cut, but she didn't say anything. Eli looked very intent on taking care of her.

And that made her feel warm and fuzzy inside, even if their conversation was frustrating. She'd let things slide a little, then. It was pointless to argue with him anyhow, especially when he was taking such good care of her. "I'm sorry if I scared you," Cass told him. "I was trying to make dinner. I thought you'd want something warm to eat after being out all day, and I certainly wasn't intending to baste the bacon with my own juices."

Eli looked surprised at her admission, and then chuckled, carefully curling her fingers over the bandage before releasing her hand. "I just don't understand how one person can be so bad in the kitchen. What do you do at home?"

"I don't know," she answered glumly. "I don't even think I can recall where my home is." Her jaw clenched and she felt dangerously close to tears. "Maybe I've sworn off everything but celery sticks and that's why I don't know how to cook." Her voice was hoarse and she gave him a wobbly smile as she stood up, her wounded hand against her chest.

"Hey," he told her softly. "None of that, now." When she wouldn't look him in the eye, he slid a finger under her chin and tipped her head up. Their eyes met, and Cass felt an electric rush move through her. God, he was handsome. It was more than just his looks, she realized—though those were incredible, with his stunning eyes and perfectly shaped mouth—it was that he was caring, and hardworking, and patient. Even when she cut her hand open and bled everywhere and then he was all gruff at her, she never felt like she was a bother to him. He was concerned, but he wasn't annoyed that she was around. That felt good. It made her feel important, and more than that, it made her feel important *to him*. Like if something happened to her, he wouldn't act as if it was just one of his cows down for the count. It would be like . . . she was someone to him.

The thought filled her with a sense of wonder. She gazed up at him and found he was still staring at her, so very intent. The air practically crackled with the attraction she felt for him. Surely she wasn't imagining this. Surely she wasn't making all this up.

Surely he felt it, too.

His thumb brushed against her chin, almost as if he were caressing her. "If you don't get your memory back, you can just stay up here forever with me."

Cass's breath caught in her throat. This wasn't in her head. He was leaning close to her, so close that if she breathed too deep, her breasts would brush against his chest. Her gaze fluttered over his face, and she wanted to put a hand on his chest, to slide it up to his neck and pull him down against her in a kiss. What would this handsome, stern cowboy kiss like? Would he kiss her gently? Or would it be full of all the passion he had bottled up inside? God, she really wanted to find out. She bit her lip with the need of it.

His gaze moved to her mouth, and she knew he was watching her with just as much intensity. A moan rose in her throat. She'd never been so full of need for someone she'd never even kissed before. Everything about Eli just called to her, though. His strength, his clean, warm scent, his smile . . . his loneliness. She suspected that even when the ranch was full of other people, he stood apart. She knew how that felt, deep down in her gut. She understood it.

And she wanted to kiss him so hard that he'd realize that he was never alone again. "Eli," she whispered, leaning in and tilting her face up.

"Cass," he murmured, and a shiver went through her at the sound of her name on his lips. It sounded so good, so right. So—

A crash from the kitchen made them both jump. Eli turned away, groaning. "That'll be the dogs."

"Of course," she said, flustered, and clutched her wounded hand to her chest as she followed him out of the bathroom and back to the kitchen. She lagged behind him a few steps. Not because she was tired, but because she wanted the mental privacy of having a few moments to herself. She didn't know what to think.

They'd almost kissed, and Eli had practically jumped to get away from her once the moment was broken. Maybe all the attraction was on her side and he was humoring her. Just being a lonely guy presented with a woman who was throwing herself at him.

Ugh. How could one almost-kiss feel like it had gone so wrong so quickly?

CHAPTER FIFTEEN

Eli wrestled the bacon package away from the dogs. Frannie had already eaten several raw strips, and Bandit had carried another chunk into the living room, no doubt to hide it away. "Good boy, Jim," he told the only non-thief, and was rewarded with a lazy tail wag. Jim was apparently the only ranch dog not ruined by Cass's kind heart. He should have told her that feeding them treats led to thieving and the like, but he didn't have the heart to destroy the pleasure that shone in her eyes when she fed them. It was clear she loved animals, even if she swore she didn't have any.

He mopped up the blood, too, and then straightened things up while she lingered behind him, a distressed look on her face. She was silent, which wasn't like her, and he cursed himself for jumping up like his pants were on fire. Sure, the timing was wrong, but he hated that he'd made her feel uncomfortable. That just made things worse.

"Thanks for cleaning up," she said softly from behind him.

"Of course." Like he was gonna make a woman with a hurt hand clean up her own blood, and then demand she make him dinner. He glanced over at Frannie, who was making coughing noises like she was about to vomit. Figured. "I'll take the dogs outside in case they yack up the bacon."

"Oh no. I'm sorry."

"Ain't your fault," he told her, even though it kind of was. He knew she hadn't meant to, and intention was everything. That was why he was so very mad at himself. If intention was everything, the fact that he'd wanted to kiss her was a problem. Didn't matter that he didn't do it. What mattered was that he'd wanted to.

"Okay." She clutched her injured hand and stood awkwardly in the kitchen. "Hey, um, Eli?"

"Yeah?" He stiffened, waiting, almost dreading what she was about to say.

"When do you think you'll be able to get my phone and purse from my car?"

That hadn't been the question he was expecting. "You want that stuff right now?"

She blushed. "Not right now. I mean, it's late. Of course not right now." She fidgeted with the bandages on her hand. "I was just thinking that it has some of my personal info on there. My address. My last name. Maybe if I get that stuff, it'll help jog my memory. Once I'm recovered, I'll be out of your hair and on my way. Win-win situation for the both of us."

Is that what she thought a win-win was? It was more like a lose-win situation for him, because he already hated the thought of her leaving. He didn't want her to go, and the realization staggered him. He'd never cared if anyone left in the past. But the thought of never seeing Cass again? It hit him in the gut and made him feel physically ill. Of course, he couldn't tell her that. Not when it was clear she wanted to go. Why else would she ask? He straightened, getting up from the floor and tossing the dirty towel in the sink. "It's the same as driving on the roads right now, Cass. Isn't gonna happen until the weather clears up."

"Ah." He didn't know if she was upset. That one syllable made it hard to tell.

"Need a few days of sunshine. Then we'll see."

"All right," she said softly, and they stood there staring at each other.

He desperately wanted to say something. Anything. He didn't want her to hate him because he was attracted to her. He didn't want her to be scared. He needed to think of something to reassure her, but nothing came to mind and so he just gazed at her, because looking at her was becoming as important as breathing.

Frannie ruined the moment by puking up the stolen bacon on the rug.

Cass slept badly that night.

Her hand throbbed, which didn't help things. And she didn't want to ask for aspirin, in case Eli thought she was being ultra wimpy and needy. So she tossed and turned, trying to not brush against her hand or dream about Eli. Didn't work. She couldn't help but think about Eli the entire time she lay in bed. How soft his gorgeous, piercing eyes had gotten when he gazed down at her. How good he'd smelled—like leather and fresh herbs and sweat—when he'd leaned in. How much she'd wanted him to touch her.

And how relief had flashed across his face when they pulled apart. That was the moment her brain kept reliving over and over again. He didn't want to kiss her. Didn't want to be attracted to her. That hurt. A lot. It made her dreams restless, and when she woke up in a cranky mood the next morning, finding Eli gone without so much as a note made things worse.

To top it all off, it was snowing again. Big, fat flakes drifted down from the gray sky, piling more snow onto an already white landscape. Cass scowled at the dawn as she went to feed the chickens. Even they were jerks to her—one pecked her hand when she was trying to spread the feed evenly in the trough, and another squawked and flapped its wings as if Cass were trying to kill her instead of feed her. She definitely was not feeling popular today. Frannie had abandoned her to remain sleeping under the Christmas tree, curled up in the skirt.

All and all, it was not starting out as a great day. Cass soldiered on, although all she wanted to do was sit down and cry. She finished her chores, ate a cold breakfast of bread and jam, and then found her crochet hook and fumbled her way through a series of stitches that wouldn't make her bad hand ache. She didn't cook anything, because she figured it would just end badly. So she crocheted and stewed over last night's aborted kiss. She glared out the window at the snow, she glared at the Christmas decorations he hadn't even commented on, and when she saw Eli distantly out in the pasture with the herd, she glared at his back, too.

The day passed achingly slow. She finished his hat and stared at the completed project for a while, not sure if she should unravel it in a fit of irritation or put it under the tree. She wrapped it anyhow, just because she couldn't stay mad.

Even if he didn't want to kiss her, it didn't change the fact that he'd saved her life. That was worth a hat at the very least, so she put it under the tree and fussed with the bow until it looked perfect. She thought about crocheting him something else, but her hand was starting to ache, so she just rubbed the bandages and gazed out the window as it grew steadily darker throughout the afternoon.

Eli didn't come inside for lunch. When dinner passed, she peered out the window to see if she could locate him in the pastures, but all she saw were the cattle's dark shapes. She made peanut butter and jelly sandwiches—because she couldn't hurt herself on those—and sat at the dining room table, waiting. Being alone all day sucked. It made her realize how uncomfortable the rest of her stay would be if he avoided her, and the thought made her ache. She didn't want that to happen. She'd apologize to Eli and get all of this out in the open, then. She'd lie that the knock on her head had really messed with her thoughts and she didn't truly like him or want to kiss him. It was just the concussion. Nothing more. Then he'd give her one of those gorgeous, relieved smiles that told her he wasn't really interested in her, just responding to the situation, and she'd tuck her easily broken heart away and try to forget about the cowboy she lusted over on a wintry Christmas holiday.

Christmas Eve was the day after tomorrow, after all. Surely the weather would break after that and start to clear up. That was how Murphy's Law worked, wasn't it? If you had somewhere to be, everything cleared up after the fact. Of course, she wasn't exactly sure where she needed to be. Cass sighed and stared out the dark window, then curled up on the couch to wait.

She drifted off and when she woke up, she realized it

was fully dark outside. The wood-burning stove was mere coals, and the Christmas CD she'd put in had ended some time ago. She rubbed her eyes and glanced around the too-quiet ranch house. "Eli?"

No answer.

She got up and padded around the house, checking all the unlocked rooms. No Eli. The kitchen was undisturbed, the sandwiches still neatly arranged where she'd left them hours ago.

He should have been back by now.

A sudden, panicky thought occurred to her. What if he was hurt? What if something had happened to him and he needed a rescue, just like the one he'd done for her? She raced toward the mudroom and started grabbing her layers.

"Frannie?" The dog was nowhere to be found, and Cass had to backtrack to find her hidden behind the Christmas tree, tail thumping as she curled up on the tree skirt. Her heart softened at the sight of the fluffy dog so comfortable in such a sentimental spot, right next to the lone present under the tree. "All right, you stay there, girl. I'll go find your dad."

With that, she bundled up and headed out into the night, determined to find him.

Of course, without the sun, it was bitterly cold and her lungs ached with every breath. Even through all her layers, she didn't feel warm. Shivering, she trudged out into the snow, heading toward the pasture.

As she got closer to the cattle, she noticed they were packed tightly together, their backs facing her as if huddling against the wind. She didn't blame them—it was fiendishly cold. "Eli?" she called out, scanning for him. She didn't see him anywhere, though, and she was a little afraid to go in with the cattle, because they were big and intimidating to someone who had never really been on a farm or a ranch before now. "Bandit? Jim?"

The wind carried her voice away, and she wandered around the edge of the fence in the dark, nearly twisting an ankle with every step. There was never an answer, no matter how many times she called, and Cass was outside for what felt like a half hour before she gave up and headed toward the barn. She wished she'd brought a flashlight, but the snow in the dim moonlight lit up enough for her to see by. Her teeth chattered as she headed toward the house, and a weird sob felt like it was close to breaking from her throat. What if she was right and Eli was gone after all?

She had to find him. If he was right and she was the only one on this side of the mountain, it was her turn to do the lifesaving. She was utterly terrified at the thought, but she couldn't leave him. No one could save Eli but her.

Choking back the sob in her throat, she went to the barn. She could saddle a horse, theoretically, and look for hoofprints in the snow . . . provided they weren't buried. Or she could take out one of the tractors. Something. All she knew was that she had to find him, and it'd go much faster if she wasn't on foot.

She'd figure out the logistics of things as she went. Did she know how to ride a horse? No. Did she know how to work a tractor? Nope. But that wasn't going to stop her. Eli needed her, and so she'd be there for him.

Cass pushed open the barn door and immediately felt warmer. There was a distinct musty, horsey smell in here, but it was comforting compared to the frosty feeling of the outside. On a brick-like stack of hay in the corner, she saw Bandit and Jim curled up, sleeping. Well, that was two less she had to rescue, though she wasn't thrilled at the sight of them. "Traitors," she whispered.

They only wagged their tails at her, and she imagined they looked guilty.

She walked past them, gazing helplessly at the stalls of the horses. There were ten of the boxy stalls, but only four horses. Eli had told her that sometimes the cattle were separated and put into the stalls, or if they had to bottle-feed babies, they were kept in the barn because they'd been abandoned by their mothers. Right now, though, she only counted the four horses. She moved toward the closest one and put her gloved hand between the bars and into the stall. "Are you the most friendly one here? I need an easy horse to ride that doesn't mind a rather unskilled pilot."

The thing sniffed her hand, and then tried to bite her glove.

She yelped and pulled back. "Not you, too. Why is everyone on this farm such a jerk?" She had a petty moment and flipped the damn horse the bird, and then went to the next one. It ignored her, hindquarters in her direction. All right, well, she'd take a calm horse over Bitey Biterson in the next stall over. "Come on, boy," she cooed at him, unlocking the latch on the stall and rolling the door back. "You and me are gonna—"

"What the hell are you doing?" Eli stormed around the corner, a dirty rag in his hand. He looked utterly furious at her, and put a hand out. "Stop right now! I mean it, damn it!"

She stared at him. He was here, alive and well and not frostbitten. He was also yelling at her like she was the one who had done something wrong. Cass stared at him in shock as he moved in front of her, shut the stall door again, and then turned around to give her the angriest glare she'd ever seen on his face.

And then she burst into tears.

"Ah, hell," Eli said, tossing down the dirty rag in disgust.

He dug through his pockets for a handkerchief, and when he pulled it out, it was oily from the stuff on his hands, and he swore again. "Don't cry. Damn it, Cass."

"Quit yelling at me," she sobbed back at him. And because she was so mad, she punched him in his shoulder. It felt ineffective and weak, so she did it again, just because.

He gave her a shocked look. "Of course I'm going to yell at you," he said, raising his voice until she was pretty sure he was yelling all over again. "You were about to walk into a stall with a horse facing the wrong direction! Do you want a hoof to the head? Do you want him to break your ribs? Because if you get in there with him, that's what's going to happen."

He was definitely yelling . . . and it only made her cry harder. "I was coming to save you, you . . . prick!" She smacked his shoulder again. "I thought you were dead!"

"Why would I be dead?" he roared. "I'm not the one constantly in danger just by walking into the kitchen!"

Cass sucked in a breath and gave herself the hiccups in her effort to stop crying. "I was scared you were dead," she repeated again, scowling at him. "Don't be mad at me!"

"*Why* did you think I was dead?"

"Because you didn't come inside! It's late!"

"Yeah, it's late! Did you notice that I'm the only one around here?" He spread his arms wide. "I'm doin' the work of four people, Cass. At what point do you think I have time to sit around the fire with you?"

"You're being a jerk," she cried. She hated that every word out of his mouth sounded so logical. She hated that she was the hysterical one in this. "I was worried!"

"So worried you decided to kill yourself by pissin' off all the horses? Jesus, Cass! Are you trying to get hurt again? Is that what this is?"

Like she was deliberately going to hurt herself? "Excuse me for caring about you," she shouted at him and clenched her fists. Of course, that hurt because her one hand was still throbbing from yesterday's cut, and she gasped at the pain that shot up her arm. It just made her angrier. How dare he be mad at her? As if it was a bad thing to care about someone! "You know what? Fine! I don't want to spend Christmas with you! I don't even like you anymore! Go and die out in the snow. See if I care! Sleep out here for the next week! It doesn't matter to me!" She turned her back on him and went to storm away.

A hand grabbed her shoulder.

Cass turned around, her temper flaring. She was determined to give him a piece of her mind. In the next moment, he cupped her face and his mouth was on hers.

Shocked, Cass remained perfectly still for a moment, unable to believe it was really happening. After all this time, Eli was kissing her. His mouth slanted over hers, hard and angry with emotion, but it was still breathtaking to feel his body against hers, the warmth of his mouth on her. The brim of his hat was shadowing both of them, and she could feel it tip back when it hit her hair. Of course, then she was distracted by his lips again. His mouth was both hard and soft against her own, and she melted into the dual sensation of it. He pulled away a scant second later, before she was even getting into the kiss. "Cass—"

No. She didn't want to hear excuses or apologies. She wanted a better kiss than that. Cass grabbed him by the collar and pulled him back down. That was too short of a kiss and she needed it to be longer, more thorough, before she was going to let him yell at her more. A nice, toe-curling kiss would make everything better.

So she kissed him before he could continue speaking,

and hers wasn't a light flutter of lips or the hard, fierce claiming that his was. She attacked him with methodical strategy. First, she bit the plump edge of his lower lip, because she'd been wanting to do that for ages, and it should have been sinful for a grumpy cowboy to have such a full, kissable mouth. She heard his quick intake of breath, and that only encouraged her to keep going. With a little lick of her tongue against his lips, she coaxed his mouth to part, and then her tongue brushed against his. Then, she wasn't kissing him—and he wasn't kissing her.

It was a mutual kissing, and it was glorious.

His arms went around her, holding her so tight against him that her bruised ribs protested, but she didn't care. All she cared about was the hot, wet heat of his mouth on hers, and the way he tasted. She loved it, loved the sensual drag of his tongue against her own, loved the way he knew how to kiss her just enough to make her pulse throb between her thighs. She'd dated both good and bad kissers in the past, but Eli put them all to shame. Within moments, she was breathless and shaking with need. When his mouth pulled away from hers so they could both catch their breath, he pressed his forehead to hers, his hands tight on her waist.

"Shouldn't have done that," he rasped, panting.

"Why not?" She sounded equally breathless. "I've been wanting you to do that for days now."

He groaned, closing his eyes. "Cass . . ."

"Eli," she teased, her gloved hand sliding up and down his arm. He wasn't wearing his coat, which told her he'd been in the barn for a while. Probably was out there the entire time she was wandering in the snow at the edge of the herd, looking for his lifeless body. Didn't matter. He was here and kissing her and that was all that mattered.

"Been telling myself not to touch you," he murmured,

and his nose rubbed against hers. There was a small twinge of pain because she was still bruised, but she didn't care. None of it mattered except the way he felt against her right now, and how close his mouth was to hers. She wanted another kiss. She wanted dozens of them.

"Why?" she breathed. "Why not touch me?"

"Wasn't right," he told her. "You're here stuck with me, alone and vulnerable. Doesn't seem right for me to take advantage of you." He pulled away again, gazing down at her with the sexiest hooded eyes. "You—"

She grabbed his collar and put her mouth on his again, kissing him fiercely. Cass swept her tongue into his mouth and then he groaned, clenching her tight against him. God, she loved the sound he made when she kissed him. It made her body do all kinds of crazy little shivers. Of course, she was doing most of the kissing, but she didn't mind that.

He gave her mouth a little lick when they pulled apart again, and Cass gasped at how good that felt. It sent a quiver right down to her thighs. "You keep interrupting me," he told her.

"You keep saying silly things." Now she was the one staring at his mouth. But really, it was just too delicious not to stare at. His lips had darkened slightly in color and were shiny from their kissing, and she wanted to taste them again.

"I'm being serious, Cass. I'm not tryin' to molest you—"

"Molest me?" She pulled back from him slightly, frowning up at his face. "Why on earth would you think that?"

"Because you're a woman alone? Because you don't have your memories?" He flicked a hand back against his cowboy hat, and she realized it was in danger of falling off his head, and he didn't seem to care. He was more interested in frowning down at her. "I shouldn't be touching you."

"I don't know if you noticed," Cass said, "but I'm really, really into being touched. I like you, Eli. I want you. Can't we just enjoy this?" She leaned in and lightly kissed his mouth again. "And this?" She nipped at his lower lip. "And this?" She slid a hand down the front of his chest, and headed toward his belt.

He grabbed her gloved hand in his. "I want to make sure it's what you want."

Good lord. "Do I need to start doing smoke signals? Morse code? What's it going to take to convince you?"

Eli frowned down at her, and she realized he was still clutching her waist, and her breasts were pushed up against his chest. Oh man, it took everything she had not to rub up against him like a cat in heat. She wanted to, though. Boy, did she want to.

When he remained silent, she continued. "I guess I'll just have to keep kissing you until you give in." Her hand was still on the back of his neck, so she reached up and took his hat off his head and tossed it to the floor of the barn. "Get ready, because you're about to be thoroughly kissed."

He gave his head a little shake, as if unable to believe how she was acting, and then hauled her against him again. This time, he was the aggressor, his kiss full of all the pent-up passion and need that she'd been feeling for days. All those little sparks between them? It hadn't been in her imagination. She moaned against his lips as his tongue slicked against hers and sent a bolt of longing straight between her thighs. Oh god, yes. Now that was the kind of kiss she was looking for.

Eli groaned, too. "You make the sexiest damn noises," he told her between frantic presses of his mouth to hers.

"Okay," she breathed. She was barely aware of him pulling her along with him, their bodies stumbling together as he guided them farther back into the barn. Where they were going, she had no idea. If he flung her down in the snow, she doubted she'd notice at this point.

"'Okay'? That's all you have to say?"

"Should I have moaned again?"

"Hell yeah," he growled, and then he was kissing her again. She was lost in the moment, her arms tight around his neck, and she was pretty sure she was seconds away from straddling his thigh and rubbing up against him. The sound of a stall door rolling back made her jump, but Eli's arm remained locked around her waist, and a moment later, they were tumbling into fresh straw in one of the empty stalls. Then she was under him and he was over her, gazing down at her with heated eyes full of need.

And oh, this was so much better than standing up and kissing. Being under him was an entirely new set of sensations and she locked one leg around his hips, pulling him down against her.

"I'm getting saddle oil all over your clothes."

"Don't care," she panted. "Kiss me again."

"I'm gonna get it in your hair, too," he warned even as he leaned in, but she still didn't care, because that sexy growl was back in his voice.

"Go for it." She raised a glove to her mouth and bit one finger, pulling it off because she wanted to feel him, and all these layers weren't giving her anything.

Eli made another one of those low noises in his throat, and then his mouth was on hers again, hot and divine. She moaned as his tongue moved against hers, and she couldn't stop her hips from lifting up against his in an age-old motion. He groaned and then his hands were in her hair, pushing off her knitted cap and tangling in her curls. There was a strange scent to his touch—saddle oil, he'd said—but she didn't care. It smelled like leather and Eli, and his mouth was on hers and that was all that mattered. A moment later, his hips were resting between her thighs and she felt the hard press of his length against her sex.

Oh yes. She whimpered, because that was what she wanted. She wanted Eli like this, with his lips on hers, his hands in her hair and his body over her. It felt better than she'd ever imagined.

He kissed her one more time, soft and sweet, and then gazed down at her face. "We shouldn't do this here."

"We shouldn't?" Disappointment crept into her voice.

"It's cold, and you're injured."

"Still don't care."

"I do." He kissed the tip of her nose. "I care a lot."

"Oh. Well, all right." Hearing that took the edge off.

Eli leaned in and kissed her one more time, as if he couldn't help himself. "And I'm covered in saddle oil anyhow."

"Me too." She didn't move.

He grinned down at her—a large, pleased grin that creased his tanned face and made him go from handsome to breathtakingly gorgeous. Oh lord have mercy on her, because she was lost when he smiled like that. Cass had to bite back the moan that was rising from her throat. "You sure we can't stay?"

"Only if you want frostbite on your pretty ass . . . and mine."

Well, as long as he acknowledged it was pretty. Cass wasn't sure she agreed with that, but when he got off of her in the next moment and offered her his hands, she let him help her up. He batted stray hay out of her hair and then handed her back her knitted cap, and she noticed that he was right—her hair had that weird smelling oil in it.

He pulled her close again, and for a wild, heart-thumping moment, she hoped he was going to toss her into the hay and give her the tumble she was begging for. The look on his face was so intense she held her breath. Then he groaned and pressed his forehead to hers. "Go inside before I do something I regret."

"I won't regret it," she said eagerly.

"Cass," he warned.

"All right." She was reluctant to leave, but it was clear he was going to wait for her to go. She wanted to stay and keep talking to him, but then she remembered what he'd said about doing the work of four people and felt guilty. "I'll go inside. I made sandwiches, by the way. Can't injure myself with a butter knife."

"I'm thinking if it's possible, you could," he told her in a teasing voice, then put a hand to the back of her neck and pulled her in for another fierce kiss that left her dazed and wanting more. "Don't wait up."

"Okay," she told him breathlessly. "I'll just go in and . . . shower." She hoped he'd take her up on that and join her.

His eyes gleamed with interest, but all he did was nod.

Drat.

CHAPTER SIXTEEN

Eli remained inside the barn for a while. It wasn't that working on the saddles was so very pressing. It was that he wanted time to sort through his thoughts. Much easier to do it with something to occupy his hands and let his thoughts work through everything that was going on. It helped that Cass was safely tucked away in the house, because when she was near him, he found it too distracting to do much other than gaze at her like some starry-eyed fool.

Couldn't help it, though. He wanted her like he'd never wanted anyone before in his life.

He rubbed oil into the last saddle for the night, thinking hard. They shouldn't have kissed. He knew that. Likely she knew that, too. It was a bad kind of situation and bad timing. She was still recovering from her knock on the head. She didn't have her memories. She was beholden to him at the ranch because she was trapped here. It shouldn't have happened, but it seemed like they couldn't stay apart from each other. He hadn't meant to give her that first angry kiss.

Instead of slapping him, she'd grabbed him by the collar and kissed him back so fiercely that it shocked him.

It also aroused him. There was something so fascinating about Cass. She was sweet and wanted so much to be helpful, even if she was terrible at it. She was a constant optimist, and she loved simple things—the dogs, music, the holidays. But she also had a fiercely determined side, and he'd seen that when she'd snagged his collar and hauled him forward to plant her mouth on his.

She didn't like taking no for an answer.

Eli liked that a lot.

He knew she didn't have her memories. He was all too aware of that. She seemed to recall lots of bits and pieces about who she was as a person and her past, but when she tried to think about her current situation, it was a blank. He knew it was wrong to get involved with her, especially when she was in a situation like this. It was a bad idea.

But he was starting not to care.

If she liked him, and he liked her, and they took things slow . . . did it matter if she didn't have all her memories? As long as he was respectful of her and her boundaries, did he care if she didn't recall what her job was or where she lived?

More than that, was it wrong for him to fantasize that she'd never get those memories back? Eli knew it was. He knew that she hated the missing parts of her mind, and he knew that she was desperate to get those pieces back. What happened when she did, though? Would she immediately pack up and leave? Would he never hear from her again once she realized just who she was? The thought was like a punch in the gut.

So yeah, sometimes he dreamed that she wouldn't get those parts of her back. That she'd decide to remain at the ranch. That she'd give ranch life a shot, and maybe life with him a shot. It'd be crowded to squeeze another person in at Price Ranch, because it wasn't a big house and there wasn't really a job for another person. But he could marry Cass. Give her his last name instead of her forever wondering what her own was. He doubted the boss would mind. Mr. Price lived down in Texas and had millions upon millions of dollars. Hadn't he just got married and had a baby himself? He'd know what it was like to want your woman at your side.

And Eli wanted Cass at his side. Forever. Didn't matter that he'd only known her a week. When you fell into something that felt right, you didn't question things. He'd known after a week of ranching that this was the life for him. Of course he'd know how he felt about Cass after a few days. It made sense.

But it still felt a little wrong to hope for such things. To hope that she'd never get her memory back, because then it meant she'd stay with him. He couldn't help thinking it, though. He'd never felt so strongly about anyone before. He thought that life with someone at his side was just a fantasy.

Maybe it was real, and maybe it could be for him after all. Maybe he wasn't meant to be alone forever.

Maybe, for once, someone would love him enough to stay.

The next morning, he woke up earlier than usual. There was a lot to do around the ranch, and he wanted to make sure that he got everything done and still had time to spend with Cass. He knew she wouldn't understand the heavy load of chores as much as someone who lived on a ranch constantly, so he made a quick breakfast of bacon and eggs, left a portion for her, and even wrote a note explaining that he wouldn't be in for lunch but he'd be back for dinner.

Felt weird to check in with someone. Eli realized that he'd been a little selfish with his time, too. Sure there was a lot to be done, but Cass didn't know how life on the ranch worked or the long days involved. He should have told her more about when to expect him back, and when to expect not to see him. He should have made more of an effort to spend time with her instead of avoiding her. Of course, he'd been avoiding her simply because he was far too attracted to her.

That kiss had changed everything, though. Now it made him race through his tasks for the day instead of lingering over them. He fed the horses and mucked stalls. He caked the cows and drove the spooler out into the pasture so he could start haying the cattle. The snow had stopped for now, and the weak winter sunlight was making everything bright and cheerful.

He didn't like it. Every day that it snowed was another day he got with Cass. Eli found himself wishing for nothing but storms for the next month. Hell, he'd take them for the next year if it'd keep her at his side. Wasn't practical, but he was quickly learning to appreciate less practical ideas in his head if they involved Cass and more kisses. When he was out in the pastures, he'd caught a glimpse of her tending to the chickens, and he'd raised a gloved hand to let her know he saw her. She waved back, and even though it was silly, it felt warm just to have that small greeting.

By the time the sun was creeping behind the mountains once more, Eli had finished the chores for the day. The cattle were doing well and eating heavily to make up for the cold, but they looked healthy. He took the saddle off his horse, brushed it down, and gave it fresh food and water before he headed through the barn, breaking ice on the other water troughs and adding warm water for the night before heading in.

He was going to get an entire evening with Cass, and he was looking forward to it. All day, he'd had visions of curling up by the fire with her, his arm around her shoulders, her slight figure snuggled under his arm. He had to admit the thought had a lot of damn appeal. Maybe she'd be hungry for more kisses. He knew he was.

Of course, the moment he stepped into the mudroom and stamped the snow off his boots, the phone in the kitchen rang. Uh-oh. That'd most likely be Doc Parsons or Maria, and he didn't feel like talking to either one at the moment. They were sure to have prying questions about Cass.

Before he could call out to let it ring, he heard Cass pick up the phone. "Hello? Price Farm."

"Ranch," he muttered under his breath. "It's a damn ranch." She still hadn't figured out the difference or realized that it was an insult to any good rancher to call him a farmer.

There was a pause, and then Cass spoke again. "It's nice to speak to you. I'm Cass." She laughed. "I guess that was obvious." Pause. "Mmhmm. Merry Christmas to you, too. No, no puppies yet. Eli? He's in the mudroom. He was just coming inside when you called. He—what? Oh no, he's been a perfect gentleman." Then there was another pause and Cass laughed again.

He hurriedly stripped off his snowy layers, not liking the idea of Cass getting grilled by Doc or Maria. Both were far too nosy for their own good. When he was in his bare socks and down to his regular clothes, he hurried out of the mudroom and into the kitchen, only to see Cass with her eyes wide, the phone held to her ear as the other person talked. Her cheeks were slightly pink, and he couldn't help but notice that the bruises and swelling were almost entirely gone today, and she looked prettier than ever. He should tell her that, too. But . . . not right now.

He held out his hand for the phone.

"Here's Eli. It was nice to meet you, too." Cass held the phone out to him, a little smile on her lips. "It's Maria. She wanted to call and wish you a Merry Christmas."

Was it Christmas already? He frowned to himself as he picked up the phone and held it up to his ear. "Hello?"

"Feliz Navidad, mijo! Are you having a good time?" Maria sounded cheerful as she yelled into the phone, a loud chatter of voices and noise behind her.

"I'm good, Maria. How're things there?" He glanced over at Cass, but she picked up a coffee mug and headed into the living room, her cheeks still pink with a blush. He wondered what the housekeeper had asked her, and he felt his own face grow hot.

"Oh, busy, busy, busy. So many babies here. I always have one in my arms and another waiting to be picked up. It's exhausting." She sounded so happy, as if the hustle and bustle thrilled her. "How about you? How are you keeping on all by yourself with no help? Everything good? Or are you ready to fall over and admit to the world that you're not made of steel?"

"Not yet," he told her, amused. "And I know I'm not made of steel. It'd be impossible for the horses to carry me if I was."

She muttered something in Spanish and somewhere in the background a baby cried. Maria made a soothing noise and Eli wasn't sure if it was for him or for the kid. "Give him to me," she told someone on the other end of the phone, and there was a rustle of air. He imagined her hauling a baby into her arms and pictured the pleased expression on her face. Maria loved to mother. "So, Eli, how are things going with your new friend?" Maria's tone grew knowing and nosy. "She sounds very nice, mijo. Very sweet. Are you getting along?"

"Yup. Great." He rubbed one suddenly hot ear. "It's all fine."

"And she's recovering well?"

"Yup."

"How's the weather up there? I saw on the Weather Channel that it's been more snow every day. You might be keeping her company for a while." She chuckled. "Maybe we'll have a nice wedding to celebrate in spring, hmm?"

Jesus, and here he thought he was moving fast. Turned out he had nothing on Maria.

"Not entirely sure that's easy to predict yet," he told her vaguely, aware that Cass was probably listening in the next room over. Time to change the subject. "How's the weather there? And the kids?"

If Maria minded the conversation change, she didn't say so. She was happy to go on and on about what the grandchildren were up to, how her daughter's new pregnancy was going, and who was coming down for Christmas dinner tomorrow. "You're going to fix something nice for your guest for dinner, won't you, Eli? Don't make me come up there," she teased in warning.

"I'll do something special," he promised her. He didn't know what, but as long as he cooked it and Cass didn't, he figured they'd both get out alive.

Maria continued to dominate the conversation, and he

was content to listen, pepper in a few responses about the ranch, and watch Cass from afar. She sat on the sofa in the living room, sipping a mug of coffee and studying the tree. Frannie was tucked underneath it again, and he could barely make out the white fluff of her fur under the green branches. Weird dog. She'd been a little distant since Cass had arrived, no doubt focusing her energies on the newcomer. He found himself far more focused on the shiny, loose curls of Cass's hair than on Frannie, though.

Man, he had it bad. Dreamin' about a woman's hair, even. That wasn't like him.

"You're quiet," Maria teased, drawing him back to the conversation. "Everything all right?"

"Hm?" He tore his gaze away from Cass's cascading hair and focused on the phone in the kitchen. Couldn't think with all the gawking at her he was doing.

She chuckled. "You know what? I'll let you go. It seems like you're busy. I just wanted to wish you a Merry Christmas, mijo. Just in case you were feeling lonely over the holiday. I'm glad that's not the case."

He grunted a response, then cleared his throat, because Maria hated it when he just grunted at her. She was the closest thing he had to a mom, so she deserved better. "You too, Maria. Happy holidays. Thanks for calling."

They hung up, and he glanced over at Cass. She turned her head from her spot on the couch, looking over her shoulder at him. He rubbed his neck, feeling a little uncomfortable and unsure about what to do now. Go over there and kiss her like he'd been dreaming of all day? Or should he take it easy? Pretend like nothing was different and not maul her the damn second he got in the door?

That was probably smarter. He rubbed his neck again. "I'm gonna take a shower before dinner."

"All right." She smiled over her shoulder at him but didn't get up.

He headed toward the hall, his footsteps creaking on the floorboards.

"Can I join you?"

Eli froze. His entire body stiffened and his eyes went wide. He turned to look at Cass. Did she just—

An impish smile curved her mouth. "Just teasing." She winked at him. "Go shower."

"I . . . okay." Heat suffused his ears. Seemed like he'd spent half the day blushing. He turned around and left, heading into the bathroom.

As he showered, he mentally cursed himself for not handling that better. Jordy was the youngest cowboy on their ranch, and a consummate flirt. He loved to get the attention of women in town, and Eli couldn't help but wonder how he would have handled that. Would he have swept over to Cass and dragged her into the shower with him? Flirted back with some funny quip?

Damn it, and all he'd done was stand there and stare like a lump. Eli vowed to do better. He'd get out of the shower, dress, and then go into the living room and give her a fierce kiss in greeting. Remind her of what they had, since it was clear they'd both been thinking about it. That brief little flirtation of hers told him that she was all right with keeping things heated between them, and he needed to take her up on it.

So after the shower, he rubbed his jaw and gazed in the mirror. He'd shaved just that morning, but there was some stubble, and he remembered how pink her face had gotten after their kiss in reaction to his whiskery jaw. He grabbed a bit of aftershave, patted it on, and then quickly wiped it off again, because now he smelled like a damned teenage boy about to head off to his first date.

You're a grown man, Eli Pickett, he reminded himself. *Act like one.*

With a glare at the mirror, he wrapped a towel around his hips and crept into his room to change, shutting the door behind him. He dressed quickly and told himself he wasn't disappointed that Cass didn't barge in and put her hands all over him. That was all right. He was probably sending her some terribly mixed signals.

Well, no more.

CHAPTER SEVENTEEN

Eli charged toward the living room with determination just as she was coming out of the kitchen. Cass looked up at him in surprise, clearly puzzled by the expression on his face. Eli moved to her side, cupped her face, and gave her the kiss he'd been fantasizing about in the shower.

Immediately, she melted against him, making one of those soft, throaty little moans when his tongue slicked against hers. It was just as good a kiss as yesterday, and her body felt incredible against his own. Like she was meant to be there, tucked against him. Her tongue flicked against his, and then he was as lost in the kiss as she was, mouths melded together and slanting over and over in a consuming dance.

Finally, he pulled away and gazed down at her, body aching with need. "Been wanting to do that for hours."

Her eyelashes fluttered and she looked dazed, which only made him hungry to do it again. "Oh wow. I've gotta say, I like this new greeting a lot more than just a 'hello.'"

She licked her pink lips, as if tasting him, and he bit back a groan. "Hi, Eli. How was your day?"

A laugh rumbled out of him. Were they doing this? "It was fine. Busy but good. I finished early." He slid his hands to her shoulders and then locked them around her back, holding her against him. He watched to see how she'd react.

She put her arms around him and leaned in, a blissfully content expression on her face as she tilted her head back to gaze up at him. "You smell nice."

Hell. Now he was going to blush again because she'd smelled his aftershave. "Soap," he grumbled. "Just soap."

She smiled. "You used soap for me? I'm such a lucky girl."

"Wouldn't use it for just anyone," he said, trying to get into the whole teasing thing. And then, because it wasn't really who he was, he got serious again. "You sleep well? How are your bruises?"

Cass chuckled, shaking her head at him. "I don't know which is worse—you, or Doc Parsons."

"Doc called?" Damn, everyone was sure friendly today.

She nodded. "He wanted to talk to you, but when I told him that you were out feeding the cows, he gave me a lengthy quiz about how I was feeling and if I had any lingering migraines or trauma or the like."

Words like "lingering" and "trauma" made Eli's gut cold. "And do you?"

"Nope! I'm good." She made a fist and pretended to knock on the side of her head. "Except for the holes up here, everything's doing great."

He grunted. He should really call Doc and thank him for checking up on Cass, but he wasn't in much of a mood to talk on the phone more. He'd worked through his chores like a wild man today so he could spend time with her, and he intended to. "You have plans for this evening?"

Her face lit up and the prettiest smile curved her mouth, and he wanted to kiss her all over again. "Is that the cowboy version of asking a girl on a date?"

"That's the 'we're both stranded up here together' version of it, yeah." When she laughed, some of the tension in his body eased. "I can make dinner, but you have to promise not to help. I'm not in the mood for a medical emergency tonight."

She gasped and mock swatted at his chest. "Not funny!"

"Pretty funny." Eli grabbed her hand, checking the bandages. "This feeling better?"

"It stings, but it's scabbed over."

"Good." He turned her hand over and pressed a kiss to her knuckles, just because he couldn't resist. "Now, for dinner, do you want spaghetti, or Hamburger Helper?"

"Those are my choices?"

He lowered her hand but kept it in his as he headed toward the kitchen. Felt nice to hold her hand. Felt right. "Just because I'm better in a kitchen than you doesn't mean much. I can make breakfast, and I can make things that come in a box. After that, I'm pretty lost."

"Spaghetti sounds good. I can help—"

"No you can't." He moved to the table in the kitchen and pulled out one of the chairs, gesturing that she should sit down. "You can sit and keep me company, though."

Her lower lip thrust out in the prettiest little pout, but she thumped into the seat. "Fine."

"Not everyone's a cook, Cass. I'm sure you have other skills." And then his ears got hot again, because that sounded pretty darn sexual to him, and he hadn't meant it like that. "I—what the hell is that?"

He'd turned toward the counter and saw a plateful of what looked like . . . well, he wasn't sure. Blobs with eyes and burned edges. They looked like something out of a horror movie. White icing slithered down the sides, like snow had melted atop each one. It resembled a creepy snowman graveyard, with all of the blobs lined up and staring at him with beady little eyes.

"Oh! Well, I tried to make gingerbread men cookies," Cass told him. "Snowman gingerbread men. Except I think the oven is broken because they got all soggy in the middle, so I had to leave them in for longer and then they burned. And they really didn't look great without icing, so I iced them and . . . and now they look like an even bigger disaster. Like a Pinterest fail."

"Like a what?"

"Do you not know what Pinterest is?" She sounded amused. "Or I guess cowboys don't hang out and pin their dream wedding stuff online."

"Hell no," he said, wondering if he should take a bite out of a cookie to please Cass. After a moment of staring down at the beady eyes of the closest cookie, he decided against it and carefully slid the plate away so it'd stop looking at him. "All right. Dinner." He got out a pot of water to boil the noodles.

"Have you ever thought about that stuff?" she asked from behind him.

"Pinterest? Not at all." He took the pot to the sink and began to fill it.

"No. Weddings, silly. Have you ever been serious with someone before? You said there was no ex-wife. Just wondering if there's a string of ex-girlfriends out there. Basically, I'm being nosy."

"Ah." He finished filling the pot and carried it back to the stovetop, not looking over at her. He was flattered that she was asking, but it also made him uncomfortable, because his answer was kind of . . . sad. "Haven't had a girl-friend in ten years. No wait, twelve. My last one broke up with me when I was in the army."

"Really?"

"Really."

"That's . . . an awfully long dry spell."

He turned and gave her a stern look. "Didn't say it was a good thing. Just said it was what it was. I guess you've never gone that long between relationships?"

Her smile turned wistful. "I can't remember."

Right. He mentally cursed himself for bringing it up. "You can ask what you want," he told her, trying to deflect away from the reminder of her lost memory. "It's not a fan-tastic story by any means. Kind of boring, really. But I'll tell it if you want to hear it."

"Of course I want to hear it. I like learning about you."

So he told her all about what a shithead of a kid he was back in his younger days. Drinking, smoking, gambling, skipping school—he'd done all of it. He talked about his wild years as he browned ground beef in the pan and threw spa-ghetti noodles into the boiling water. It wasn't much to tell. He'd had a wild-tempered girlfriend back in high school who'd been exciting and bold. Then he'd gone away to join the army, and when he was stationed halfway across the country from her, things soured. Her fast-paced and free-wheeling lifestyle hadn't changed just because he was gone, and so he told Cass all about the things that embarrassed him for so long—like when he'd come home on leave for Christ-mas and found his girlfriend in bed with two men at once.

"Oh wow," was all she'd said, her eyes wide.

It was funny, though—it didn't feel weird or shameful to tell Cass about these things. He'd kept them to himself for so long that they'd started to feel like ugly secrets. Now, in telling them, he realized they were just things in his past. Hurtful then, but not now. It did explain why he wasn't a big fan of Christmas, though.

He kept talking, telling Cass about how he'd been disgusted with how the relationship had ended and that when he'd returned to his post, he'd sworn off relationships for a while. Then when he'd come to Wyoming and started ranching, he hadn't really had another relationship since. Couple of dates here and there, but they never went anywhere.

A long dry spell, indeed. But it was one of those things—not good or bad. Just was. It had never bothered him before. He told himself he was living a life that most women didn't want. He told himself that the mountains and valleys of the Price Ranch land were enough to make up for the fact that his love life was anemic. And he'd been happy with it for a long, long time.

But that was before Cass. She'd changed everything.

"I just can't believe you haven't dated much in the last twelve years, Eli." She told him as he served up plates of spaghetti with meat sauce.

"Why's that so hard to believe?" He sat down across from her.

A little smile curved her mouth. "Because you're polite, and handsome, and hardworking? You've got a great body and a fantastic smile and you're a cowboy. Women should be falling all over themselves to get to you."

Eli stared at her in surprise. The flood of compliments made him uncomfortable, but it also made him feel pretty damn pleased that she thought of him that way. "So you think I have a great body, huh?"

She reached over and lightly smacked his hand. "Hush."

They ate in companionable silence and he suspected he'd embarrassed her. Eventually, Cass asked what he'd done that day and he told her all about the particular cattle he'd been rounding up. Houdini had gotten out again and this time hadn't wandered far. It had been annoying, though, and then he'd had to search the fences for the problem and repair it. Another cow had to be watched closely as she looked as if she was sick, with extra mucus hanging from her nose, so he'd taken her into the barn to keep an eye on her. She'd been given some additional vitamins and he planned on monitoring her progress tonight to see if she perked up or got worse. If she didn't show signs of eating, he had antibiotics to administer and failing that, he could always call Doc Parsons and get his advice.

Even though the topic wasn't the most appetizing one, Cass listened with interest. Before he knew it, he'd eaten two helpings of food and she'd cleaned her plate. They did the dishes together while she told him about the chickens. She'd found two eggs today and had been so very excited. Cass admitted it felt like finding buried treasure, which struck him as funny and sweet all at once.

It felt good to spend this time with her, even if it was just doing simple domestic things around the house. Maybe some women would be bored with that sort of thing, but she didn't seem bored. She seemed happy, and that made him happy. He liked seeing her smiles, and they were more frequent as the days passed.

After cleaning up, they headed into the living room and Cass put on more Christmas music. A man's smooth voice rolled out over the room and sang about white Christmases. Cass smiled at him and sat on the edge of the couch, the nervousness returning to her body. He supposed he was a little nervous, too. After all, he wanted to grab her and kiss her, and he wondered if that'd be too much too soon, or if she was hoping for it, too. He'd already kissed her once today. Maybe she didn't want to be mauled by a cowboy at every turn.

But then again, she had told him he had a good body, and then she'd blushed after saying that.

"Do you mind the music?" she asked, looking over at him from her end of the couch as he sat down on the opposite end. Cass frowned at him as he leaned back, and then slid down until she was next to him, her thigh brushing against his. "Is something wrong?"

"Something wrong?" He frowned at her. Or tried to, anyhow. He was having a hard time concentrating on anything other than her nearness.

"I just thought that after you kissed me . . ." She shrugged. "That maybe you'd want to sit with me instead of as far away as possible."

Well hell, he was messing this up, wasn't he? "I didn't want to crowd you."

"Crowd me?" Cass gave him an incredulous look. She grabbed his arm, lifted it over her shoulders, and then snuggled in under his arm. "If you don't want to touch me, say so."

"Why would you think I don't want to touch you?" He'd been dreaming of touching her all day. Even now, it took everything he had to keep his hand on her shoulder and not let it roam. He'd love to explore her body and touch her soft curves, but only when she was ready.

"Because you're being weird. I . . ." She gazed up at him speculatively. "Eli, are you shy?"

He didn't think of himself as shy. Maybe not outgoing or pushy, but shy seemed such a . . . girly word. "Naw."

She rolled her eyes and settled in against him. "You're shy."

He grunted.

With a little sigh, she put her head down on his shoulder

and they were quiet as the music drifted through the room and the fire crackled with warmth.

It was nice. Peaceful.

But only for a few moments. Cass touched his shirt, resting on his stomach and distracting him. "Do you have a favorite Christmas song?"

"Me? Nah. I'm not much for Christmas." He rubbed her shoulder absently, unable to resist touching her. It was either that or he was gonna be very focused on that hand right above his belt.

"Why not?"

Eli wanted to tell her about his childhood, but the words stuck in his throat. The bitterness and misery of those years rushed back to him and he forced it aside. He didn't want to think about bad things with someone as pure and happy as Cass in his arms. "Just wasn't a big deal for my family. What about you?" He nudged her shoulder with his hand. "Favorite?"

She sighed dreamily, tilting her head back and gazing up at him from her spot on his shoulder. Her dark hair spilled over his shirt and he thought he'd never seen anything so damn pretty. "I have so many. But if I had to pick one, maybe . . . 'O Holy Night'? It's just so lovely and peaceful." A smile immediately curved her face. "Though I'm partial to the Mariah Carey album, too. Anything with jingle bells and a beat is fun."

He had no idea what she was talking about, but if she liked it, then he liked it, too. "Sounds great." One stray curl tickled his skin and he tugged on it, unable to resist its lure. "This is your favorite holiday, then?"

"Oh, absolutely. Hands down."

"Can I ask why?"

She looked surprised at his question, and then shrugged

her shoulders. "Gosh. I've never been asked 'why' before. Why do you love anything that's wonderful?" Cass pursed her lips and gazed at the tree, thinking. "Maybe it's because at Christmas, everyone's so full of joy and hope. They're thinking about how to make their loved ones smile with gifts, and how to bring family together. No one's sad or lonely. I guess I like that about the holiday most of all. It's a time for everyone to be kind to each other instead of jerks."

He grunted at her words. *No one's sad or lonely.* Obviously they'd had very different Christmases. "You're an optimist, you know that?"

"I do." She wiggled her eyebrows at him. "Is that a problem?"

"If you don't mind me being a bit of a Christmas grouch, I can live with your optimism."

"Grinch."

"What?"

"It's a Christmas grinch, not a grouch. Boy, you really are bad at this holiday, aren't you? Did you grow up in a bubble?" She tilted her head, gazing up at him, and her fingers danced on his stomach in a light tickle.

"Not a bubble, no." Eli put his hand over her wiggling fingers, stopping them. He laced his fingers with hers, because that felt right. And when her lips parted as she gazed up at him, he leaned over and kissed her, because that felt right, too.

She met his kiss eagerly, as if she'd been waiting hours just for that moment. He'd held back from being too pushy with her, too overbearing, because he didn't want to intimidate her. Clearly, Cass wasn't intimidated in the slightest. She was ready for more, and when her tongue touched his with a teasing flick, he knew that he didn't have to be cautious around her. Hell, maybe she was right. Maybe he was shy and just coming up with excuses so he wouldn't fall for her too quickly.

Too late for that.

Cass made a soft noise of pleasure, her hand going to his hair as the kiss deepened. He groaned against her, his tongue licking against hers as they kissed, and his hand went to her waist. He pulled her against him, dragging her forward until, in the next moment, his enthusiastic Cass was in his lap, straddling him. Her breasts pushed against his chest and her arms were around his neck, and it was the best moment he could remember in a long, long time.

Between soft, quick kisses, he pulled his mouth from hers, mindful of the way her hips straddled him. "Am I going too fast for you?"

She gave her head a little shake and then rocked down against him, rubbing her sex along his aching length. "I've been waiting for you to go fast. Speed up as much as you want, Eli." And then she bit his lower lip, gently sucking on it.

Damn. She was a vixen. His vixen. He'd been ready to give her a great big speech about going slow and taking as much time as she needed, but all of that went out the window with her sexy little bites. She didn't want slow. She wanted this as much as he did—and the thought was as mind-blowing as it was exciting. Eli tangled his hand in her long, silky hair, knotting at the back of her head and pinning her against him as he swept his mouth over hers again. She gave a little whimper as he possessed her with his kiss, using his tongue and lips to pleasure her and urge more of those tempting little noises from her throat.

Of course, Cass was fantastic at one-upping him when it came to flirting. Her hands slid to his chest, and she rocked back and forth against him again, moving her hips in a way that was going to drive him mad. He certainly wasn't thinking about Christmas now. He wasn't thinking about anything but the gorgeous woman on his lap. With another hot, sultry kiss, he slid his hands to the curves of her ass, squeezing. God, but she had a pretty ass. Round and bouncy and just the right handful for him. He bet it'd look amazing naked.

He'd bet all of her would look amazing naked. All sweet curves and pale skin and enthusiasm. Dear god, his cock strained against his jeans as he thought about that. He'd never met anyone like Cass.

No wonder he was half in love with her already. Maybe more than half. Maybe he was already fighting the inevitable and his mind—and heart—were already gone. She'd snatched them up in her lovely hands.

Her mouth was on his once more and he couldn't think about anything except how good Cass's lips tasted on his, how her tongue brushed and rubbed against his own in a way that made him crazy with need. Had he thought that he was fine without relationships in his life? That he didn't need anyone else? Clearly he was an idiot, because he couldn't picture a day without kissing Cass. Already he was addicted to the feel of her sweet mouth against his. His body ached fiercely with need, but he didn't want to push her if she was hurting or wasn't ready. She'd just been in a car accident, after all. He kissed her hard, until she moaned, rocking down against him. Then he pulled back and met her dazed eyes. "I wanna make this good for you."

"It's good," she promised.

"We can go as slow as you want—"

She made an exasperated sound in her throat. She grabbed one of his hands on her waist. "If we go any slower, I'm going to start screaming." And she put it on her breast.

Lust, hot and wild, surged through him.

She wanted faster? More? He'd give her all of that. With a groan, he locked his grip around her waist and lifted her off his lap, pushing her gently backward onto the couch. Heat and determination poured through him, and she must have seen it in his gaze because she gave an excited shiver. He laid her down gently and then moved over her, cupping her neck even as he kissed her again. God, he loved her kisses. They were so hungry and full of anticipation and need both. It was as if he was giving her a gift each time their tongues met, and he felt the same way. Kissing Cass was never boring, never unemotional. Then, he began to kiss lower. He moved along her jaw, pressing light kisses as she gasped and clutched at his shirt.

He grabbed the front of her shirt—his, really—and pulled it apart, not caring that buttons flew everywhere. She was tired of waiting? Him too. He'd show her just how impatient and demanding he could be. He nipped at her throat, loving the moan she gave him. He wanted more than just a moan from her, though. He wanted to see her lose control. To tug at him with her frantic hands. To scream out his name as she came. His thoughts grew greedier by the second, and he welcomed it. Cass wanted more?

He'd give her everything.

Eli kissed along her collarbone and then pushed the shirt open, exposing a delicate, lacy bra. It was white against her skin, and he was surprised to see a smattering of freckles along her breastbone. It was so damn charming and perfect, just like her. He leaned in and pressed his mouth to one freckle, and was pleased to see her breasts heave in response.

"Please," she whispered. "Touch me, Eli. I'm dying for it."

How could a man refuse something like that? He put his hand on her breast again, his thumb giving the soft skin that swelled above the cups of her bra a light caress. She moaned, her head going back, and he pulled the fabric down, exposing her breast even as he kissed lower. Her skin was creamier here, her nipple a dusty rose color that wasn't quite pink or brown, but a mixture of both. He still thought it was the prettiest thing he'd ever seen, and he kissed the tip. "Beautiful."

Cass's hands moved to his shoulders, gripping him tightly. "Oh god, do that again."

With pleasure. Eli rubbed one knuckle along the smooth curve of her other breast, teasing it through the material of her bra as he leaned in and lavished attention on her nipple. He explored her with his tongue, gliding the tip along her skin and feeling her responses quivering through her body. She went wild with every graze of his mouth against her breast, every time his thumb skated over her other nipple, still concealed. He kissed and nipped and sucked at the exposed skin until it became pink with his attentions and she was writhing and moaning under him, pleading for more.

"I can't believe you haven't had sex in twelve years," she panted, arching up against his demanding mouth.

"Maybe I was waiting for something special," he told her as he palmed one breast, then licked the tip of the other and gently blew on it. "Didn't want just anyone."

"You can't be real." Cass's hands moved over his hair, roamed along his shoulders, as frantic and desperate as the rest of her. "I must have hit my head too hard and this is all a delicious dream."

"Nah," he told her as he nipped at the tip again. "In your dream, I'd probably be rich." He dragged his tongue along the underside of her nipple. "And have softer hands." He could feel the calluses on his thumb scrape against the satiny material of her bra as he caressed her.

"I love your rough hands." Her fingers tangled in the short strands of his hair and she pulled his mouth to hers for a fierce kiss. "Love that you work hard. That all of this is real." She squeezed his arm. "And I don't like rich guys. They're too pushy."

"And I'm not?" he asked, lowering his head between her breasts again. "I've got you half naked and under me."

"You're pushy in a good way," she told him, clutching hard at the throw pillow under her head. "And you can get me fully naked under you and I won't mind."

"That so?" He kissed his way up that freckled skin and back to her pretty, pouty mouth. It was slightly swollen and darker pink from their kisses, and he loved the sight of it. He studied her face to see if she was just saying that to please him. That she truly didn't want more than just kissing and petting for now. But the look in her eyes was nothing but eagerness and need.

A thought flashed in Eli's head—where were the condoms? He wasn't sure he remembered and also wasn't sure he wanted to ruin this moment between them by a birth control scavenger hunt.

Tonight would be all about her, then. If she wanted more after that, he'd be happy to oblige. But for now, he could pleasure her and get his own enjoyment out of that. So he helped her sit up, wordlessly, and she followed his lead eagerly, her gaze riveted to him. He brushed his lips against hers even as he pulled the shirt off her and then undid the clasp on her bra, tossing the clothing to the ground. Then she was truly half naked and just as beautiful as she was in his dreams. With a happy sigh, Cass put her arms around his neck and kissed him, as if she couldn't get enough.

He couldn't, either. He'd never have enough. But for now, if she was hungry for more, he'd give it to her.

Eli let his fingers skate along the waist of her jeans, gauging her reaction as they kissed. When her mouth on his grew more enthusiastic, he undid the button at the front and slipped his fingers into her panties. "You want more, baby?" he murmured between kisses. "Because I've got plenty to give."

She moaned, rocking against his hand. "I do want more." Her mouth trembled against his as he carefully caressed the curls he found between her thighs, and then stroked his fingers up and down her slick heat, exploring her. She was hot and wet here, so wet that it made his mouth water with need. He dragged his mouth along her neck, sucking lightly at the soft skin there, even as he touched her and caressed her slick folds, seeking one spot in particular. Cass gasped and shifted against his hand, rocking against him and making soft, wordless cries.

Just as he found her clit, he bit down on her neck. Not hard, just enough to excite her. She gasped his name, her fingers clenching in his shirt, and then she moved against his hand, pushing her hips against him and pressing her clit against his fingers with intense need. "Please," she whispered. "Please, please, Eli."

"I've got you," he told her, nipping at her neck. "I'm here."

She whimpered, rubbing up against him even as he rubbed her clit, trying to find the movement that would make her wild. Every girl was sensitive in different ways, he knew, and every one liked to be touched just a little bit differently. When she cried out as he slid a finger against either side of her clit, he knew he'd found the answer. He murmured words of encouragement as he stroked her. She clung to him, the tension building in her body, and her nails dug into his shirt as she shuddered and came. He kept stroking her, holding her tight against him as she rode the waves of the orgasm. She was beautiful like this, panting with her release, her features soft. She—

A yip from one of the dogs across the room made them both jerk out of their reverie.

Reluctantly, he pulled his hand from her panties as she slid off him. "What was that?" Cass asked.

"Sounded like Jim. Come here, boy," he called, slapping a hand against his jeans. He'd have the scent of her body there now, he realized, and wondered if it was too strange to fold up the jeans and keep them in a drawer so he could breathe it in every now and then. Probably.

Jim came out from behind the Christmas tree, and Cass made a strange sound in her throat. "Is Frannie still back there?"

"Is she still back there?" he asked, curious. He gave Jim's head a scratch and then pointed at the kitchen entrance, where Bandit waited, relaxing on the tile. The dog wagged his tail and headed to curl up next to Bandit, and Eli followed Cass. She'd moved toward the Christmas tree, naked to the jeans sagging around her waist and showing the dimples in her lower back that led to her buttocks. He watched the delicate line of her back, fascinated by her movements as she knelt in front of the tree and pressed her face to the floor.

She gasped. "I think Frannie's having her puppies under the tree!"

"She is?" He got down on the floor next to her and pressed his face to the floorboards as well.

There, at the very back, tree skirt bunched up and hidden behind the thick branches of the oversized tree he'd gotten for Cass, was his dog. She lay on her side and wagged her tail at the sight of them. Eli could barely make out a squirming bundle moving against her belly. "I'll be damned. I didn't realize . . ."

Cass chuckled and nudged him, her cheek still pressed to the floor. "We were a little busy, if you hadn't noticed."

He laughed, because the roof could have caved in and he probably wouldn't have noticed anything but Cass. "Guess you're right."

"What a wonderful early Christmas present," she said in a soft voice. "It's been a magical night."

"Indeed." It had been pretty damn magical for him, too.

CHAPTER EIGHTEEN

Eli gave Cass the shirt off his back and she curled up in it, unwilling to leave her post near the tree in case Frannie needed her. She put out some leftovers and set them on a plate, along with a fresh bowl of water, and sat and waited. Eli joined her, shirtless and in nothing but his jeans and socks, and it was a curiously intimate moment. She found herself reaching for his hand as they sat next to each other, and was pleased when he linked his fingers with hers. He didn't seem like the type to hold hands, but she liked that he would anyhow.

"I think I count five balls of fluff," she told him, barely able to see movement through the branches of the tree. "Two of them look white like her, but the others have the same coloring as Bandit, the scamp."

His laughter made her feel warm. The squeeze he gave her hand? Even warmer. "Don't be too hard on Bandit. Ever since I got Frannie, it was the plan all this time for her to have one litter before I got her fixed."

"It was?" She looked over at him, surprised. She also really, really liked his laugh and tucked their joined hands against her leg, because she loved his touch just as much as that delighted laugh. "You've been planning this all along? Is it doggy true love, then?"

"Dunno about that." Eli gave her an amused grin. "But when I bought Frannie, she was the last pup the breeder had, and the last one she'd have for a while."

"This is the part where I should tell you to adopt instead of buy, right?"

He shrugged. "I bought her because I needed to make sure she was a ranch dog. I'd have loved a mutt just as much, but not every mutt has the herding instinct. With Frannie's breed, I knew she'd be a good cattle dog. Those are just as important on the ranch as any of the horses."

"Oh. I didn't know."

"I know you didn't." His thumb rubbed against the seam of her jeans on the inside of her thigh. "And Old Clyde had a pair of Great Pyrenees for the longest time. Big fluffy white monsters. Could herd cattle like nobody's business. Frannie looked downright petite next to them. They died about a year ago within a few days of each other, and Old Clyde was just devastated. Had those dogs for over a decade, and I think he loved them more than most people. They were getting on in years, of course, so he knew it was coming, but to lose both at once was a real blow. I'd just gotten Frannie and she was nothing but this adorable white bit of fluff, and Old Clyde just looked so sad every time he saw her. So I suggested we let her have a litter, and then I'd get her fixed. One of those little guys is gonna be for him. Maybe two if he wants."

Her heart stuttered. If that wasn't one of the sweetest,

most thoughtful things she'd ever heard. "You're a good man, Eli. That's lovely of you."

"I wasn't the one carrying it, so I don't know that I can take the credit." He winked at her. "But it made Old Clyde real happy, and he's been waiting a long time to see these little ones born. He'll be thrilled when he gets back."

"I can imagine. Who wouldn't want a puppy?" Even now, just seeing those little balls of fluff moving around behind the tree made her heart squeeze. Every time Frannie licked one, Cass's heart squeezed again.

Of course, every time Eli looked over at her, her heart squeezed, too. Lots of squeezing going on.

"What about the rest of them?"

He considered for a moment, and then pulled her against him, until she was tucked under his arm. "We'll figure it out."

He'd get them good homes, she knew. He wasn't the type to abandon someone in his charge. Her hands went to his waist and she laid her head on his shoulder. She was still half naked, because she hadn't buttoned his shirt, and her jeans were still undone, but it didn't matter. She felt pretty. Cared for. Loved.

Happy.

Gosh, when had she been so happy? She racked her brain, desperately wishing that memories would pop up, but nothing came forward. No last name. No job. No idea why she'd been heading into the mountains. At some point, those memories would return—she refused to think otherwise—and she'd have to deal with real life. The idea made her stomach knot, as if real life were something she desperately wanted to avoid, and she didn't know why. She wouldn't think about that tonight, though.

Tonight, it was Christmas Eve, and she was going to spend it in the arms of the cowboy she was falling for.

They watched Frannie and her puppies for hours. Once Frannie emerged to eat, Eli carefully moved the tree away from the wall and Cass squeezed in to rescue the newborns from the corner. She wanted to wash the tree skirts and get the dog fresh blankets, and she was a little worried that all those pine needles that dropped from the tree might land on the puppies. Eli prepped a large box and she padded it with blankets, and then one by one the delicate little bundles were moved to their new bed. Frannie hovered while Cass gently moved them, and once they were in the new box, she climbed in and began licking them again.

The three pups that looked like Bandit had the splotchy gray and gold and white coloring that Eli said was typical of the breed—Australian shepherd. They had Frannie's thick coat, and Cass bet they would be gorgeous when they got older. The two smaller puppies were pure white miniatures of their mother, and she suspected those were the ones that Old Clyde would want. Since it was Christmas Eve, she named the three big ones Gold, Frankincense, and Myrrh— or rather, Goldie, Frankie, and Myrtle. The two tiny ones would be Joy and Noel.

Eli just rolled his eyes at her names, but she didn't think he minded. She threatened to name them after reindeer, and that got a belly laugh out of him.

It was a lovely evening, Cass thought. When the dogs were settled, she and Eli curled up on the couch together and talked of anything and everything. The weather, politics, television shows, books they'd read. Cass found that she had more memories than she thought, because she was pleased to find out that she'd read the Harry Potter books just last year, and Eli never had. She made a private vow to get him copies, because she thought he'd like them. The last book he said he'd read was *Lonesome Dove*, and so she called him a cliché. That had brought a fiendish gleam to his eyes and they'd ended up in a tickle fight on the couch.

The tickle fight had ended up in more kissing.

So much kissing.

And god, she loved kissing him. The way his mouth fit against hers was perfection, and she loved the way he tasted. It felt weird to think of people having a "taste" but there was something about him that just made her crazy with lust, and she couldn't get enough of his touches, his kisses, his everything. They'd made out on the couch for hours, mostly just slow, lazy kisses, exploring each other from the waist up. He'd played with her breasts until she was whimpering, and she'd ran her hands all over that delicious, tanned body of his. She'd tried to push him for more, to have sex, but he'd simply put his hand in her panties again and made her come twice in short succession, and well, she couldn't really complain after that. She was too dazed.

The last thing she remembered was his arms around her and his mouth pressed to her forehead as she went to sleep.

Cass woke up to a puppy's mewling yip sometime close to dawn, and scrubbed a hand over her eyes. She squinted at the watery gray sunlight leaking through the windows and tried to figure out where she was. Not Eli's bed, but the couch. They'd slept on the narrow length, tangled together all night. It was wonderful. She wondered if they'd be sleeping together every night from now on. Even if there wasn't sex, she just liked cuddling up next to him.

And, okay, the cuddling would hopefully lead to sex. Fingers crossed. She was pretty sure he wanted her—hours of kissing couldn't lie—but she was also pretty sure he moved a lot slower than she did. And that was all right, as long as they met somewhere in the middle.

She wasn't even upset that he'd gone out on Christmas morning and hadn't woken her up. If there was one thing she'd learned over the last week, it was that the ranch didn't wait for anyone to sleep in, and it certainly didn't wait for holidays. She could appreciate that, though, and she appreciated how hard Eli worked. There wasn't a lazy bone in his body. He was far too responsible. And, goodness, when had responsibility become so damn sexy? But it was, and it made her want to do something other than sit around all day.

Well, at least she had chickens to look after. And now puppies. Between that and keeping the house tidy, it was something. Cass went through her chores, hoping for a glimpse of Eli out in the pastures. He'd left her a note in the kitchen, telling her that he'd wrap things up early and to wait for him to eat. He'd signed it with a big "E," and she'd dreamily traced that "E" over and over again as she ate breakfast.

The day was bright and sunny, making the snow so shiny it almost hurt her eyes. She wondered if it was going to melt soon.

She wasn't sure if she wanted it to ever melt.

After the chickens were fed and the laundry was started, she checked on Frannie. The dog was happily nursing her pups, her tail thumping at the sight of Cass. She scratched the fluffy head and let her be, wandering into the bathroom. After staring at her reflection in the mirror for a bit, Cass decided that the big gash on her forehead had healed up pretty nicely. It'd leave a scar, but hopefully not a dreadful one. Someone would hate it . . .

Someone.

Someone.

She squeezed her eyes shut and tried to concentrate. A face floated at the back of her mind, but disappeared as quickly as it had flickered through. That was progress, though. She'd take it. It was a flash of memory, returning in less than a week.

Who knew where she'd be in another week?

For some reason, the thought wasn't comforting. There was something she was hiding from, Cass sensed. Something that she was running away from. Some sort of confrontation she was avoiding. That had to be why she dreaded the thought of getting on the Internet and looking herself up.

Maybe in another week she'd be ready to confront it.

Maybe.

Cass was flipping through a cookbook in the living room when the mudroom door opened. She glanced at the clock and was delighted to see that it was indeed early. Just a little after lunch. She threw the book aside and raced into the kitchen to greet him. "You're back early, all right. What—"

She'd expected to see him in the mudroom, pulling off his boots or peeling off layers. Instead, she was greeted with a fierce kiss, his cowboy hat smacking her forehead and tipping backward as he pulled her against him. Cass was thoroughly kissed until she was dazed and panting, and then he released her with one more small peck on the lips. "Merry Christmas," Eli murmured.

"Hi," she breathed, clinging to his coat for support. "Did you miss me?"

"Hell yeah."

"I missed you, too," she told him, and felt herself blushing.

"Luckily we have the rest of the day together," he said,

giving her another smacking kiss and then releasing her. "Let me undress and I'll join you."

"I'd love to help you undress," she told him breathlessly, and was rewarded with a heated glance over his shoulder. She fanned herself with a hand as he headed back toward the mudroom, because that wasn't the greeting a guy gave his girl when he wanted to go slow.

She was totally getting laid tonight.

Her pulse thrummed with anticipation as she watched him take off his outer layers. She picked up his hat from the kitchen floor, and it reminded her of her Christmas present for him. Excited, she rushed into the living room and snagged it from under the tree, then returned to the kitchen to wait for him. She set it down on the table in front of her, proud of the wrapping job she'd done on it. It had taken two tries (and several paper cuts) before she was able to make a pretty box, but the end result was rather professional, if she said so herself.

When Eli stepped into the kitchen in nothing but a sweaty white T-shirt and jeans, scratching at his chest, she sucked in a breath. It was unfair that a man should be that handsome when he was dirty. There was a smear of dirt on his forehead and his hair was slick with sweat, but he still looked good enough to eat. "I should shower before . . ." He paused, noticing the present on the table in front of her. "What's that?"

Cass held it up triumphantly, excited. "Merry Christmas!"

He blinked at her, unmoving. "That's . . . for me?"

"Who else would it be for?" She chuckled and pushed it toward him. "Open it!"

Eli took one step forward, hesitated, then took the box from her. The smallest smile curved his mouth, as if he couldn't believe what he was seeing, and it broke her heart. Somehow, she thought he hadn't gotten many presents in his life. His incredulous reaction followed by shy pleasure was that of someone who expected nothing, and who always expected nothing. Her poor, sweet cowboy. Now she wished she'd somehow figured out something else to make him instead of just a stupid hat.

But what was done was done. He took the box from her and she clasped her hands in front of her chest, brimming with excitement. "I hope you like it."

His gaze flicked to her and his smile widened. "How can I not?"

"You don't even know what it is yet. Let's hold off judgment until you see it."

With careful hands, Eli pulled the ribbon off of the top and peeled the wrapping paper back as if he wanted to keep it all without a single crease. He lifted the lid off the box and then pulled out the red hat she'd made him, with the silly white edging and the earflaps. Mentally, she cringed. This wasn't what you gave a big, sexy man. "It's not much," she began.

He set the box down and held the hat in his hands, rubbing the yarn and just staring at it for so long she began to feel anxious. "You . . . made this?" Eli looked up at her.

"I did." She squeezed her hands together tightly so she wouldn't wring them in nervousness. "I know how to crochet, apparently, and I saw the yarn there and I wanted to make you something as a thank-you for saving me. I felt like you should have something to open on Christmas day, even if you're not a big fan of the holiday. It didn't seem right otherwise." Cass bit her lip. "It's just a hat, but it was all I could do. And I'll pay Maria back for the yarn—"

"You knitted this for me?" There was a husky note in his voice.

"Well, it's crochet, but yes. I know it's kind of bright but

I figured you could wear it under your cowboy hat, maybe, and . . ." Her voice died as his jaw clenched. "It's not much."

When he looked up at her, his eyes were curiously shiny. "You didn't have to do this."

"I wanted to do this, Eli."

He crushed it to his chest. "Best damn present I've ever gotten," he told her in a gruff voice.

She laughed, because it was either that or start sobbing, and she suspected he wouldn't be a fan of the sobbing. "Oh, come on. You had to have gotten better than that in the past. Your parents—"

"Didn't have any."

"—Must have . . . wait, what?" She stared at him in surprise.

He shrugged. "I mean, I did. I don't remember them, though. They sent me to a state home at age seven and then from there, I was bounced around between foster homes. Some were good foster homes, of course, but I never stayed in those for long." His smile was thin, brittle with old pain. "Not a lot of people want a troublemaking older boy with abandonment issues. They want a cuddly baby. I eventually landed with a very strict family who didn't believe in personal wealth and who thought Christmas was just an excuse for commercial greed and excess. I told you I joined the army right out of high school—it was because I couldn't wait to get away from them." He stared down at the hat in his hands. "No one's ever taken the time to make me something because they cared. So . . . thank you."

"Oh, Eli—"

"Don't," he told her with a small shake of his head. "Hard enough to talk about. Let's not make it weird." He gave her a small, crooked grin and her heart melted all over again.

"All right," she said softly. "I'm just glad you like it."

Eli turned it over in his hands, thoughtful. He glanced up at her and his face was more composed, the raw openness of a few moments ago gone. "I didn't get you anything."

She waved a hand in the air. "It's not about getting. It's about giving."

"Well, maybe I want to give. What do you want?"

"You," Cass said softly.

He gazed at her with a thoughtful expression on his face. Slowly, he reached up and put the red floppy hat on his head, the flaps curling up against his ears. It looked a little ridiculous, and she was about to tell him so when he leaned in and kissed her again. He smelled like sweat and horse and cattle, but she didn't care. This was Eli, her big, sweet cowboy with a crusty exterior and a wounded heart, and she was utterly crazy about him. So she flung her arms around his neck and kissed him back with all of the emotion she had bubbling up inside her.

"You want me," he murmured as he pulled back. "You've got me, Cass."

CHAPTER NINETEEN

He showered first. Of course he did. Eli was nothing if not clean, and Cass fluttered around the kitchen and the bedroom, straightening things and staying busy while he cleaned up. She gave Frannie and the other dogs more food, just in case she was occupied for the rest of the day, and gosh, wasn't that wishful thinking? She fed the chickens one last time, and then she went into the other bathroom to fluff her hair and make sure that her freshly shaved legs were smooth. She'd shaved earlier that day in hopeful anticipation, and she was glad she was an optimist about these sorts of things.

Of course, she'd been pushing for this moment for what felt like days—and now that it was here, she was a little nervous.

Sex was a big step between two people. Cass didn't really worry that there would be something about Eli that would be a turnoff, but it was still a big change in how they'd been together, and so she had nervous butterflies in her stomach. There was no going back after sex. Everything changed for good.

But she was likely worrying over nothing. Eli was a great kisser. He had an amazing body. He'd given her orgasms yesterday that made her thighs clench together in memory. Sex would be great. If she didn't stress out over where it led them, she could enjoy herself. So Cass gave herself mental pep talks as Eli showered, and fluffed her hair again and made sure she had nice sheets on the bed, because she could control those kinds of things. She didn't have extra panties or bras, because hers were still trapped in her car. She'd been wearing his boxers and rewashing her one pair every day, and she hoped they didn't look too pitiful. She wondered if guys noticed a sad-looking bra and panty set like girls did.

The bathroom door opened, and Cass practically jumped, her heart pounding. She pressed a hand to her chest as Eli emerged from the bathroom, all dewy, tanned skin and wet hair. He wore nothing but a pair of plaid sleep pants, and she forced herself not to stare at that rock-hard browned chest. He frowned at her startled expression. "Everything all right?"

"Yes. I . . . just jumpy." She smiled at him. "Nervous, I guess." Even the little laugh she made after saying that sounded like a high-pitched trill of anxiety.

"Nervous, huh?" He rubbed his hair with a towel and then tossed it aside, moving toward her.

Maybe she was. How could she not be with such an attractive, masculine man in front of her? Time to play it cool so he wouldn't know just how nervous she truly felt. So all she said was, "Do you have condoms here?"

His ears flushed red and he nodded, pulling two out of a pocket in his pants. "Found them in the bathroom."

"Not expired, I hope," she teased, trying to make the mood lighter.

Eli rubbed his ear and shook his head. "I imagine they're Jordy's. He fashions himself a bit of a ladies' man."

"Well then, I'm glad I was stuck up here with you and not Jordy." Cass moved forward, shoring up her courage, and put her arms around his neck. "I wanted to say thank you, Eli."

His hands slid down her back, rubbing her lightly. "Thank me? For what? Showering?"

"No, for finding me that day and bringing me here. I couldn't have asked for better treatment or a more handsome protector."

"Anyone would have done it," Eli told her, looking uncomfortable at her praise.

"Maybe." Maybe anyone would have done it, but she also wouldn't have fallen for just anyone. There weren't many people like Eli, with his rigid code of ethics and his stubborn determination. There wouldn't have been anyone with those piercing eyes and protective nature. It was as if someone had decided she needed a cowboy for Christmas and given her the best present ever. "I still feel lucky to be here with you, though."

"I feel the same. I wasn't looking forward to being here alone," he admitted, his hands sweeping up and down her back in slow stroking motions that made her feel petted and adored. "Figured it'd just be really quiet, but having you here has been . . . amazing. Normally I'd take my time outside, do everything I could to try to get ahead, and instead, I find myself racing through my chores so I can get back to you." He grabbed a handful of her hair and let it spill over his fingers. "Might say I'm obsessed."

"I'm okay with that," she teased. "Obsess away."

"It's new for me," he admitted, twining one of her curls around his fingers. "Never cared if anyone stayed or went before, and now I can't stop thinking about what'll happen when you leave. What happens to us." The look in his eyes grew wary, as if he were afraid of getting hurt. "Cass—"

"Let's not think about that right now," she whispered, because hearing him voice the same worries she had wasn't helping things. She put a hand on his chest and slid her fingers down the lines of his pectorals, following their delineation with a fingertip. "Let's just think about us and we can see where this leads."

"Pretty sure it's leading to bed," Eli said.

"I certainly hope so." Cass dipped her fingertip into his navel. "Otherwise, I'm going to be mighty disappointed."

"I'd hate to disappoint you," he told her, voice husky with need. He tightened his hand in her hair and lowered his mouth to hers in a searing kiss that made her toes curl. His tongue swept into her mouth with such ownership and authority that it only took moments before she was panting, her pulse throbbing between her thighs. How did he manage to get her so aroused so very quickly? It seemed like all he had to do was press his lips to hers and she'd turn into a puddle of need. Their mouths met with wild, hungry kisses, and it felt like it had been days since he'd last touched her, when in reality, it was only a few hours.

Too long, she decided. Her body had forgotten what his hands felt like and she needed to learn it again. She slid her hands to his waist, playfully tugging at the string at the front of his flannel pants. "Can I unwrap my Christmas present now?"

His eyes grew hot with arousal. "You want to go first? I thought I'd lay you down on the bed and get you all nice and naked for me. Put my mouth on a few places it hasn't had a chance to go yet."

"Oh, I'm absolutely looking forward to that," Cass breathed. "But I want my turn first." She moved down to her knees, gazing up at him, and then carefully pulled on his pants until they slid down his thighs and he was naked before her. And mercy, what a sight that was. His cock was big and thick, straining with his arousal, the skin flushed. His hips were a pale white compared to the tan of his chest, and she could only imagine how deep it would be in the summer. It made her smile to think that she was the only one who'd seen this delicious sight in a long, long time. Not even the sun got to glimpse what she was about to put her hands—and mouth—on.

"Merry Christmas to me," she murmured, and then wrapped her fingers around his length.

He groaned the moment her lips touched him. "Cass. Damn. Your mouth. I . . . can't . . ."

"Shhh," she told him as she moved her mouth along his length, exploring him with her tongue and lips. The heat of him seemed to be magnified here, and it made her shiver to feel just how hard he was under all that velvety soft skin. Cass let her lips whisper up and down his shaft before she took him in her mouth and gave the underside of his head a slow lick. She loved the sounds he made as she worked his cock, because it just made her more excited to touch him. She flicked her tongue against the head and then took him deeper into her mouth, trying to pull him in as far as she could.

"No," Eli breathed, pulling Cass away from his length. "I want to come inside you. I'm not ready to be done yet." He pulled her to her feet and caressed her cheek, just staring at her as if she were the most precious thing he'd ever seen.

Cass sighed dreamily up at him, sliding a hand against his neck and holding him close. "I love touching you. I want to put my mouth all over you."

"We've got time," he reminded her, and then pulled the shirt knot at her waist apart, loosening her top. "All the time we need."

She bit her lip and let her arms fall to her sides, allowing him to undress her. He kissed her over and over again as he unbuttoned the shirt, then pushed it off her arms and onto the floor. Next went her bra, and all the while, his mouth made sweet love to hers. Then she was in nothing but her jeans and he was working on those, too. When he slid them down her thighs, she shucked her panties too, impatient.

Then they were both naked, arms twining around each other, skin to skin as their kisses grew more intense. Cass moaned as he lifted her into his arms and hauled her onto the bed. He caressed her breasts as she lay back, and then gave her another hot, sultry kiss of promise before he straightened, standing tall over her.

"Condoms," was all he said.

Right. Condoms were definitely important. She slid her hands over her breasts as she waited for him, aching with need. Cass watched him from her spot, prone on the bed, as he opened the package and rolled the condom down his length. He glanced over at her and she caressed herself again, just because he was looking.

Eli groaned. "A man would die happy at the sight of you right now, Cass."

"I don't know how happy he'd be," she told him playfully, reaching for him with one arm. "Because he'd be missing out on all the good parts."

But he didn't respond to her quip. He just moved to her side, and while she touched him and caressed his chest, he ran his gaze over her body. "No bruises or pains from the accident, right?"

She snorted and tweaked his nipple. "You should have asked about that last night when we made out."

He flicked her hand off his chest, which told her that he was sensitive there . . . which meant she wanted to touch him in that spot even more. "I was distracted. I'm askin' now."

"I'm fine. Really. Look, no bruises." She cupped her breasts and jiggled them. "Everything's working as intended."

"Can't help a man if he worries about you," Eli told her in a low voice. He leaned over her, his cock prodding against her thigh, and grazed his thumb over her brow, on the mark that was sure to leave a scar.

"I promise I'm fine." He was making her ache with how thoughtful he was. She skimmed her fingers up one arm and down the center of his chest. "But I know something that would make me feel finer."

Eli cocked an eyebrow at her, and it took her breath away how sexy he was. "I do believe you have a one-track mind."

"I do believe you're right."

"I'll see what I can do about that, then." He moved onto the bed and covered her body with his. Cass automatically put her legs around his waist, encouraging him to slide closer. He gave her another deep, soulful kiss even as his hand slid to her thighs, pushing them farther apart. "I love the way you feel, baby," he whispered as he sank into her. "So soft and warm, and all mine."

Cass moaned at the sensation of him filling her. He'd pierced her so deep that she swore she could feel him inside her all the way to her heart. It felt incredible, and she tightened her legs around him even more.

He remained stiff over her, arms propping up his weight

on either side of her shoulders, his face full of tension. He didn't move, and she gave him a curious look, caressing his shoulder. "What is it?"

"Too good," he gritted, closing his eyes. "Give me a moment."

Was he close to losing control? She loved the thought of that. It made her feel so sexy to think that this big, delicious cowboy was close to pushing his limits just at touching her. She wanted to test that theory. So she dug her nails into his shoulders and lifted her hips against him, sinking him deeper.

The breath hissed from his throat. With a low, sexy growl, Eli buried his face against her neck and began to thrust, hard and sure. Oh god, yes. This was exactly what she wanted. She moaned encouragement even as he pushed into her, making their bodies rock on the bed as they came together. She tried to meet his thrusts with her hips, but it was too much for her to keep up with, and all she could do was cry out and tremble against him as he ruthlessly made love to her.

An orgasm built inside her belly, far too quickly. She tried to mentally push it aside, to focus on the pleasure of his body surging over hers. It was so good, she wanted it to keep going forever. But her body had other ideas. Within minutes, she was clenching tighter with every thrust, a low keening building in her throat. "Eli," she panted, full of a need that couldn't be defined.

"I've got you, Cass," he murmured into her ear. "I've got you."

She shattered. Her body curled in on itself as the orgasm rocketed through her, and she cried out at the intensity of it. Eli called her name hoarsely, his movements becoming erratic even as they grew fiercer. Then he shuddered atop her, and she knew he'd come, too.

She held him against her, panting, and realized her skin was dewy with sweat. His was, too, and she leaned in and breathed deeply of his scent. Even after all this, he smelled wonderful. He also looked good enough to eat, and she was still frisky, so she nipped at his shoulder and then swiped her tongue over the tiny mark.

Eli chuckled, and she could feel it deep inside her. "Give a guy a moment to rest, Cass."

"Just a moment," she whispered, and licked his shoulder again. "The day is young, remember?"

"I haven't forgotten." He lifted his head and gazed down at her, then brushed a sweaty lock of hair from her brow. "You're beautiful, you know that?"

She could feel herself blushing, which was silly, given that the man's cock was still buried deep inside her. Her fingers skimmed over her brow and the big, nasty mark there. "I looked better before."

"Not to me."

"You didn't see me before—"

"Precisely." He kissed the tip of her nose. "So don't argue."

"You're impossible."

"Ah, but I'm yours."

Cass liked the sound of that, a lot.

CHAPTER TWENTY

One week later

S he never thought she'd be so unhappy to see snow melt.
Cass sipped coffee from a big red mug and tried not to
glare at the sun shining down from the pale blue skies. It
wasn't the first sunny day since Christmas, but just the lat-
est in a string of pleasant (well, for winter) days that were
slowly but surely reducing the heaps of white snow on the
ground. Snow melting meant changes.

She didn't want changes.

She wasn't ready for them.

Everything in Cass's life felt perfect. She had a few holes
where her memory was, but it bothered her less as the days
went on. It'd come back, or she'd make new memories to fill
the holes. She was becoming more used to the idea as time
passed. It had been enjoyable to be here at the ranch, even
if there was a lot of work to be done. She'd graduated from
just helping with the chickens to now helping to feed the
horses and muck out stalls. Eli allowed her to help only if
she didn't seem tired at the end of the day, so Cass made

sure she looked fresh and cheery even if it was exhausting work. She enjoyed helping him out, though. It was hard, but satisfying. She loved feeding the horses, because they were always so excited to see their food. In a way, it was like Christmas for them every day, and that was fun.

Of course, there were also the puppies. Frannie's pups seemed to get bigger every time she saw them, and at a week old, their eyes were still closed, but they were fat and fuzzy, and made the most adorable little whines and grunts as they nursed from their patient mama.

And then there was Eli. Even as she stood at the window, she scanned the pasture looking for him. He wasn't out there, of course. Since the weather was better, he'd moved the cattle to a less muddy pasture because the one they'd been in for the last while was destroyed, and it was farther away from the ranch. She still searched for his horse, though, because she was addicted to the sight of him. Even a glimpse of her cowboy from afar set her heart to fluttering.

And, ahem, other parts to fluttering, too.

It was New Year's Day, and they'd been sleeping in the same bed for the last week. Maybe there was a tiny, worried part of her that feared that the sex wouldn't stay great. That something would happen between them and the spark would melt away, just like the snow was. She supposed that would make things a lot easier. It was the opposite, though. With every day that passed, she fell for Eli just a little more, craved his kisses a little more. Daydreamed about touching him and being in bed with him that night. She fantasized about new ways for them to explore each other, and she loved surprising him with caresses in the middle of the night. There was nothing better than a cowboy shocked to find his girlfriend's mouth on his body at three in the morning. She loved doing it, and he loved receiving it, so what was the harm?

Cass supposed she was his girlfriend. They hadn't really discussed labels. That hadn't seemed necessary. She was his and he was hers, and that was all there was to it. They couldn't keep their hands off each other. He laughed at her corny jokes. He ate her terrible attempts at cooking and made her breakfast because he liked to let her sleep curled up in the blankets for a bit longer than him every morning. They shared showers. He washed her hair. They even played cards together. Last night, he'd read aloud from his copy of *Lonesome Dove* with his head on her lap while she worked on crocheting him a matching scarf.   •

It was nice and homey and simple, and she loved it. Maybe she'd never been this person in the past, but she was now.

It was easy to not think about the world outside of Price Ranch when your life consisted of a snowbound house in the mountains. She didn't call anyone or get on the Internet. She figured that somewhere out there, someone would be looking for her. She knew that, and she felt guilty about it . . . but she just couldn't force herself to Google things and somehow trace back her information. It felt like if she did, it'd ruin everything.

Cass didn't know why she felt like that, just that she did. It was a gut feeling, an instinct. Happiness was fragile, and she was determined not to be the one to screw it up.

She hadn't confessed her worries to Eli. He was afraid of nothing, and she didn't want him to worry with just what it was that she was afraid of. She didn't want to put doubt into his mind. But late at night in bed, sometimes she worried. She worried about the kind of person she was.

What if she had a criminal record?

What if she was some deadbeat mom that had abandoned her kids?

What if she was a corporate-ladder climber who would

hate everything she'd found happiness with in the last two weeks?

What if . . . what if she was married?

That thought was the worst one, and it was the one that tended to float into her mind the most often. She touched her unmarked ring finger to reassure herself, but it still went through her thoughts every now and then. Not everyone wore wedding rings. What if she'd married some hipster that didn't believe in jewelry and that was why she didn't have the mark of a ring?

Cass knew most of it was in her head. She didn't think she was married—another gut feeling. But she didn't know for sure. If she even had the slightest suspicion that she was, she'd have never touched Eli, because cheating was a terrible thing. But . . . what if she'd lost those portions of her memory so completely that she didn't even realize? The thought had occurred to her a few days ago and now she couldn't shake it.

So she avoided reality and lost herself in Eli's arms. It was easy enough. All she had to do was close her eyes and kiss him. Lose herself in the feeding of chickens and the mucking of stalls and nights spent by the fire with the dogs and her man. And if she worried about things, well, she just wouldn't let him know.

A *thump thump thump* caught her attention, and Cass glanced over at Frannie, who was lounging in her box, five wriggling puppies attached to her. Her tail was wagging, smacking against the side of the box. "What is it, girl?" Cass asked, but she knew the answer.

Two seconds later, she heard the door to the mudroom even as Bandit and Jim shot into the house, dancing around with glee and tracking mud all over the floors. She wasn't even mad. They were far too cute. She bent over to rub Bandit's muzzle, calling out to Eli. "Hey, babe. You're done early." It was barely three, and sometimes he was out much, much later. Of course, ever since they'd started sleeping together, he'd found a way to finish up a lot quicker.

It gave them a lot more time for kissing . . . among other things. "Everything all right?"

"Just callin' it an early day today," he told her as he came into the kitchen. He pulled off his hat and underneath was the silly-looking crocheted cap she'd made for him. It was a little too small and left a waffle-weave texture on his forehead, but he wore the damn thing every day like it was the best thing he'd ever seen, and every time she saw him in it, her heart melted a little more.

Eli was just so easy to love.

"Well, I certainly don't mind," she began, and her words ended in a squeal when he grabbed her around the waist and hauled her over his shoulder. "What are you doing?"

"Taking you into the shower with me." He gave her ass a slap through her jeans. "Heard you were a dirty girl, so I thought I'd clean you up."

Wild giggles erupted from her, and she squirmed atop his shoulder as he carried her through the house, making her feel as if she weighed nothing. She loved this side of him. She was always a playful, teasing sort, but Eli was far more serious. That he was starting to play back with her was amazing, and she adored it. Besides, them in the shower together usually led to good things, so she was all for a quick wash. "You're in a good mood," she called to him as he entered the bathroom. "How are the cows?"

"The *cattle* are fine. I'll give them your regards." He always thought it was funny that she asked about them, as if they were pets. She couldn't get into her head that these were products and beef. They were just silly, smelly cows to her. She wasn't quite a rancher just yet, it seemed. "And besides, I thought we'd make other plans today."

"Wild shower sex followed by more wild shower sex?"

"Wild shower sex," he agreed, "followed by a ride out to your car to get your purse. You ever been on horseback?" He gently set her down on the tile floor and then began to undress her.

"Oh," she said. She tried to think of something else to say, and nothing came to her. The unpleasant knot returned to Cass's stomach.

Eli gave her a curious look as he worked the buttons on the front of her borrowed shirt. "That all right?"

"It's fine," she told him brightly. "And no, I've never ridden a horse before, but they make it look easy in the movies. So the weather's cleared up that much?"

He snorted, giving his head a little shake. "Movies. Riding a horse is not like they show it in the movies, Cass. You'll have to hold on to me. On second thought, maybe we should wait another day and take the Gator, because I don't trust you not to fall off the back of one of the horses unless I strap you to my back."

"How rude," she told him, mock offended. "And I don't mind waiting another day." In fact, she'd prefer it. It gave her one more day with him. One more day of bliss and no worries. When his hand went to her breast, she captured his mouth in a hot, hungry kiss.

She could convince him to go tomorrow, she figured. It'd be easy enough to distract him and buy herself another day.

S he managed to keep Eli (and herself) happily distracted for the rest of the evening, and she prayed for snow the next morning. If it snowed again, she'd buy herself a few more days. Unfortunately, the next morning dawned as sunny and crisp as yesterday, which meant there was no delaying the inevitable.

It wouldn't be that bad, she reasoned with herself. If she got her stuff back and was able to piece together who she was, great. It didn't mean things had to change. It just meant that the missing gaps would get filled in. She told herself that over and over again, but in the end, she still wasn't convinced. Something about this felt unsettling, and when Eli drove the Gator to the front of the house, she bundled up and then got in, forcing a smile to her face.

"You feeling all right, baby?" He pulled her against his side, tucking her under his arm. In the back of the Gator, Jim and Bandit paced, excited about the ride.

"I'm great," she lied. "Just anxious to get my stuff from the car." It wasn't a lie, exactly. After all, there was good anxious and bad anxious. She moved closer to him, though, because being snuggled up against him was nice, and she told herself to enjoy the ride. The farm vehicle they called the Gator was something like a small Jeep or an overlarge golf cart, designed to truck through the worst sort of terrain, and the thing had a flatbed for hauling stuff. The dogs raced around as it puttered over snowy hills and through muddy slicks. Cass noticed that most of the snow was turning to patchy brown and revealing the wet earth underneath. The trees were uncovered from their white blankets, and everything around them was very pretty and very drippy and depressingly snowless. It meant that she couldn't delay the inevitable any longer.

It also meant that the others would probably be returning soon. Eli had mentioned that they'd be coming back after New Year's and that if the weather was bad, they'd just stay in town for a few days until the road cleared. If the road was clear, it meant their private idyll was over. That made her really sad. Like it or not, this felt like an end to what they'd had. She put her hand on Eli's knee, just needing to touch him, and noticed that he wasn't wearing the thick layers he normally did. He had on a coat over his jeans but no thermal pants—another sign that the weather was warming up.

It would no longer be an excuse to keep her here.

They traveled in companionable silence for a while. It must have been at least a half hour by Cass's estimation, though she didn't really have a good idea. She didn't know this territory, but when Eli moved the Gator off the snowy hills down to a gravel road, she knew they were getting close. The road wound down into a ravine of sorts, the rocky cliffs of the mountains rising around them, and the snow grew higher here. "Almost there," Eli told her.

She nodded, silent.

Then, a few minutes later, a beige and white mound came into view. Cass held her breath, realizing that it was her car. The front end was folded around the trunk of a tree, and she was shocked that she hadn't been hurt more than she was. Her hand went to her breastbone and she rubbed it, thinking of the bruises that had been there until recently. She was so lucky.

The car was still covered in mounded snow on the top and the hood, though it had melted off of part of the window. Eli parked the Gator nearby and the dogs flung themselves onto the ground, running around with excitement as if there was nothing wrong. To Cass, everything felt wrong and strange. Her head felt floaty as she got out of the Gator and moved toward the car. Did she remember this vehicle? Or was it all still a blur? She couldn't tell. The outside of the car was as bland and familiar as any sedan, so that didn't help. She ran a hand over the trunk and noticed a rental company bumper sticker. That seemed . . . familiar. She'd rented a car. Right. Because . . . because . . .

Oh. Because she didn't live in Wyoming. She'd flown in to stay for the holidays.

Cass held her breath, tense with anticipation. That was a new stray thought. She couldn't even call it a memory, because now that she'd put it out there, it felt like it had always been there. It wasn't a missing piece, but what were the missing pieces supposed to feel like? Were they supposed to be surprising or just feel like this? She didn't know. She didn't have anyone else that had lost their memories that she could ask. Cass glanced over at Eli. He leaned against the Gator, his long legs crossed at the boots, arms folded over his chest. His hat shielded his eyes so she couldn't see his expression. She didn't know what he was thinking. Was he as weirdly nervous as she was?

"You all right?"

She nodded.

"Want me to get anything out for you?"

"No, I'm okay." For now, anyhow. Cass trailed her gloved fingers on the snow that clung to the sides of the car, sending it sprinkling down to the ground. She found the door handle and tried it, but it was iced over. With a few yanks, she was able to get the handle to move, and the door of the car creaked and groaned as if in pain before it opened up. The car interior yawned before her, and Cass stared at it.

It looked like a mess. The steering wheel had something that looked like a deflated balloon sagging out of the center of it. *Airbag*, she mentally told herself. There was no glass shattered, at least, but there was a bloody spot on the windshield where she'd smacked her head and somehow torn it open. She touched the scar on her brow, then leaned in, peering at the rest of the car. Her purse was on the floorboard on the passenger side, and the contents were spilled all over the car. She hesitated a moment, then slid inside the car, sitting in the front seat.

Her things were everywhere. They must have gone flying when she hit the tree, and she gazed out of the windshield, trying to recognize this spot. Didn't ring a bell, but would it? If she'd known the tree was there, she wouldn't have hit it, of course. Cass picked up a lip balm tucked in the seat, knew it was vanilla flavored before she opened it, and put it into her pocket. The car wasn't familiar, but the things she was seeing were. That blue wallet was hers—given to her by her parents two Christmases ago. That mirror compact she'd won at a fair when she was twelve and had used ever since. Her favorite sunglasses. Her cell phone in its pink, girly case. She picked it up and held her breath, then clicked the button at the bottom to activate the screen. Here it was, the moment she'd started to dread.

The phone's screen remained black.

Dead.

She let out a deep breath she hadn't realized she was holding. Of course it was dead. It had been out here uncharged for almost two weeks. Leaning over, she picked up her purse and started to put things inside it. As she did, they felt familiar, and the twinges of memory in her mind grew stronger. She'd gotten this package of almonds at the airport. She'd packed extra hand lotion in her purse because her fingers got chapped in the cold and she'd known . . .

She'd known she was going to the cabin for the Christmas holidays.

Her parents' cabin. Memories flashed through her mind, filling in the blanks. Of summers spent running through the woods with her cousins, of campfires behind the house and roasting marshmallows. Of the time she'd twisted her ankle and had to spend the entire week sitting on the ugly plaid sofa in the cabin while her parents and aunts and uncles skied. She knew that cabin. Knew this road—well, kind of.

And she swallowed hard, because the vague feeling of unease was returning. She'd gone up to the cabin for the holidays alone, because she'd wanted to hide. The answer of why she wanted to hide was somewhere in her phone, because just holding the damned thing filled her with dread. She ran her fingers over the screen absently, lost in thought. She didn't come to this cabin often. It seemed odd to want to spend Christmas alone—but that was right, her parents were in Italy and she couldn't stay in New York.

Aha. New York. Of course. She lived there! And all at once, she could see her tiny apartment just above the corner bodega, the trees on the sidewalk, the subway stop just a short block away. It was as real as the breath frosting in front of her face.

"Cass?"

She jumped, startled—and a little guilty—at the sound of Eli's voice. He leaned in the open driver's side door and peered down at her. "Everything all right? You're quiet."

"I think so." She let out a long breath. "I'm starting to remember things, Eli. I'm from New York!"

"Well, I won't hold that against you, baby." He gave her a little grin. "But I'm real glad you're starting to get your memory back. Sounds like it won't be gone for good."

"No, I don't think so."

"You want to take this stuff back to the house with us?" He gestured at the back seat, and she turned around. There were boxes of supplies back there, junk food of all kinds, packages of cookies and snack cakes and packets of hot cocoa mix. Off in one corner, she saw the CD wallet that held all her Christmas music, and her favorite ugly Christmas sweater. She was a few days late for all that stuff. "It's okay. I don't think I need most of it. It was supplies because I was going to stay at my parents' cabin up the road." She pointed off behind him, where the narrow gravel-covered road forked in the opposite direction of the ranch. "We have a cabin up there."

He got a funny look on his face. "The Horns' cabin? Greg and Martina?"

Horn. That was her last name. Her eyes widened. "Oh my god, that's me, Eli! I'm Cass Horn. Those are my parents!" She fumbled her way out of the car, because she wanted to throw her arms around him and hug him. He stepped backward to let her out of the car, and as he did, she dropped the contents of her purse all over the slushy ground. He put a steadying hand on her elbow and she stumbled into his embrace. "You know my parents?"

"Met 'em a time or two. They had car trouble a summer or two back. Needed a jump, so I came over to help them. Didn't know they had a daughter."

"That's me," she breathed, giddy. Even now, she could picture her parents' faces. Oh, they'd be so worried . . . well, actually they probably wouldn't. If they got her voicemail, they'd just assume she was out having a great time for the holiday and go back to their vacation in Italy without thinking too hard about it. They weren't due to return until the middle of January, and if she wasn't back by then, they'd worry. But someone else was expecting her to check in . . . She frowned and rubbed her head.

She didn't know who. Or she didn't want to know who. And that bothered her almost as much.

Eli leaned in and snagged the keys off the floorboard and handed them to Cass. She put them in her purse and then began to scoop up the contents from where they'd fallen on the ground. "You want anything else from this thing, baby? Clothes? Shoes?"

"Oh. Yeah." She shoved her hairbrush back into her purse and stood up, frowning at the car. "You think we should call a tow truck?"

"Not yet. Give it another few days to melt. No one's going to come up the mountain until then."

"All right." She bit her lip as he picked her phone up from the ground and offered it to her. "It's dead."

"You have a charger?"

"In my suitcase."

"Let's get your suitcase and head back, then." When she didn't say anything, he paused. "You all right, baby?"

For some reason, that made her eyes well up. She loved it when he called her baby . . . and she was terrified she wasn't going to get to hear it very often anymore.

"Cass? What is it?" He moved toward her, cupped her face in his leather gloves. It wasn't the same as being touched by his warm, callused hands, but it was still nice. "You don't seem like yourself."

She swallowed hard, then forced herself to shrug as if it were no big deal. "I guess I'm . . . afraid."

"Afraid?"

"That something's going to change between you and me." She dropped her gaze, clutching her purse to her chest. Her eyes blurred, and she realized with horror that she was about to cry. Oh damn it, not now.

"Hey," Eli murmured, and his gloved thumb stroked her cheek. "Do you like what we've got?"

"Yes," she managed to choke out.

"I do, too. I love you, Cass. Doesn't change if you're Cass Nobody or Cass Horn. You're still my Cass, all right?"

She looked up at him in surprise. "You love me?"

He gave her one of those crooked half smiles. "Well, yeah. I thought that was pretty obvious." When she shook her head, he leaned in and gave her a fierce, brief kiss. "I love you, Cass. I know it's sudden, but I feel like that doesn't matter. I love you, and whatever happens after this, we'll figure it out."

"I love you, too," she whispered, her heart thudding. She didn't know if it was fear or pleasure. She loved his words—loved him, too—but she couldn't rest easy. Not yet. Not until she knew what it was on her phone that filled her with so much dread.

But when he grinned and leaned in to kiss her, she lost herself in the magic of his lips on hers. The phone could wait. Reality could wait. When she was with Eli, she wanted time to stand still, forever.

CHAPTER TWENTY-ONE

Cass stared uneasily at her phone. It sat on the dining room table, plugged into the wall. It was silly to be intimidated by a piece of technology, but she couldn't help it. She knew that whatever weird, unhappy feelings she'd been having had to do with that damned phone and the information it contained. Finding out her last name and piecing together her memory had thus far been more like a welcome reminder, a pleasant blanket that she could wrap up in. She didn't have guilt or anxiety associated with her parents, or New York, or any of the other small bits of information that had been filtering in as she rummaged through her purse and wallet, or as she dressed in her own clothes for the first time in almost two weeks. Those things didn't make her anxious.

It had everything to do with whatever information her phone held. She knew it was the key.

Maybe that was why she was terrified of it.

Cass swallowed hard and made herself another cup of

coffee as the phone charged. Every now and then, it would buzz with some sort of activity, information flashing on the screen now that it had a bit of juice to it.

She didn't go check it out. She didn't even cross the room to make sure everything was going well. She avoided it.

She finished her coffee, checked on Frannie and the puppies, and snuggled them for a while. The puppies were the most adorable, delicious little furballs. She adored them and could spend hours petting them and watching them snuffle against their mother's side. If she had to pick one in particular, she was drawn to Joy, just because she was the tiny, white little runt of the litter. Frankie, Myrtle, and Goldie were fat little nuggets, while Noel was all fluff. Joy was petite and tended to get overwhelmed by her bigger siblings, so Cass spent a little extra time with the pup every now and then, making sure she got enough time nursing.

Of course, because a ranch didn't wait on anyone's anxiety, then it was time to feed the chickens again, and change out the hay in the stalls, so she spent the afternoon pleasantly tending to animals. It was warmer now—still freezing, but not so cold that her breath felt like dry ice—and so the chickens could hang out in their yard for a little while and soak up sunshine. She moved the horses from stall to stall as she cleaned each one out, petting noses and giving them some wilted carrots saved for this sort of thing. Eli had worried she'd not pay attention around the horses and get stepped on, but the big animals were gentle and well trained, and she suspected that they were more cautious of her than she was of them. Once everything in the barn was taken care of, she had nothing else to delay the inevitable.

Reluctant, Cass returned to the house . . . and then took a shower, because she could buy herself another twenty minutes that way. She dressed, braided her wet hair, and then went back to the kitchen and stared at the phone for a good, long while.

Might as well get it over with.

Cass inwardly cringed as she picked up the phone and clicked the button. There were a million messages showing on the screen but she ignored them and clicked the button again, which prompted her to the password screen. Automatically, she started to type in a password and wasn't surprised when the phone unlocked. It was like her reflexes knew all the pieces were there even if Cass herself didn't.

The screen was a picture of herself and another woman—a blonde—with their faces pressed together and a beach behind them. They had silly grins on their faces and sunglasses obscured their eyes, but Cass hated that she still had no idea who the woman was. Why was it that she had pieces of her memory in regards to other things, but this woman—who was clearly in her life in a big way—was a blank? It didn't make sense. Maybe one of the text messages in her phone would fill in the details.

She flipped to them and scrolled through the alerts.

Immediately, her stomach clenched in a sickening way. She had twenty-two messages from the same person recently. Not just any person, but Ken.

Who the heck was Ken? She racked her brain, trying to put a face to the name, but there wasn't a picture attached to the profile in her phone, just the name. She swallowed hard and flicked over to "Recent Calls" and was dismayed to see that there were at least five attempts to contact her from Ken, for five days in a row. After that, he'd stopped. She switched back to "Messages" and went through the list. Message after message was from the same person. Ken. Ken. Ken.

Ken really, really wanted to get in touch with her.

KEN: You're not answering me. Are you mad?

KEN: Don't be like that, Cass. You know you're my girl.

KEN: Cass?

KEN: Call me.

KEN: You little tease. You're making me chase you, aren't you?

KEN: Haven't heard from you in a few days. Come on.

KEN: Thinking about you. Merry Christmas.

KEN: Thought about sending you a pic but didn't want to get myself in trouble. But if you asked nicely . . .

KEN: I hate that we're not spending the holiday together. What's up with that?

KEN: You not here has me all sad and lonely. I feel abandoned. That's not right.

KEN: You totally ran out on me, didn't you? And here I thought we'd be spending the holidays together.

KEN: I miss seeing your face.

On and on the messages went, and it was very clear.

Ken knew her, and knew her well. He knew her enough to know that she was going out of town for the holidays . . . it was obvious she was in a relationship with Ken.

The realization was utterly devastating.

She'd *cheated* on this guy with Eli. She'd sworn up and down that she wasn't in a relationship, but this phone was the damning proof that she was a ho and a liar. Oh god. Cass felt sick. Was this why she was so full of dread every time she thought about answering her phone? Because she *knew* deep down that she was a cheater and secretly didn't care? Eli would hate her.

Hell, she hated herself.

Pressing her fingers to her mouth. Cass raced to the bathroom and managed to get there moments before she vomited into the sink. Her lunch heaved up, and once she was done, she pressed her face against the cold tile of the counter and willed herself to die. Right there. Right in that moment. How could she be this person? How could she be in a relationship and allow herself to fall in love with Eli?

Oh god. Eli.

What would he say? How could she ever face him after seeing this? He'd never want to talk to her again. But it wasn't like she could keep this a secret. It was something that she had to share. She couldn't just pretend like nothing had happened, because it felt as if her world had come crashing down around her ears the moment she'd opened the phone screen and saw those texts.

Cass burst into tears. She felt like she'd lost Eli. No, she *knew* she had. She was the worst person ever and these messages just confirmed it.

* * *

Collapsed on the bathroom floor, Cass sobbed for a good half hour, utterly miserable. She didn't look at her phone. She didn't want to. She didn't want to see the evidence that she was already in a relationship when she was in love with Eli. He'd never understand how she could do something like that—and she didn't blame him, because she didn't understand it herself. How was she this person? How could she just be so utterly convinced that she was not in a relationship? How did her brain forget something so very important? She sniffed and rubbed her finger. She wasn't engaged, but it was clear she was with someone else. Those text messages made a liar out of her and wanted her to be with him. Th different story than what she'd s

She'd told him she'd kno she Well, she wasn't. But that didn't mean she wasn't already committed, and the thought was heartbreaking.

She didn't know what to do.

She stared dully at the bathroom wall, sniffling and feeling sorry for herself. Her stomach churned, but there was nothing left in it. She knew she should get up and feed the chickens, or clean the place. Maybe give the horses a few treats or see if she could help Eli out. He'd promised to show her how to use the Gator the other day. But she didn't move from her spot on the floor. What was the point? This farm person wasn't who she was. This Cass wasn't the right Cass.

This Cass didn't get to stay. She didn't get to be with Eli. The Cass she was already had a man, one named Ken, whom she'd apparently run out on without telling him where she was going.

She swallowed hard and reached up, snagging her phone from where she'd left it on the counter. She unlocked the screen and stared at the picture of the woman in the photo with her. *Think, Cass*, she demanded. *Think of who this is. You know her. You know you do.* But when she tried to recall who it was, the spot in her mind was just blank. It was the same with Ken. She tried to picture his face, but all she got was a big fat nothing. How could she forget such important pieces in her life?

She had no answer. It was utterly distressing and she wanted to vomit and cry all over again. Sniffing, she swiped a hand over her face, wiping away her tears. She had to pull herself together. "Come on, Scooby-Doo," she muttered aloud. "Solve this stupid mystery." Absently, she flicked through some of the icons on her phone, hoping that they would provide clues. There was a diet app, and Instagram, and Facebook, of course. She clicked on "Photos," and scrolled through them, looking for Ken's face. Who was her boyfriend? How long had they been dating? Maybe the photos would provide answers.

But most of the photos were useless. There were pics of locations she didn't recognize. Pics of birds in Central Park. A few pictures of the smiley blonde in workout wear. One of her in a slinky dress, her hair in curlers.

There were no pictures of this Ken guy.

Her Ken guy.

She swallowed hard.

It didn't make sense. Why wouldn't she have pictures of her boyfriend?

Cass stared at the pictures on the phone, then flipped to the text messages. She thought she should probably write Ken, to tell him that she was fine. That she was alive and well and just hadn't been able to come to the phone. But she couldn't bring herself to do it. How could she possibly explain herself? He'd hate her.

And he'd have every reason to.

Choking back the next round of tears, Cass scrolled through the list of names in her contacts. Her parents were there, but she'd feel weird calling them to let them know she'd been recently hurt. Her memory pinged her about a long-awaited vacation to Europe, and she didn't want them to cut it short. Them returning home wouldn't solve any of her problems, anyhow . . . and she didn't want them to find out what a horrible person she was.

Even as she sat, staring at the phone, an incoming message pinged.

> ROSE: FYI I should be back on Thursday. Ran into Corvelli here on vacation, and he asked to dress me for Oscars. Need you to call my ppl and see if we already have someone lined up so I can tell him no. His shit is fug and I don't want to be known as the chick who showed up at the awards show w/ shoulder pads the size of boats.

A frowny emoticon followed that note and Cass stared at it. Was she expected to respond? This Rose person made it sound like Cass should know what she was talking about, but she had no clue. Was she invited to an Oscars party, then? Did they know someone famous? She hesitated, then typed a response.

> CASS: Corvelli . . . like the designer?

Three dots showed up on the screen, indicating that a message was coming in. They disappeared, and then a moment later, Cass's phone rang. She nearly dropped it in surprise, and managed to fumble it to her ear. "Hello?"

"Are you fucking with me?" The woman's voice on the other end was young and hard with irritation.

"No?" Cass said timidly. "Is this Rose?"

"Who else would it be?" A pause. "You *are* fucking with me. Well, I don't find it funny, Cass. God. I am stressed out of my mind. I don't want to go to the damn Academy Awards in some avant-garde potato sack shit that Corvelli thinks looks unique. I want to look like the hot piece of ass that I am." She sounded furious.

"Lily," Cass began.

"Rose!" The voice on the other end was incredulous. "What is *wrong* with you?"

"Right. Rose. Sorry." She rubbed her forehead, because she was getting another headache. "So this is going to sound crazy, but apparently I was driving up to my parents' cabin for Christmas and I crashed into a tree and hit my head and lost my memory."

She paused, waiting for the inevitable flood of questions such as, "are you all right," "how badly were you injured," "is there anything I can do to help," and things of that nature.

Rose made a sound in her throat. "And?"

Cass was baffled. "What do you mean, 'and'?"

"And I mean, that's terrible, sweetie, but what does this have to do with me?"

Cass swallowed hard, surprised. "Um, that's just it. I don't exactly remember you?"

"Really?" Rose sounded fascinated. "At all?"

"Well, your picture is on my phone but I'm not ringing a bell. I'm sorry." Her voice was small. "I can remember some things, and others are huge blanks." Things like *boyfriends* and *cheating*.

"Oh wow. That's crazy." The crankiness had gone out of her voice. "Does it hurt?"

"My head?" Cass rubbed her brow. "Not now, but it was really bruised up for a while. I have a cut on my forehead, too. A long one, about three inches over my left eyebrow. I'm pretty sure it's going to leave a scar."

"Ew. Glad I'm the model, then."

"You're a model?"

Rose laughed. "Wow, you really don't remember? Rose Gramercy? I was on the cover of *Vogue* for their Spring Fling issue? *GQ*'s Hottest Woman of the Year? *Sports Illustrated*?"

"Good job," she said faintly, because what else could she say? It filled in some of the gaps, though. Like the memory she'd had of watching a TV show live. That must have been . . . because of Rose? "Do I work with you?"

Rose giggled. "Well, not as a model. You've got really wide hips. I don't mean that as an insult. You know I have to smoke my way down to a size two for fashion week every year. You're my assistant."

"Oh."

"So why were you going into the mountains for Christmas?"

"I don't know."

"By yourself?"

Did Rose know Ken? "Looks like it. I rented a car and everything. A nice cowboy saved me."

"A cowboy? Oh brother." She laughed again. "Wow, you are just having all kinds of adventures out there, aren't you? Hanging out with a bunch of hicks, banging your head . . . you're probably even wearing flannel right now."

Cass glanced down at her clothes. She was wearing one of her dark sweaters that her suitcase was full of, but she also had on a bright red plaid flannel shirt she'd borrowed from Eli and couldn't bear to return. She flushed. "Just a little flannel."

Rose laughed again, and someone murmured something in the background. "Oh my. You are going to have to tell me all about your adventures when you come back. I could use a good laugh. My vacation has been positively dreadful. Is this vegan?"

"What?"

"Not you, dummy. I'm talking to the waiter here. Vegan?" Another murmur of conversation and then Rose gave a long, gusty sigh. "Didn't I tell you that I wanted vegan cheese? I'm pretty sure I did. I don't eat animal products." Her voice was stiff with irritation. "I was on a fucking PETA poster last year. Why would I shove my mouth full of cow leavings? Get me cheese made from cashews. I don't care how long it takes, just do it."

For some reason, Rose's constant switching between imperious and chatty seemed familiar . . . and it made Cass feel small and unsettled. She was Rose's assistant? Did she even like the job? Or did she constantly exist in this state of anxious hopefulness, waiting for a kind word from Rose and flinching at her cruel ones?

If so, she didn't like herself very much.

Again.

"So, ask me about my Christmas," Rose said brightly, her attention back on Cass.

"Oh. Um, how was your Christmas?"

"Well," Rose said primly. "You will never believe who I ran into in the Riviera." She launched into a long story involving the fashion world and a friend that was snorting lines in the bathroom at a soiree, and Cass tuned out. Rose was nice enough, she supposed, as long as the conversation was on Rose. Cass didn't know whether to be annoyed by her or amused. She didn't seem to care about how Cass was feeling at all. She just wanted to know when Cass would get back to work . . . probably because it affected her. It was like the vegan thing. Cass hadn't been vegan since Eli had rescued her, and she realized now that she wasn't vegan because she liked it—it was because Rose was vegan and Cass was her assistant. She suspected Rose didn't like animals much, either, because Cass had fallen in love with the horses and the dogs and even the silly chickens in the short time she'd been on the ranch. Some of the things she was learning about herself didn't match . . .

And some she wanted to change forever, because she hated them.

"And so I told Ken that—"

"Ken?" Cass echoed, tuning back in. "My Ken?"

"Your Ken?" Rose tittered on the other end. "Are you serious? Cass, that's so cute. I'll have to tell him you said that. He'll get a real kick out of hearing that."

Oh. This was another thing that wasn't adding up. "My brain's scrambled. I'm having a hard time remembering names and faces. Rose, who's Ken again?"

"Hmph. My boyfriend, silly. Ken Wallis? Star of *The Eyes of the Queen*? The *Titanic* remake? He was also in that stupid space movie. What's it called?" She snapped her fingers, the echo on the other side of the phone. "*Space Avengers*? Something like that. The one all the fangirls scream over."

"*Starship Avengers*," Cass said faintly, and a face slid into her memories. A handsome, bronzed god with blond hair and a megawatt smile.

Oh my god. *That* was Ken. Cass was a cheating ho two

times over. Not only was she lying to Eli, but she was lying to her friend Rose, too.

What kind of monster *was* she?

"I'm going to throw up again," Cass blurted into the phone.

"What?"

"I have to go," she said quickly, getting to her feet.

"Well, call me back once you're done purging—" Rose began, but Cass hung up on her before she could finish the sentence.

Hysterical, she threw the phone down on the sink and watched it skid across the counter. She regarded it like she would a snake. She'd known that picking it up again would ruin the fragile peace she'd found, and she was right.

The Ken that was texting her had to be Rose's Ken. And it was clear from the texts that they had a rather personal relationship. You didn't text your girlfriend's assistant and tell her that you *missed her face* unless there was something shady going on.

She was clearly cheating on Rose . . . and Ken . . . *and* Eli.

Cass buried her face in her hands and sobbed.

CHAPTER TWENTY-TWO

Eli was in a pretty damn good mood that day.

He whistled as he unspooled hay for the cattle, hummed a Christmas song (even though the holiday was over) while he repaired fences, and basically thought about Cass all day long. He'd never been so happy with another human being. He'd dated, sure. But none of them quite compared to Cass. Heck, even thinking about them right now, the details in his head were fuzzy because they weren't Cass. She'd ruined him for other women, and happily so. She was kind, sweet, thoughtful, and beautiful, and she seemed to take to ranch life. He'd caught her talking to the chickens and sneaking carrots to the horses, and each time he did, it warmed his heart a little more.

Cass was the one for him. He had no doubt. He got tired of most people, but he never got tired of her. That was pretty incredible on its own. The explosive yet tender sex between them? Icing on top. He'd never been happier, and so when Doc Parsons pulled up to the ranch in his truck and waved, instead of groaning, Eli greeted him with a return wave.

"You're in a good mood," Doc called as he exited the truck. "I take it that our patient is doing well?"

"Cass is great," Eli said. "Unless by 'your patient' you meant one of the cows. In that case, I've got one in the barn that can't shake her cold." He gestured at the building behind him.

Doc squinted. "I'll be damned. Did you just make a joke, Eli Pickett?"

Normally he would have scowled. Today, he just grinned.

Doc's eyes widened. He gave Eli a knowing smile. "I take it the company wasn't too much of a burden over the last while, then."

"Nope," Eli drawled, swinging his leg off the side of his horse and dismounting. "It's good to see you, Doc. How's things over at Swinging C?"

"Can't complain, can't complain," Doc said easily. "All the cattle are alive and so am I, so it's been a good month." He rubbed his jaw, stroking his wiry white beard. "How about over here? I bet you're more than ready for the others to come back from their vacations so you can have a breather."

He considered that for a long moment. Was he? There was no doubt that the workload was enormous when it was only him. But at the same time, it was nice to have the time alone with Cass. He envisioned them a few years down the road with their own small ranch. Less cattle, so he could run things on his own, but just the two of them and a couple of dogs. The idea filled him with such intense longing that he swallowed hard. Turning back to Doc, he gestured at his horse and then patted it on the nose. "Let me get Betsy into the stable and I'll introduce you to Cass."

They entered the house, and Eli didn't see Cass in the

living room. Normally, this time of day, she was curled up on the sofa, watching the puppies as Frannie tended to them. "Babe?" he called out, ignoring Doc's raised eyebrow. He didn't care if the man put together that he and Cass were a couple. Let the whole world know—Eli was fine with that. Cass was his and that was all there was to it.

A muffled sob met his ears.

Frowning, Eli headed for the hallway toward the bedrooms, Doc at his heels. As he approached, Cass emerged from the laundry room with a pile of clothing in her arms. Her eyes were red and swollen, and she took one look at him, burst into tears again, and then rushed into the bedroom.

"Cass? What's wrong?" Eli forgot all about Doc and followed her into his room. His stomach clenched when he saw that her suitcase was out on the bed and she was hastily stuffing clothing into it.

"I can't stay," she choked out. "I have to go. Today. Tonight. Now." Her shaking hand fluttered over her face, swiping at the tears on her cheeks.

Eli tried to think of something to say. All that came out was, "What?"

"I have to leave," Cass stated again. She didn't look him in the eye. Instead, she shoved a pair of jeans into her suitcase and crammed a shoe—items she'd just unpacked hours ago—on top of it. "I need to get out of here. I called a tow truck and it's meeting me in an hour and—"

"Wait, a tow truck?" He didn't understand. Just this morning, they'd woken up before dawn with kisses and caresses, and he'd stayed in bed with her far longer than he should have, simply because he couldn't bear to leave her side. She'd been full of soft smiles and promising glances, and when they'd made love, she'd come so sweetly that he'd wanted to spend all day in bed with her. This turnabout made no sense. "Cass, what is it? Are you hurting? Doc's here, he can take a look at you—"

Cass shook her head, almost violently. The shoe she held in her hand wouldn't fit into the suitcase, and she shoved it twice before pulling it out and then clutching it against her breast. "You don't understand. I just—I can't stay, all right?" Her voice rose a hysterical note, and fresh tears poured down her face. "I just can't stay here! I just can't!"

"Baby—"

"No! No baby," she sobbed and collapsed on the floor, still holding her shoe. "I can't be your baby."

"Why don't I just wait outside while you talk?" Doc said in a mild voice. "Call me if you need me." He edged out of the hallway and Eli could hear his boots as he moved into the living room and then out the front door.

Then Eli was alone with Cass. He sank down onto the floor next to her, putting a hand on her back as she sobbed against her shoe. "Cass, honey," he began, careful not to use the word "baby" lest it set her off again. "Tell me what's bothering you. Tell me what's wrong. I don't understand."

"I need to g-go home," she managed through chest-shaking sobs. She wouldn't look at him, her head bent and her shoulders slumped. It was like all the life had gone out of his vibrant girl. Just this morning, her blue eyes had gleamed with amusement and fun. Just this morning, her smile had been bright and cheery. What had happened? What had changed between now and then?

"You can go home soon enough," he told her, even though he hated saying the words. Truth was, he didn't want her to go home. Maybe ever. Of course, that wasn't realistic. Even if she wanted to stay with him, she'd still have to wrap up things wherever she lived, he imagined. She couldn't just disappear into Wyoming forever. "If you need to make some calls or make arrangements, I can help you with that—"

"No," she said firmly, and the shaking eased from her voice. She flicked her fingers over her cheeks again, dashing away tears. "I need to go home today, Eli. I can't stay. It's wrong."

His stomach clenched with dread, but he didn't plead with her to change her mind. He needed to understand this, even if his soul was icing over at the thought of her leaving. "What's happened that made you need to leave today? Is it your parents? Is someone sick?"

For the first time since he came in the room, Cass looked up at him. Her eyes were so full of sadness and hopelessness he was taken aback. This wasn't like her. She never looked, even when she was dazed and injured, as hopeless as she did now. "I can't tell you, Eli."

"Why?"

Her lower lip trembled and she looked ready to collapse again. "Please don't ask me."

An exasperated sigh escaped him. "Cass, you know I'm going to ask. I love you. I'm worried about you. How can I not want to know what's going on?"

At his words, though, she just started crying even harder. "I'm the worst person ever." She hunched over as if physically in pain, her shoulders shaking.

He rubbed her back. "No, no, baby, you're not. You're the best person I've ever met. You're sweet and you're generous." When she shook her head silently, he continued. "It's true. You're not much of a cook and you tend to not pay attention, but I don't think those are bad things. That's just who you are. You're just so eager to experience things you get distracted." He forced a chuckle out of his throat to make his words seem lighter. "The animals love you. Look at how much Frannie adores being around you. The horses get excited every time you come in the barn now, because you give them carrots and sugar. You have such a good heart. I can't believe that you're this awful person that you're convinced you are. You'll never get me to believe that, Cass. Never." He rubbed his hand up and down her back, trying to soothe her. When she shook her head silently, he continued. "That doesn't matter, though. If every animal on this damn ranch hated you, I'd still love you because you're you, Cass. I've never felt this way about anyone before. I love you. I love your smile and your heart and the way you're determined to see sunshine in every day. That's why it's killing me to see you cry like this. Let me help you. Tell me what's wrong."

"I'm a bad person," she whispered.

"From what I've seen of you, that's just not true."

"But you've only known me two weeks," she said brokenly. Her shoulders slumped even more and she wavered, as if she wanted to lean on him but didn't trust herself to do so. "That's not enough time."

"It's enough for me," he said stubbornly. "You're not going to convince me that you're a bad person, because I'm just not going to buy it, sorry."

"You don't know the real me," she insisted. "The real me might be an animal hater. An asshole of the highest order. The real me might be a con artist and a horrible person all around. You don't know the real me because she's been gone from my head for the last two weeks." Cass pressed a fist to her brows. "When she comes back, you'll realize what a mistake it was to get involved with me—"

"Bullshit," he said, his voice firm. "You think that you're going to find out all these awful things about yourself the moment you get your memories back? People don't change,

Cass. You are who you are, and I think the person I know, the person I've spent the holidays with, is the same person I see before me. She's loving and kind and eager to please. She's thoughtful and sweet. She's—"

"She's not me," Cass said softly, heartbreak in her eyes. "You may think she's me, but she's not. And it's because you've only known me for two weeks, Eli."

"I've known you long enough to fall in love with you." He reached up and stroked her hair, then put a finger under her chin, trying to get her to lift her gaze to his when she dropped it again. "I've seen enough to know who you are inside, and I love that woman. Nothing you can say can convince me that I don't love you."

"You don't know me, though," she insisted. "You don't know who I am. I'm not even sure I know who I am."

"Then stay with me and find out." Eli took the shoe out of her tight grip and placed it on the bed. He took her hand in his and felt it trembling, and he wanted to crush her against his chest and hug all of the terror out of her. He simply held her hand for now, though. "You can stay here at the ranch with me. Your memories can take all the time they need to come back. We'll figure out who you are together. You can help out with chores if you want to earn your keep, and you can have little Joy. I wanted to give her to you, but I wanted it to be a surprise. Now seems as good a time as any." Especially if it could bribe her to stay. "I know it's a late Christmas present, but I figured you'd be all right with it." He lifted her hand to his mouth and pressed a kiss to her knuckles. "Stay, Cass. If you find out something about yourself that you don't like, we can talk it through. We can work on things together. And if your memories don't come back, we can create new ones. Together."

She lifted her eyes to his again, and there was such longing and misery in them. He didn't see the hope that she normally carried with her, and the pit of his stomach felt like ice. It didn't surprise him when she shook her head again, or when she pulled her hand from his. "I wish I could stay, Eli. I really wish I could. But I can't. I need to leave, no matter what, before I make things worse."

"I love you," he told her again, desperation in his voice. He cupped her face and tried to kiss her. She pulled away, turning so her mouth wouldn't meet his.

In that moment, he felt like he lost her. He didn't know how or why, but she was gone.

And there was absolutely nothing he could do about it.

S he didn't kiss him goodbye. She couldn't.
As much as she wanted to give Eli one last kiss, to tell him how much she loved him and how much the last two weeks had meant to her, she didn't dare. If he knew who she really was, he'd look at her with loathing instead of sadness. She couldn't take that. It would destroy her inside if her last memory of him was one of him looking at her with disgust.

Cass knew he didn't understand why she was leaving. She knew he blamed himself, no matter how many times she said it was her and not him. She couldn't make him understand, though, not without spilling the truth. Maybe when she was ready, she'd tell him all about what a horrible person she was and how she'd pretended to be someone virtuous for about two weeks, just long enough for them to fall in love. He'd realize that he'd dodged a bullet and be grateful instead of frustrated, and that would be the end of things.

But right now, it was all too fresh, and all of it hurt.

She packed her suitcase and put it in the back of Doc's truck, since he'd volunteered to take her to meet the tow truck at the pass. Eli had volunteered, too, but she'd opted to go with Doc. Maybe it would hurt less if she did. The parting would be less brutal. There'd be less crying.

Oh, who was she kidding? She was on the verge of tears and she hadn't even left the ranch.

It was because Eli stared at her, his heart in his eyes, begging her to stay. To explain to him. To help him understand. He didn't move from his spot in the doorway, just watched her with an intensity that made her skin prickle with awareness even as she got into the truck across from Doc. She calmly put on her seatbelt and set her purse in her lap.

"Ready?" Doc asked.

"Sure," Cass said, her voice brave . . . and then she crumpled. She pressed her hands to her face and tried to stop the sobs from erupting from her chest.

A hand was at her side, suddenly, and she looked over to see Eli. He'd reached through the window of the truck and grasped her hand tight in his. The expression on his face was intense, and when he tipped his hat back, she saw the look in his eyes was only for her. "I don't know what this is, Cass, but I know how I feel about you hasn't changed." He squeezed her fingers. "You do what you have to do, but know this—I'm going to be here. I'm not going anywhere. And I'm going to keep Joy, because she's yours. When she's old enough to leave Frannie, you can come and get her, or have someone come and get her for you, if you like."

Did he think she was upset about the puppy? Her heart was breaking and it was entirely his fault. She'd fallen so hard for him but the person he thought she was didn't exist. Instead, she was the worst kind of liar—a cheater. "You don't have to do that," she told him, aching.

"She's yours," he stated again, voice firm. "Just like I am. And when you're ready for me, I'll be here, too." He lifted her hand to his mouth and kissed her knuckles, and Cass felt like her heart was breaking all over again. She wanted to tell him she loved him, but the words wouldn't escape.

She didn't trust herself not to hurt him more than she already had.

If Eli was disappointed in her silence, he didn't show it. He gave her fingers one last squeeze and then gently put her hand down. "No more crying, baby." He thumped his hand on the truck door and nodded at Doc. "Be here if you need me."

Or if she changes her mind, was the unspoken addition. They all knew it.

But Cass wasn't going to change her mind. Eli deserved better than her. It might not seem like it right now, but he'd thank her later on.

CHAPTER TWENTY-THREE

New York City didn't feel like home, which was weird since it truly *was* her home. But Cass didn't feel settled or at peace when she took a taxi to her building, went up the elevator to her floor, and opened the door to her apartment. This didn't look much like home, either. It was neat and clean and gray, the walls painted a slate shade and the flooring a pale white. Artful decor was placed on the decorative shelves built into the wall, and her sofa had carved legs and tiny lace throw pillows. It looked chic and together and wholly unlived in.

She thought of the ugly couch on the ranch, and how easy it had been to curl up and relax on it with a mug of coffee. The multicolored quilts tossed on the furniture. The rag rugs strategically placed on the floors because the dogs liked to get muddy. How cozy and lived in and well loved it all felt despite the rustic decor. Her apartment had none of that, and for a long moment, she stood in the doorway, wondering if she'd somehow wandered into someone else's place.

But the key opened this door, and there were her clothes in the closet, so this had to be her apartment. Cass set her suitcase down on the bed, and couldn't help but notice that her entire apartment was the same size as Eli's room back at the ranch. She told herself it didn't matter and that she needed to stop comparing things. She was just going to make herself even more miserable.

Then she opened her suitcase and saw the sweater on top was covered in white dog hairs from a Frannie petting session, and Cass wanted to cry all over again.

That night, she lay in bed and stared up at the ceiling. The city seemed noisy after being on the ranch for a few weeks. Down below, she could hear the traffic in the streets. Somewhere up above her, a dog's feet pounded on the floor, and a neighbor yelled. Even though she had her own space, it felt crowded compared to Wyoming.

She just had to get used to it again, she told herself. She'd settle in and get back to normal.

Cass couldn't sleep, though. Either it was the noise or her own restless mind, but she tossed and turned, and eventually gave up, just staring at the ceiling. She thought about Eli. Last night, she'd been in his arms. They'd curled up in bed together, talking about the day. Talking about just small things, like the number of eggs she'd gotten from the chickens in the last week, to her favorite horse in the stable, to how many cattle he'd run if it was just him. She'd been hopeful last night. She'd felt like she had a future.

Now she felt like a stranger. Like the real Cass had been left behind in Wyoming and she was forced to live someone else's life.

Did Eli miss her? she wondered. Was he sad that she

was gone? Heartbroken, like she was? Or would he just get over it and go on with his life? Cass didn't think she could move on easily . . . or at all. There was a big hollow spot where it felt her heart should be. Part of her hoped that he'd miss her, but that was selfish. She wanted him happy more than she wanted him sad and miserable.

Cass kind of felt like she had sad and miserable cornered already. No need for both of them to be unhappy. Hot tears slid down her cheeks as she thought of her cowboy. She missed his body, his smile, his scent, his laugh. She missed him. To think that she'd ever thought Eli was stern. Strong, yes. Stern, no. He'd been so gentle and loving with her, so protective. She missed that.

She missed him.

Grabbing her phone from her nightstand, she Googled his name, looking for a phone number. When that didn't work, she looked for a Facebook page. Nothing. Depressed, she flung the phone aside again. Of course Eli didn't have a Facebook page. She hadn't seen him use the computer much when she was there. He didn't like social media, and he said all the people he wanted to talk to were at the ranch. And he'd given her such a heated look that she'd blushed. Now, though, she wished he was a little less of a ranch hermit so she could Facebook stalk him. She had no pictures of him from the time they'd spent together over Christmas. It was such a weird thing to realize. In this day and age, people took pictures of their food, their pets, things they saw on the street . . . and she didn't have a single picture of the man she loved.

Because she still loved him. Even knowing what a horrible person she was didn't stop her from loving Eli and wanting to be the Cass he'd thought she was.

She swallowed hard and wondered if she should contact

Ken. Tell him she was back and confess what she had done. But if she was confessing, shouldn't she also confess to Rose that she'd slept with her boyfriend? It was an ugly, tangled situation and try as she might, she couldn't figure out a way to untangle it.

Cass picked up her phone again eventually, and then texted Rose.

CASS: I'm back home.

CASS: New York. I'm in my apartment. At least, I think it's mine.

She felt needy and vulnerable. Maybe she needed to have girl talk to get some of these feelings off her chest. That would help, even if her relationship with Rose was . . . troubled over the whole Ken thing. When the three dots flashed on her screen, indicating a text message was incoming, she felt a little less lonely. It might be two in the morning, but Rose was there for her. That was something, at least.

ROSE: Gr8. Pick up my dry cleaning in the morning, plz.

Well . . . it was definitely something. Not something good, but something.

Days passed and Cass started to settle back into a routine that felt familiar. Memories slowly filtered in as she immersed herself into her daily life.

She'd expected to be a lot happier with their return. That all the missing pieces would feel filled in and she'd be whole again. She didn't feel like that at all, though. She just grew more frustrated with her life as it was.

There wasn't anything wrong with her life. It just didn't feel like a great fit for her anymore. When she stopped by the corner bodega and picked up a few snacks, she'd see the cats hanging out in the back, and instead of avoiding them—because Rose was allergic—she'd bend down and try to coax one over to pet it. She didn't spend much time in her apartment but wandered the streets of New York in her downtime, desperate to do something with herself. Her place was far too quiet, too lonely. So she shopped and went to the park and ran a lot of errands for Rose. She actually didn't have much spare time because Rose lived two floors up from her and wanted Cass on call at any time, just in case she needed something. So Cass worked ten to twelve hours a day, getting cashew-milk lattes for Rose or picking up clothing or fielding calls from Rose's agent, whom Rose didn't want to talk to because she was mad. She got cigarettes for Rose and yelled at Rose's favorite tailor and managed Rose's busy schedule. She screened interview questions and fetched makeup brushes. One time, she even went to Rose's apartment and got Rose a drink from the kitchen because Rose was in the bathtub and didn't want to get out. It was easier for her to text Cass to come up two floors and do it for her.

And since it was what she was paid to do, and she had nothing else to do with her time, Cass did it.

Friendship with Rose—if you could call it that—was odd. They were something more than just employer and employee, and something less than friends. Rose was hot and cold. She was sweet and funny when she wanted something, vivacious when she had an audience, and whiny and petulant when she didn't get her way. She was lazy and wanted Cass to do all of her errands—even cleaning her refrigerator. Sometimes she just wanted another person to gripe at.

And when she griped, she tended to snipe at Cass.

At first, Rose was pleased that Cass was back. She rattled on and on about her vacation in Europe as she sat in hair and makeup for a photo shoot, and Cass sat nearby and listened as she held Rose's drink. Rose's only comment about the bright red scar on Cass's forehead was "ew," and she then quizzed her makeup artist on what could possibly cover Cass's "unsightly" wound. Rose didn't ask how she was feeling. She didn't ask why she was sad, though she did occasionally scowl if Cass was "giving her a depressing vibe."

In addition to being a gofer, Cass needed to be an entertaining one, it seemed.

And that was fine, too. For a while. She let Rose take the spotlight because Rose obviously needed it. And if she sniped at Cass and told her that she looked like shit and to put tea bags under her eyes to get rid of the dark circles, she endured it. If Rose had a boho scarf for Cass to wear over her forehead the next day because Rose didn't like looking at her scar, she put it on. If Rose wanted Cass to put on a sweater because Rose wanted it "stretched out" and Cass was bigger, she did it. Rose was a jerk, but not in a malicious way. She was just incredibly self-centered, and after seeing how everyone fawned over her, Cass didn't blame her. She constantly had people gushing over her, from fans on the street to paparazzi to the makeup artists and hair stylists who wanted to get in good with an in-demand model. Rose's sniping didn't bother her, because it didn't matter.

None of it mattered.

The thought that this was her life was becoming more and more depressing by the day. Was this what she had to look forward to for the next who-knew-how-many years?

Being told to change out of a brown sweater because it made her look sallow? To stand next to Rose in a photo so she'd look thinner? To have her employer slowly eat away at her confidence with small thoughtless comments and then want Cass to come up to her apartment at eleven at night for girl talk?

The temporary loss of her memory had made her dissatisfied with her life, it seemed, and she didn't know how to get that joy back. It was like it had all disappeared the moment she knew she couldn't have Eli.

Cass didn't text Ken, either. As days passed, he would text her every now and then, accusing her of avoiding him or playing hard to get. No matter how demanding his texts got, though, she ignored them. She didn't know what to say to him. Rose was self-absorbed and kind of a jerk, but she didn't deserve to have her assistant sleeping with her boyfriend. She had to come clean to Rose, and if Rose fired her, then Cass deserved it. And she had to tell Ken Wallis that whatever they'd had was over, because she didn't want to be this person.

She wanted to be Eli's Cass. Even if she didn't deserve Eli, she still liked that version of herself better than this one.

Three days after she'd returned to work, she got a call from her parents.

"Milan is wonderful," her mother gushed into Cass's phone. "I swear I've put on ten pounds just from the food here. And the scenery! It's just divine. I think your father and I are going to stay a few more weeks. We're retired now, you know? We can do what we want! And right now we want to stay."

"You absolutely should," Cass told them, happy that someone in her life seemed to be content with where they were. And because she couldn't put it off any longer . . . "So did I tell you guys I was in a car accident over the holidays?"

Her mother gasped loudly into the phone. "*What?* Are you okay?" Her voice got muffled, as if she'd put a hand over the receiver. "Honey, Cass was in a car accident. No, I don't know. I'm asking."

"Tell Dad I said hi," Cass said, amused, and then launched into a brief description of what had happened to her. Or at least, the parts she remembered. She told them about waking up and not remembering who she was, and her mother clucked unhappily. She told them about Eli and how he'd saved her, and how she'd had to stay on Price Ranch over the holidays.

She avoided the part where she'd slept with Eli. Or the part where she'd fallen in love with him.

"But you're okay now? Do we need to come home?" Her mother sounded terribly worried.

"I'm totally fine, I promise." It was gratifying to have someone worry over her, at least. "Please don't come home. I would feel terrible if you cut your vacation short for me. My memory's mostly back now and I have a scar on my forehead, but other than that, I'm just fine."

Her mother exclaimed again. "Well, you should write that nice cowboy a thank-you note, sweetie. It was so thoughtful of him to let you stay at the ranch over the holidays. Your father and I have met the men that live over on that ranch a few times and they're just the nicest, most polite young men. So definitely write him a thank-you note."

"I'll keep that in mind," Cass told her drily.

"Did you make an appointment with your doctor just to check things out?"

"No, but—"

"No buts, young lady. You get him to check you out. Your mother says so."

She sighed. "All right. I'll let Rose know I need a few hours off."

Her mother snorted with irritation. "Is she still running you ragged and you with a head wound? You know I don't like that job for you, Cass honey."

Cass didn't like the job much for herself, either. But maybe it was because she was just too fixated on the things she couldn't have. Things like a peaceful life on a ranch in the mountains . . . and a cowboy in particular.

When Old Clyde's truck pulled up to the ranch, Eli felt a mixture of relief and frustration. Relief because there would be others to handle some of the chores and give him a much-needed break.

Frustration because it wasn't Cass.

He hugged Maria as she returned, then slapped Jordy and Dustin on the back as they grabbed their bags and hopped out of the flatbed. Old Clyde shook his hand and then bent down to give Bandit and Jim extra attention. Everyone looked good, happy, and refreshed.

It made Eli tired. He didn't feel happy or refreshed. He felt lonely for the first time in his life, and even the return of his ranch family couldn't fill the hole that Cass had left.

"Glad to be home," Dustin drawled. "Heard we're due for another whiteout soon. Probably a good thing we already have all the cattle in a close pasture." He nodded at Eli. "How were things while we were gone?"

"Fine," Eli said.

"Frannie have her pups?" Jordy asked.

"Yup. Five."

Old Clyde lit up and got to his feet. "Can't wait to get a look at them." He headed for the house.

"The smallest one is Cass's," Eli called after him. "It's taken."

Maria gave him a sly look. "Cass is the lady friend, yes? Is she not coming out to meet us?"

"She's gone."

The housekeeper looked surprised. "She is?" When all Eli did was nod, she frowned. "Well, that explains your unhappy expression, mijo. You couldn't convince her to stay?"

"Don't want to talk about it," Eli told her. He walked away. "Chores to be done."

"You want to come inside for coffee?" Maria called after him. "We can catch up. I have pictures from Christmas—"

"Later," he told her, and he hated that his voice sounded more abrupt than he meant it. He just . . . needed time by himself to see how the ranch felt with everyone else back and Cass gone.

So far, he didn't like it.

Then again, he didn't like much with Cass gone. He missed her too damn badly and there was not a thing he could do about it.

After Cass had been back in NYC for a week, she decided that she'd delayed things long enough.

She needed to tell Rose about Ken and how she'd betrayed her. She knew she'd get fired, and she'd deserve it. She'd fooled around behind Rose's back with her boyfriend, and that made her the worst kind of person. She hated herself for who she'd become, and so whatever punishment Rose meted out, it'd be fair.

In a way, she wanted to be fired. This life wasn't satisfying to her. It was lonely and shallow and boring. She no longer enjoyed the hustle and bustle of the city. When she dreamed, she dreamed of a quiet countryside covered in snow. She dreamed of horses and dogs romping in the fields.

And, okay, she dreamed of Eli.

If she had a fresh start, maybe she could become the Cass he'd thought she was. It didn't excuse what she did, but maybe he'd forgive her anyhow . . . eventually. And if he didn't, she had money saved up in her bank account. The large amount had surprised her at first. Then, it made sense. Rose was so needy and demanding that Cass didn't have time to spend it on herself. If she shopped, it was for Rose. If she went on a trip, it was because Rose needed company. So the money piled up.

It was probably enough money to buy a bit of land, Cass figured. Not much, but enough to start, maybe. A nice down payment.

Provided Eli ever forgave her. Just worrying over it made her queasy.

So . . . she needed to tell Rose. Rip the Band-Aid off, confess her sins, and get one thing off her plate. She'd lose Rose and her job, but she'd gain some self-respect.

Cass contemplated when to tell her as she went and got Rose up that morning for another photo shoot. This one was for a big denim brand, and Rose had been stressing over it for days. She'd smoked three packs of cigarettes a day and lived on black coffee and celery, and had bleached her teeth twice last night. She'd also yelled at Cass a lot, but Cass was starting to remember that was part of the job— scapegoat.

Yet another reason she wouldn't mind being fired.

Still, as she woke Rose up, gave her clothes so she could

dress, and hurried her into the waiting taxi, she figured to-day probably wouldn't be the best day to confess. Rose was already stressed out of her mind. She had a zit coming in on one perfect cheekbone and had wept and railed at the absent makeup artist for not cleaning her brushes (even though Cass was pretty sure she had). Cass murmured sympathy, of course.

When Rose got to the shoot, she was sweet as sugar to everyone involved, gushing about how much she loved the company and how she'd always worn their jeans. She had a "set" personality that was charming and affectionate, and she worked hard. It was just to Cass that she unloaded. Again, part of the job.

As Rose stripped down to nothing so they could airbrush makeup on her body, her phone rang. Rose pointed at her purse, in the seat next to Cass.

Cass dug out the phone and eyed the screen. She swallowed hard. "Ken's calling."

"Tell him I'm in makeup but he's welcome to come by if he wants to meet for lunch." She raised one arm over her head and frowned at her pale armpit. "Should we get under here or will it look creased?"

"You need to dry first," the makeup artist told her. "Turn."

Rose obediently turned. "Text him, Cass, and tell him I'm on set with Denim Darlings but we can do dinner at six."

"Right." She unlocked Rose's phone, quickly texted Ken, and tried not to vomit. She needed to be casual, even though there was a sick clench in her gut. "So . . . Ken's in town?"

"Yeah, he finished shooting his new movie," Rose called over her shoulder. "It's been forever since I've seen him. That man owes me an apology and some jewelry!"

Again, the entourage tittered.

Ugh. If Ken was showing up here, Cass didn't want to be around. She didn't think she'd be able to hide how she felt, and a photo shoot wasn't the best place to have a confrontation. So she asked, "You want me to run and get you another black coffee?"

"Make it a latte. Lunch, you know." She winked at Cass, and the other handlers chuckled with amusement.

"Right. Be back soon." With a little wave, she returned the phone to Rose's purse and escaped the set.

Even though there was a coffee place just down the street, she took her time. Cass knew that Rose was going to be busy for a while, so she had at least an hour or two to clear her mind and try to de-stress. If Ken was showing up, Cass needed to be somewhere else. She'd been avoiding his calls and had blocked his phone number so he couldn't keep texting her. Cowardly, maybe, but she could only handle so much while being brokenhearted over Eli. For the hundredth time in the last week, she wished she had Eli's phone number. She desperately wanted to talk to him, if only to hear his voice.

She paced up and down the street, window-shopped, and then eventually headed in to the coffee shop. The line was long so she took her place at the back and gazed at the chalkboard menu without really seeing it. Her thoughts were back in Wyoming, with a tanned cowboy who had a dazzling white smile and callused hands that knew just how to touch her—

"Fancy running into you here," a smooth voice called against her ear, so close she could feel breath whisper against her skin.

Cass yelped and jumped, because that was *not* Eli. She turned, but she already knew who it was. Knew before people started raising their phones into the air and taking pictures and recording. It was Ken Wallis, and she'd been found. As she turned, she realized three things.

One—Ken Wallis was just as Hollywood handsome as he was in the movies. His smile was blisteringly gorgeous, his slightly ruffled blond hair charmingly perfect, and his eyes as bright green as they seemed in photos.

Two—Ken was also really short. As in, they were the same height, and when Cass wore heels like she was today, she loomed over him.

And three—she remembered this guy.

Maybe it was the sight of his face as he smirked up at her, so pleased with himself for hunting her down. Maybe it was the fact that he was short and that made him a little more flawed and human. Or maybe it was the last piece of the puzzle finally sliding together, but she remembered.

She remembered *everything*.

She wasn't the jerk.

She wasn't sleeping with this guy. She would *never*. He made her skin crawl. Always had. As she stared into his gorgeous face, a deluge of memories slid into place. Of constant text messages that skirted inappropriateness. Of him trying to put an arm around her waist while Rose was on a shoot. Of him coincidentally showing up places when he knew Cass would be there and Rose would not. And the more she turned him down, the more he pursued her. She knew it wasn't that he found her beautiful—he liked the thrill of the chase.

She knew that, and because of that, and because he was Rose's, and because she found him too pushy, she'd always, always, always turned him down.

Cass wasn't a home wrecker. She hadn't cheated on Eli. She didn't have to give him up.

Relief as strong as a tidal wave rushed through her, and she burst out laughing. She wanted to cry with joy. She wanted to sag with boneless relief. All she did was laugh and laugh, because her heart was suddenly light again. She wasn't an irredeemable monster. She wasn't the worst kind of human for stealing her friend's boyfriend behind her back.

And she was free to fall in love with Eli. Her heart had known even if her mind didn't.

Oh, *Eli.*

"I take it you're glad to see me," Ken said charmingly, interrupting her thoughts.

"Huh?" Cass blinked at him. Someone cleared their throat, and Cass realized the barista was waiting on her. Oh. "An extra-large iced latte, please, double shot, cashew milk, no sugar, splash of cinnamon."

"I see my lovely Rose has sent you out to run errands for her," Ken said, leaning in over her shoulder and standing so close that her skin prickled uncomfortably.

"Now's not the time, Ken," Cass said, keeping her voice light. She paid for the latte and then moved to the far end of the counter to wait for the order.

"It's the perfect time, actually," Ken continued, following her. He smiled at a few people and waved off autographs. "Sorry, guys, I just got off of a very long set. No autographs. I'm just meeting an old friend." He slid in next to her.

"We're not friends," Cass murmured, keeping her gaze straight ahead. Her thoughts were racing a mile a minute. Eli was still at the ranch. She knew he was. He had no plans to leave it. Would he want to see her if she showed up again? She hadn't told him a thing about why she'd left, and that was wrong of her. What if he held it against her? What if he didn't forgive her? She'd be heartbroken. But she thought of her cowboy and his protective nature, the way he'd held her hand so carefully after she'd cut it.

He loved her. He might be upset, but he'd forgive her.

Full of hope for the first time in days, Cass sighed dreamily.

"We could have spent the holidays together, you know," Ken said, undeterred. "I had the perfect little place picked out for us. Nice and quiet and discreet."

He still stood next to her, and Cass clenched her jaw. He wasn't touching her, but he was still too close. Ken was always careful to make sure that the paps wouldn't catch him being indiscreet. It was another reason he chased her—she was an easy excuse. That woman he was seen standing near? That was his gorgeous girlfriend's mousy assistant. Of course he wasn't hitting on her.

Ha.

Ha ha.

"Look, Ken, I'm sure you're a nice guy." She half choked on the lie. "But I'm really not interested. I don't know how many more times I can tell you that I'm not interested." She carefully shifted a foot or two away. "You should really focus on Rose."

"Rose is busy," he murmured, nodding and waving at a few fans still filming him nearby. "And I'm pretty sure I can convince you that we could have fun together."

"I'm pretty sure you can't—"

"I'm an excellent partner." He kept his voice low as he leaned in again. "Very . . . giving. And I'd love to give to you for a while if you'd let me."

"Your latte," the barista said, holding it out to Cass from over the bar. He froze and stared at Ken, then his gaze flicked back to Cass. "Is that . . ."

She nodded and took the drink, dropping money into the

tip jar. "Thanks." She turned and Ken was right there, blocking her path ever so slightly. Not enough for it to be noticeable to anyone . . . except her.

And for once, she'd had enough.

She'd dealt with Ken and his creepy advances for months. To him, it didn't matter that she wasn't interested. He was a movie star, and so he felt like he should get her in his bed no matter what. He thought it was a game between them. He really, really didn't seem to grasp that she wasn't interested.

It was harassment, pure and simple. And she'd never touched his foul self. Joy burst through her again, bright and shining. She was clean and free and she could love Eli without guilt.

Ken noticed her smile and wiggled one eyebrow at her. He reached out and stroked a curl of her hair on her shoulder, as if she belonged to him.

For some reason, that set her off. It was the straw on the camel's back. He was destroying her happiness. He'd been the problem all along. He'd nearly cost her everything.

That . . . *jerk*.

Furious, Cass tossed the latte at him. The cup smacked into his chest and the lid went flying. Coffee splashed everywhere.

The people gathered around them took a visible step back and gasped. Ken remained perfectly still, coffee dripping down the front of his pale designer shirt.

Cass swallowed. She looked around the coffee shop and saw people were still filming. This would be everywhere by tomorrow, every tabloid, every gossip rag, and the headlines would all be how handsome, friendly Ken Wallis was attacked by a crazed woman in a Midtown coffee shop.

Well, shit. "Accident," Cass said loudly. "I stumbled." And she pushed past him out into the street.

Already she felt a hundred times lighter. She hadn't solved her problems, of course, but she was taking control of the situation.

And she was one step closer to returning to Eli.

CHAPTER TWENTY-FOUR

Cass raced back to the set, determined. This time she didn't dawdle or take her time on the streets. She marched back into the studio, looking for Rose. She was still standing in front of the paper screen, topless as the fan blew her hair into a windswept mess and she posed, one arm over her naked breasts. Off to one side, Rose's phone bleated over and over again with her ringtone.

"About time," Rose snapped as Cass marched in, glancing over her shoulder and managing to look sultry through her annoyance. "My phone's blowing up. And where's my coffee? Where—"

She yelped as Cass marched onto the set itself and grabbed Rose by the arm, pulling her away.

"Hey," the photographer protested, looking up from his tripod as Cass dragged his subject off the set. "We're busy here—"

"You can wait a few minutes," Cass told him in a firm

voice. She was tired of everyone pushing her around. It was time to push back.

"Should I get my phone?" Rose asked as Cass tugged her to the side. "It keeps ringing—"

"Don't bother. I know who that is." Cass ignored the dirty looks the assistants on the set were sending her. "This is going to be everywhere in about five minutes so you need to be aware." At Rose's wide-eyed expression, Cass continued. "I ran into Ken at the coffee shop and threw your latte on him."

"You *what*?" Rose crossed her arms over her bare chest, incredulous. She didn't care that she was topless, only that Cass had insulted her boyfriend. "Do you know who he is?"

"Yeah, movie star and huge dick and I don't care. You should know what he's up to." Cass pulled out her phone and found the messages Ken had been sending her. She offered it to Rose. "Your boyfriend is constantly harassing me. He calls me at all hours. Shows up where I'm at. Hits on me nonstop. In other words, he's crap and you deserve to know. I threw the latte on him because he showed up and started hitting on me again. He's constantly making disgusting suggestions and I've had enough."

Rose blinked at her. She took the phone and scrolled through the messages, pausing to read one or two. "Huh. He's very good."

"Good?"

"At not incriminating himself. These could all be considered all right if taken out of context. They're easy to explain off."

Cass stared at Rose in horror. "I'm not making this up. I—"

"I know you're not." Rose shrugged and handed the phone back. "I know he's a cheating asshole."

"You do?" That wasn't the answer she'd expected Rose to give her. She'd expected protests. Mocking. Something along those lines. She expected Rose to believe Ken over her. This was . . . rather surprising.

"Oh yeah. His last girlfriend warned me. Said he banged her assistants. Plural. I figured as long as you didn't take him up on it, it'd be a nonissue."

"A nonissue?" Cass's voice rose a squeaky notch as she stared at Rose. "Are you serious? He's been harassing me."

"Just ignore him and his roving dick. That's what I do." Rose shrugged again and tilted her head. "Was there anything else?"

Anything else? Was she serious? But as Cass studied Rose's calm face, she realized that Rose was serious. She just didn't care. "Let's just ignore the fact that he's gross and harassing me. You don't mind that he's a cheater?"

"Of course he's a cheater," Rose said patiently. "He's good-looking, rich, and extremely famous. Women throw themselves at him all the time. You really think I expect him to be loyal to me?"

"Yes!"

"Oh, come on, Cass. This isn't a fairy tale." Her smile was brittle-edged and hard. "That's not how real life works. You should know by now that all men are assholes."

They stared at each other for a long moment. In the background, Rose's phone rang and rang. Cass knew it was Ken, trying desperately to get ahold of Rose to do damage control. The sad thing was, he didn't even have to. Rose didn't care.

"Not all men are assholes," Cass said quietly. "Some are good, and kind, and loving. Some would never look twice at another woman once they gave their heart. I know. I've met one."

Rose snorted, her eyes narrowed. "If that's the case, then what are you doing as my lonely assistant with no life of her own?"

That was a very, very good question. It was something Cass herself had been wondering for the last few days. Finally, though, she had an answer. She smiled and straightened her shoulders. "I quit."

Later that evening, Cass called her parents as she packed her bags. "I quit my job and I'm leaving New York City," she told them.

"Is everything all right?" her mother asked, worried. "You're feeling okay?"

"I'm fine. I just . . . I couldn't work for Rose anymore."

"Good! You deserve better than to be at the beck and call of someone who puts you down all the time."

Cass was surprised to hear that. She'd thought Rose's constant thoughtless comments were harmless, but maybe they did wear her down. Maybe others had noticed it, too. Either way, she felt lighter and happier. She'd changed the wallpaper on her phone after quitting, because she didn't want to stare at Rose's face. She'd changed it to a mountain scene since she didn't have a picture of Eli, and at least the mountains made her think of him.

She'd blocked Rose's number, too. Rose had said she'd understood Cass's decision, even though it was clear she didn't. Then a few hours later, she'd texted Cass asking her to bring hummus from the corner market, as if nothing had changed between them.

So she'd blocked her. In a few weeks, maybe she'd unblock her when Cass was ready to talk, and when Rose had time to realize that no, Cass really wasn't going to be at her beck and call anymore. Maybe it was cowardly, but she didn't care. She needed time to clear her mind and start over.

"Mom, I was thinking . . . the cabin in the mountains?"

"The summer cabin?"

"Yeah. I was thinking I'd go live there for a while. Maybe I'll write a book or something." She wouldn't, of course. But if her family thought she needed the peace and quiet for a while they wouldn't mind her using it.

"Oh. Gosh, I don't know, honey. It's so remote. And the Chiltons wanted to use it this summer for a few weeks."

"I'll be out of there by then," Cass said quickly. "And I don't mind the remoteness. It'll be like Thoreau and Walden Pond."

"Who?" She could practically hear her mother wrinkle her nose.

"Never mind. I just need to be in Wyoming for a little longer, I think." She sat on the edge of the bed and tried not to feel like a child asking her parents to go on vacation. She was an adult. If her parents said no, she'd rent from someone else and figure things out.

"Does this have something to do with a certain cowboy?" her mother asked, voice shrewd.

Cass swallowed hard. "Um, what?" How did she know? She'd deliberately avoided telling her mother how she felt about Eli because she hadn't wanted her feelings to be associated with the hit she'd taken on the head. She didn't want others to doubt how she felt, because she had no doubts herself.

"I know a woman named Maria that works at Price Ranch. I pay her to go and clean up the cabin a few times a year to dust and keep things tidy. Anyhow, she called me a few days after you did and asked if my daughter was all right. She'd heard all about the hit on your head from one of the cowboys there. Maria tells me he's a very handsome young man named Eli, and that he's been very mopey since you left."

Cass felt herself blushing. "Is he?"

"Maria wanted me to pass that along." She could hear the smile in her mother's voice. "But if you want to go and live alone in the mountains in a cabin, I guess I can't stop you. Just make sure you bring lots of food and drink and call your mother once a week."

She found herself smiling. Even though she was an adult, her mother still fussed over her like a child. "Will do." Cass thought for a moment, and then asked, "Say, can I have Maria's phone number?"

She had an idea.

"Can you sit down for a minute, mijo?" Maria asked as Eli headed inside the house. It was barely early afternoon and he should have been out on horseback, working the cattle with the others. Instead, he'd been in a foul mood all day and had snapped at Jordy when one of the cattle had turned up missing. It was Houdini, of course. It was always damned Houdini, and he should have expected it, but it still pissed him off something awful because Jordy was in charge of mending fences. Jordy had sniped back, implying that maybe Eli hadn't handled things as he should have over Christmas, and then he'd nearly gotten into a fight with the younger man. Old Clyde had intervened, separating the two of them. Instead of taking Eli's side, he'd sent Jordy to mend fences and told Eli to go inside and let off some steam.

That only made him even more surly. He knew he was being a bit unreasonable and hard to get along with lately. He also didn't much care. It was hard to lose himself in a hard day's work when it just gave him even more time to think about Cass and how much he missed her. How he let her leave without telling him what was wrong. How he should have pushed harder to keep her. What if she'd just wanted him to fight for her and he hadn't? Eli didn't have answers to any of it, but all he knew was that he was miserable without her and life on the ranch didn't feel as calming as it used to. It was missing something.

Or, rather, someone.

He threw his hat down on the kitchen table and ignored the cross look that Maria sent in his direction. "I'm a mite sweaty at the moment, Maria. Can it wait?"

"No," she told him in a firm voice. She flicked his hat to the side and then patted the seat at the table across from her. "Sit. Now."

He scowled in her direction but did as he was told. She was the closest thing he had to a mother, and even if she was a little pushy at times, he liked her well enough. Maria didn't often insist, so when she did, he supposed he should listen. "What is it?"

"You haven't been yourself since we got back, mijo." She took his hand in hers and patted it. "You're unhappy. It's like you don't enjoy being here anymore. I see the restlessness in you again. Remember when you first got here? You were such a sulky boy, fresh out of the army with a chip on your shoulder." She gave him a gentle smile. "And then one day it fell off and there was such joy and peace on your face. You loved being a rancher and it showed. I don't see that in you anymore, and it worries me."

"I'm fine." He wasn't, but he also didn't want to worry Maria.

"Mmhmm. You're a bad liar." She patted his hand again. "Look, I know what it's like to miss someone. To not feel whole when they're gone. It just gets worse and worse every day that you're apart from them. I get that." She leaned back and studied him. "That's why I'm leaving."

Eli frowned. "You're what?"

"I'm leaving. I already turned in my resignation to Mr. Price's people. They're giving me a retirement package, which is very generous, and I'll be gone by the end of the month."

"You're leaving?" he echoed, surprised. Maria had been working at this ranch for over twenty years. Her husband had been one of the cowboys until he'd passed, and she'd stayed on even after her daughters moved away. He thought she'd always be a fixture here, like the mountains in the distance, unchanging.

But that was unfair of him, wasn't it? Just because he didn't want things to change didn't mean they were his to decide. Maria was getting older. Her hair had gone from deep black to salt-and-pepper gray in the last few years. There were creases on her face that he didn't remember seeing, and the hands calmly clasped on the table were worn and wrinkled. But still, he asked, "Why?"

The maternal smile she gave him was sweet. "My Cristina is pregnant with twins, remember? She's got two young babies already, and my other daughter isn't close enough to help her out. I'm going to move in with Cristina and help her with the babies. Cook and clean and control her life instead of the lives of a few cowboys for a change." She chuckled. "It'll be nice to fuss over a few girls instead of a bunch of messy boys."

Boys. Like they were ten-year-olds. He gave her a reluctant smile. "It won't be the same without you."

"I know." She shrugged and her eyes looked a little misty. "I'll be sad to go, but I miss my daughters, and my grandbabies. They need Abuela around to spoil them. It's time, I think. I'm not getting any younger, and being around the little ones over the holidays made me realize how needed I am. I hope you understand."

"I do." He understood what it was like to feel needed by someone you loved. He understood what it was like to crave that. Eli forced a smile to his lips. "Ranch won't be the same without you. Guess we'll have to get used to Old Clyde's cooking."

The look on Maria's face turned a little smug. "You won't. I hired someone else to take over house duties here at the ranch. I'm going to train her for a week or two before I go, but it's already been approved by Mr. Price's people."

He arched an eyebrow. She'd already gotten a replacement and hadn't talked to him or the others at the ranch? That struck him as a little . . . strange. "You did?"

"I did. She definitely needs training but she's got the right attitude." Maria laughed, and when the doorbell rang, her eyes lit up with an expression he could only define as glee. "There she is right now."

The entire situation seemed mighty convenient.

"Why don't you come with me, mijo? Say hi?" The look on Maria's face was downright calculating.

A feeling of dread built in his stomach. Eli had a sneaking suspicion this was a setup on Maria's part. That she'd hired some pretty, useless little thing for them to moon over. That she wanted to try to heal his broken heart. Thing was, he didn't want it healed. He didn't want anyone but Cass. And she'd made it clear that she didn't want him. "Maria, I don't think—"

"Don't think, mijo. Just come with me." She stood up and grabbed his hand, trying to drag him to the front door. And because Eli was a pushover for Maria, he went, reluctance in every step. As they crossed the living room, he noticed Frannie was at the door, wagging her tail. Her puppies whined and yapped for their mother, but Frannie kept her nose to the door, obviously smelling the stranger on the other side.

The housekeeper was all smiles as she opened the front door. "Hello and welcome!" she called out to the woman standing there, then looked back at Eli smugly, waiting for his reaction.

He remained in place, stiff with disbelief.

The new "housekeeper" standing on the doorstep was a young woman, all right. She had dark, curly hair that tumbled around her shoulders, and big blue eyes a man could get lost in. She stood on the doorstep with a small suitcase clutched to her chest, and her face lit up as Frannie bounded out to greet her. "Hi, girl," Cass said softly as she bent down to pet the fluffy white head. "Look at you! I missed you!"

It was Cass.

His Cass.

CHAPTER TWENTY-FIVE

S he was here. She'd come back. He didn't know what to think. Hope surged in his chest, even as he tamped it down. No sense in hoping for something that might not be. She might have come back because she liked the mountains, not him.

But damn, she looked pretty. The scar on her forehead had softened to a faint pink line, and she was wearing a hint of makeup, her lips glossy and pink, her eyes bright. She wore a plain black peacoat that didn't look warm enough for January Wyoming weather. Typical city girl.

And he couldn't miss the longing in her eyes as she gazed up at him. He imagined the same longing was in his own eyes, because he'd been dreaming about her day and night . . . and now she was here. His heart tripped.

Maria cleared her throat, and he realized he'd been staring at Cass, devouring her with his gaze without saying a word. He clenched his jaw, trying to think of something to say. Eventually he settled on a firm nod and her name. "Cass."

"Ay," Maria said, shaking her head and throwing up her hands. "Stubborn fool. I'm going to go and feed the chickens. You two catch up." She headed away, muttering something in Spanish.

Eli probably should have said something about that, or chided her for her matchmaking. But all he could do was stare at Cass as she stroked Frannie's head and gazed up at him with her big, sad eyes.

"I came to get my puppy," she said after a moment, and then flushed. "I mean, among other things. I know she's not old enough yet, but I thought I'd throw that out there. I was hoping the offer still stood."

"Of course it stands. I don't change my mind."

She swallowed hard and straightened. Bit her lip, and he wanted to groan at the sight of her small teeth tugging on that plump pink mouth. "About anything?"

His throat felt tight. "I never changed my mind about you, if that's what you're wondering. It was you that changed your mind."

She gave him a pleading look of longing, hope in her gaze. "What's funny is that I didn't change my mind. I still wanted to be with you . . . I just couldn't. Not when I thought I was that person."

"What person?"

"It's a long story."

The blood roared in his ears and his heart raced. "Is this your way of apologizing?"

"I'm pretty terrible at it, aren't I?" Cass looked chagrined.

"Yeah."

"I've been thinking about what I'd say for days and now

that I'm here, I can't seem to make the right words come out of my mouth." She swallowed hard. "I know I messed up. I should have talked to you, but I didn't think you'd want me. Not after what I'd found out."

"Found out?" He wanted to cross his arms over his chest and scowl at her. He wanted to storm in frustration at how angry and betrayed he'd felt when she left. How worried he'd been over her. How he'd replayed their last few days together in his head, over and over again, wondering what he did wrong to make her leave him behind after what they'd shared. He'd never stopped loving her, but he was frustrated with her. Instead of letting him help her, she'd run away, crying. He was still haunted by that.

"I thought I was . . . a bad person." Her expression fell. "And that I'd lied to you."

He didn't care about any of that. She was here. She'd come back. That was all that mattered. "And have you changed your mind?"

"Changed my mind?"

"About loving me?"

"No, never. But—"

Eli took the suitcase out of her hands. "Then the rest doesn't matter."

She let him take it, a bewildered expression on her face. "But, Eli—"

He turned and went inside. He had a mind to take her suitcase and lock it up so she couldn't leave again. Of course, that'd mean he'd have to take her keys, too, but with a few kisses, Cass would forget all about them. Then he wouldn't let her leave again until . . . well, ever. No, he amended. She wasn't a prisoner. He wanted her to stay because she wanted to stay. Because she loved him and wanted him as much as he wanted her.

He needed her to want him back. The realization was a hard lump in his chest and he stared down at the suitcase he'd taken from her. He turned around and offered it out. "Did you want this back? I can't keep you."

"I'm really confused right now, Eli. I need to explain myself. Why—"

Eli shook his head. "Just tell me why you came back."

"Why? I thought that was obvious. I love you." The words caught in her throat, and her beautiful eyes shimmered with unshed tears. "I love you and I hate that I left. I didn't want to. I wanted you more than anything but I didn't feel like I deserved you."

"Deserved" was a stupid word, he decided. All that mattered in love was showing up for the other person. And trying again even when you knew it might be hard. Here she was, her heart in her eyes, asking him to give her another chance.

He loved her. Nothing today had changed that. He carefully set the suitcase down and turned to Cass. She gazed at it, confusion in her eyes.

So he picked her up.

She yelped in surprise, and Frannie barked in unison. The puppies near the fireplace whined and yipped, joining in with their mother's call.

"Not now," Eli told them as Cass wrapped her arms around his neck. "I'm taking my woman to bed."

"You—you are?" Cass gave him an astounded look. "Don't you want to hear my apology? My reasons?"

"Go ahead and give 'em to me," he told her, even as he headed down the hall to his room. Sly Maria was feeding the chickens, he knew. She'd probably linger out there for at least an hour to give them privacy. Smart woman. The other cowboys wouldn't be in until dinnertime.

That gave him and Cass a few hours of alone time. Good.

So he listened as she told him all about the phone, and getting more pieces of her memory back, and some creep named Ken who made her think terrible things about herself. Made her think he was her boyfriend when he really wasn't. And how she'd felt awful at the thought of cheating on him and had left because she didn't feel worthy of his love. By the time she finished her confusing explanation, he'd carried her to his room, shut the door behind him, set her on the bed, and was taking her boots off her feet.

"Well?" she asked.

"Well what?" Eli glanced up at her.

"Do you understand why I left?" Her gaze pleaded with him.

He slipped one boot off of her foot and then went to work on the other. "Cass, I'll never understand why you left instead of talking to me. But if you had your reasons, you had your reasons. What matters to me is that you came back."

"But, Eli—"

He shook his head. "No buts. You realized you made a mistake and came back. Why did you come back?"

"Because I love you—"

"And I love you, too." He set her foot down and then moved forward until his stomach was pressed against her knees as he knelt before her. He put his hands on her waist and gazed up at her beautiful face. "And I'm gonna make mistakes. You'll make more mistakes. But the point is that you came back."

Her eyes gleamed with tears. "I never wanted to leave."

"Then don't. Don't leave. Next time, talk to me and we'll work it out."

"I didn't think you'd want me. The real me I thought I was."

"I understand that. But running away from the problem didn't fix it. All it did was part us for a few weeks. And I'm a selfish bastard because I missed you something awful, and I want to keep you at my side forever."

She sniffed. "I love you so much, Eli. I want to be here forever. When Maria offered me the job, I took it. I didn't care if you hated me forever. If I could just be around you, it'd be worth it."

"And that's why you're crazy, Cass." He got up and sat on the edge of the bed next to her, cupping her face in his hands. "As if I could hate you forever. I can't even hate you for a single day. You're a good person, no matter what you might think. If you had told me all that nonsense about being a cheater, I would never have believed it. That's not the kind of person you are."

"But you don't know me—"

"Don't I?" He leaned in and kissed her. "I know you're a terrible cook. I know you get distracted easily." Between each sentence, he nipped at her pretty mouth. God, he'd missed her. "I know you steal the blankets when you sleep. I know you love Christmas. And I know you have a soft heart when it comes to animals."

"And cowboys," she added, breathless. She parted her lips and tilted her face up, waiting for the next kiss.

He slicked his tongue against hers in the next one, teasing her just a bit more. "That's right. And you have a strong sense of right and wrong. Of hope. You're an optimist, and you'd never do all that stuff because it's not in your makeup. It's not who you are, and I fell in love with you. The heart of Cass, not the trappings. I don't care what your job is or how much college education you have. That doesn't matter to me. What matters is you."

"I love you," she whispered. "How can you be real? How are you so very good to me?"

"Because I love you, too." He gently kissed her again, a sweet brush of lips against lips. It felt so good, so right to have her in his arms again. "And it took guts to come back here and confess how you felt, Cass. That says more than you'll ever know." He paused and studied her. "So is Cass short for Cassandra? Or something else? I remember you wondered."

Her smile was beautiful. "It's Cassandra. Nothing strange. Just plain and simple Cassandra."

"I like plain and simple." He rubbed his nose against hers, because he wanted to rub all of himself against her. "And I'm glad you came back, even if it was just for your puppy."

She blushed crimson. "That was just the excuse I was going to use if you didn't want to see me. I spent days trying to think of a way to be near you even if you didn't want to see me again. I had a couple of different ideas, but the puppy one was the one I was hanging my hat on. Plus," she continued shyly, "I really wanted her. Not as much as I wanted you, but if I couldn't have one, maybe I could have the other."

"You can have them both," he told her, and pulled her closer, wrapping his arms around her waist. "You can have everything you want, all you have to do is ask."

Cass smiled up at him, her expression beautiful and as full of hope as he remembered. "Will you be my Christmas present again, cowboy?"

"This year and every year," he promised. He pushed her back into the bed, mouths locked in a heated kiss. Her hands tore at his shirt, and it was clear she was eager to undress him. He wanted her naked, too. It had been weeks since he'd made love to her, and he craved the feel of her body. "I should probably shower, Cass. I'm sweaty—"

"Later," she murmured between kisses. "You can shower later."

All right then, later it was. But if she didn't want to let him go long enough for him to shower, he was going to take the lead so his girl wouldn't have to get her mouth on his grimy skin. He was going to put his mouth on *her* instead. "Undress," he told her, leaning back and tugging off his shirt.

She wiggled on the bed, sliding her arms out of her coat and then pushing it aside. Next went her shirt, and then she had her jeans unbuttoned and lifted her hips, hauling them down her thighs without getting out of bed. He'd noticed that the bra she was wearing was a bold, racy red, but when he saw the matching lace panties, he realized she'd worn them just for him.

Eli groaned at the realization. "I love you, you damn tease."

Cass paused, her eyes going wide. Then she giggled. "I love you, too." She winked at him as she dropped her jeans to the floor. "Hurry up and get naked."

"Give me a minute," he told her. He'd taken off his shirt and flannel undershirt and kicked off his boots, and had been focused on pulling off his jeans. The sight of those panties had completely derailed him, though. "Here I was thinking Christmas was over for the year." Eli leaned over Cass and slid his hand over the gentle curve of her belly. "Seems like I get to keep on celebratin' every time I'm with you."

"Seems that way," she said in a soft voice, her eyes shining with love. "Merry Christmas again. Want to unwrap your present?"

"Do I ever." He put one callused finger underneath the

silky band and gently tugged it downward. He wanted to pause and admire the sight of her dark curls peeping into view as he pulled the panties away, but he was growing impatient to touch her, to put his mouth on her.

To put his mouth everywhere.

Carefully, he guided the slinky material down her legs and then tossed the scrap of lace aside. Now his lovely Cass was bare from the waist down, and he could love her like he wanted to. He put a hand under one thigh and hauled it over his shoulder, kissing the inside of her thigh. She gasped, her eyes lighting up with realization. "Oh, Eli." Her voice was breathless with need. "You don't have to—"

"Hush, woman," he murmured, and bent his head to take a long, slow taste. He ran his tongue over the seam of her sex, and she was wet with need and delicious. Cass's moan of arousal was heady and made his cock ache with need, but he wanted this to be about her. This part had to be about her, because everything after she came was about him, and he wanted to make sure she was well pleasured first. So he licked and explored her with his mouth, kissing and tasting sensitive flesh, teasing and learning the spots she liked. Every time they'd made love before, they'd never gotten to this. They'd been too eager, or she'd been too shy. Even now, the soft little cries she made were muffled by a pillow she'd grabbed, and she hid her face from him. She didn't need to be shy about this, because he thought she was beautiful everywhere. He'd just have to make love to her between her thighs and show her that, though.

He found her clit with his tongue, and the moment he lapped that small bead, she came off the bed, arching and crying out. She clutched at his head, twining her fingers in the short strands of his hair to anchor him there. "Eli," she panted. "Oh god, Eli. Your tongue . . ."

He wanted to grin with the fierce pleasure of her response. He wanted to laugh at the wild little cries she was making. He wanted to sink into her, so deep that he'd lose his mind. Instead, he just kept tonguing her, determined to drive her over the edge.

She pushed her hips against his face, trying to find a rhythm as he lapped and sucked at her sensitive flesh. A soft keening noise broke from her throat, and he could feel her thighs tensing around him as he worked her.

"Don't stop," she breathed, her entire body quivering.

Stop? Never. Not until she came for him.

So he continued, doubling down on his efforts. He'd heard that consistency was the trick to make a woman orgasm hard, so he pushed onward, despite her urgent cries and shuddering responses. He didn't speed up his pace but kept leisurely dragging his tongue over the sweet spot that made her cry out, and when her voice rose with a low cry, he knew he'd been successful. Cass shivered against him, her thighs tight against his ears as she came, her hips undulating with the force of her orgasm.

Eli gave her sex one last lick, and then lifted his head. He was breathing hard, but she was dazed from his efforts, and he loved the soft, flushed look on her damp skin. Somewhere along the way she'd lost the pillow she'd been clutching and had taken to tearing at the bedsheets. They lay in a rumpled mess on both sides of her head, her hair spilling every which way. It was the loveliest thing he'd ever seen. "You're beautiful."

She moaned, reaching for him, and he went into her arms and gave her another kiss, his tongue lazily dragging along hers in a mimic of the loving he'd just given her. When her sated kisses began to have a hungry edge once more, he left the cradle of her hips to head to the bathroom and quickly shucked his jeans, then put on a condom. Then, sheathed, he returned to his sprawled, lovely woman and moved over her. She wrapped her legs around his hips, her arms going around his neck.

"I love you," she whispered again as he sank into her. "I love you so much, Eli Pickett."

"I love you, Cassandra Horn." He began to pump into her, and as her sighs of response grew to excitement, he realized that he'd been wrong all along. He'd thought that home was a place. When he was in foster care, he'd never felt like he had a home. In the army, he'd felt rootless. Even the ranch was not quite "home" despite the fact he'd been there for ten years.

But with his body sunk deep into Cass's and her arms around his neck, Eli finally understood what he'd been searching for. Home was a person.

And he'd found her.

EPILOGUE

Five years later

"It's gonna be a project," Eli declared as they studied the small, run-down ranch they were considering purchasing.

"It's going to be perfect," Cass told him. She shifted the toddler on her hip and pointed at the house. Ahead of them, oblivious to the conversation between their humans, Joy and Frannie frolicked in the long grass. Just the sight of the grass itself was a sign that the ranch hadn't been taken care of in years. No cowboy worth his salt would let it get this high without putting cattle to it or haying it for winter.

"It's a dump," he told her. "The house is a mess. The barn's falling in on itself."

"Oh please." Cass grinned up at him. Her curls were tied back into a wild ponytail that fluttered over one shoulder, and she was just as breathtaking today as the day he'd met her. The tiny faded scar over her left brow was the only sign of that day, and it didn't mar her beauty in the slightest. "It's not a dump. The roof only needs a few shingles. The exterior needs a coat of paint. The interior just needs a few cosmetic things. Those are easy. The house has good bones, though, and the land is fantastic. The barn needs repairs, but it's spacious and you've got more than enough acreage to run a hundred cattle. And you said a hundred was the number you wanted to go with."

That was his Cass, always such an optimist. She saw the good in things even when he didn't. "I did, didn't I?"

She nodded, beaming up at him. "I love it."

Only his Cass could see the beauty in the run-down ranch they were thinking about buying. He'd objected to spending their nest egg—well, mostly hers, because the amount he had saved would be going toward purchasing the cattle themselves—on the ranch, but she'd insisted. It was a bargain and a sign that they needed to jump on their dream of running their own small ranch. It didn't matter to her that the house was a huge step down from the one they'd been living in over on Price Ranch, or that they'd be sinking a lot of their savings into it. All Cass saw was the potential.

It was one of the things he loved most about her.

It definitely wasn't her cooking. After five years running the house over at Price Ranch, Cass still tended to get distracted midmeal and her results were . . . iffy at best. He and the boys ate sandwiches a lot of nights, but no one ever complained. They loved Cass as much as he did.

She beamed up at him as she juggled their small, squirming son in her arms. "Well," she told him impatiently. "Shall we go check it out?"

Frannie barked, followed by a higher-pitched bark from dainty Joy.

Cass laughed again. "That's a sign for us to hurry up."

"Well then," Eli said, and hauled little Travis out of her

arms and into his. "Come along then, Mrs. Pickett, and let's check out this ranch."

She slid her hand into the crook of his arm and leaned against him, and they headed toward the house.

Keep reading for an excerpt from
Jessica Clare's novel

DIRTY MONEY

Available now from InterMix

A familiar tweed suit passes by the print room while I'm standing over the copier. I immediately abandon my task and race after him. "Oh! Jack! I didn't realize you were in the office! Wait up!" I hate that I have to scramble after him—in heels, no less—but the bastard's not slowing down an iota. I hobble after him on the marble floors of Three Jacks Real Estate's swanky office, hoping I don't fall on my ass and make a fool of myself in front of the others. When Jack doesn't stop, I have to speed up just to catch him. "Jack!"

He finally stops, right at the front doors of the office, and frowns at me like I'm an annoying puppy. "What is it, Ivy? I'm on my way out the door, as you can see." He gestures at the large glass double doors like I'm an idiot. "Let's make this fast."

"Of course!" I put on my fake, cheeriest Realtor smile. "I was just going to say that my day is clear, and I know LaDonna had that big house on Forsyth that was scheduled to have a showing. I've made flyers—well, actually, they're on the copier right now—and I can go handle things, maybe pass out a few cards—"

He narrows his eyes at me. "Is LaDonna out?"

"Um, she's having an emergency appendectomy, remember?" I bite my lip as he continues to look blank. "It was emailed out to everyone?"

"Mmmhmmm?" The look on his face tells me he didn't read it, or doesn't care.

"So I thought I'd pitch in and help with her listing for today? It's a really great house and I've researched the neighborhood, and I can chat with some prospective buyers and—"

His lips purse and he holds up a finger. "The house is on Forsyth?"

"Yes."

"In the Twin Oaks development?"

I nod. It's the hottest area in the suburbs at the moment, and there's a waiting list for properties. This one's a little pricey but I also know it'll fly off the market within days. It's such a big opportunity.

"How much is the list price?"

There's a sinking feeling in the pit of my stomach, but I ignore it. I have to. I'm this far in. "It's listed as one point one million."

Jack pulls out his phone and starts to type. "Street address?"

I give it to him.

"Great. I'll take care of it."

"Oh," I say, fighting the crushing disappointment I'm feeling. "But I can do it, really. I've done comps and I've got flyers ready and—"

"Now, Ivy. You said it's a million-dollar house, right? It's been a lean month for the company and we need to make sure we land all the commissions we can." His tone goes condescending. "And I just don't know that you're the right person to take on such a big task."

"I can absolutely do it, Jack—"

"Now, if I wanted an ice cream cone, you'd be the first one I'd call." He winks at me, the jerk. Winks. Like it's a funny joke. "But for a million-dollar listing? Let's make sure someone with a lot more experience handles it, all right? Oh, and I'll take those flyers, too." He gives me an I'm-the-man-around-here look. "And can you grab me a coffee while you're in the copy room? Super. I'll wait right here." He winks. "Make it snappy. I've got an open house to handle."

"Right. Sure." I force a smile to my face and turn on my heel, heading back toward the copy room to retrieve the flyers I've been working on all morning.

It's not fair. It's so not fair. Every time something decent even comes close to landing in my lap, one of my bosses is there to snatch it away again. I'm stewing as I snatch the stack of copies from the machine and tuck them under my arm, then head to the coffeemaker. Get him a coffee while I'm at it? Like I'm his freaking secretary? But he's also the boss, so I'm stuck. I eye the two coffeepots on the burner. One's nothing but dregs, and the other's a fresh pot. I grab a paper cup, tip the dregs into the cup, and then march back out the door to hand Jack the flyers about the house I know I could sell today, if I was given the chance.

He gives me another wink as he turns to go. "Thanks for the tip, Ivy. Good work."

I watch him leave, my fists clenched. I'm stewing with helpless frustration. Thwarted yet again. *Thanks for the tip.* Like it was a freaking tip? That was my hours of hard work. That was my opportunity that he snatched away. And if I keep thinking about it, I'm going to puke with anger. So I take a deep breath, smooth a hand down the front of my suit, and calmly walk back to my desk in the back of the office, tucked near the bathrooms. A client is strolling out of the men's room and I keep a poised smile on my face. I'm composed until I sit down and put my hands on my keyboard. Calm. Rational.

The moment the client disappears? I bury my face in my hands.

"Uh-oh," Farah says from her desk across the way. "What happened? You were on cloud nine ten minutes ago! Did something happen to LaDonna?"

I take a deep breath and lift my head to look over at my friend. "Jack happened."

She wrinkles her nose. "Dumb Jack, Jack Jack, or Winky Jack?"

"Winky Jack," I say miserably. "He stole that open house from me and said he'd handle it. What could I do?"

"Tell him no?" Farah raises one dark brow at me. "Tell him to do his own work instead of stealing yours?"

"He's the boss," I tell Farah with a sigh. "I like being employed."

"I don't see how," she says drily, pulling out a stack of folders on her desk and flipping through them. "They don't leave you enough clients to make a living."

"Oh, they do," I say glumly, and cross my arms, staring at my laptop. The screen still has a dozen comp listings pulled up from this morning's work, all gone to waste. "They leave me all the clients with bad credit and no money. You need to buy a house with nothing down and a spending limit of fifty grand? Go talk to Ivy."

She snorts.

That's all she can do, because we both know I'm not wrong. Farah's been with Three Jacks for ten years—no clue why she stays. Me, I've been here for one, and a lot of the time I feel lucky to have that one. They hired me, fresh off the streets after I got my Realtor license, and I didn't have a lick of experience to my name. I was working at an ice cream shop prior to Three Jacks . . . something that the bosses like to remind me about all the time.

Three Jacks is a boys' club. I knew it was when I got hired. It's run by Jack Farrington (Dumb Jack), who's older than the hills and has a silver spoon in his mouth; Jack Jackson, who's a snake oil salesman if there ever was one; and Jack Richards (Winky Jack), who thinks women aren't born with two brain cells to rub together and he'll have to rescue us from ourselves. They're nice enough, as far as bosses go, I suppose. After all, they did give me a job. I make half of a percent on any house I sell. That means on a regular 3 percent agency commission, they get the other 2.5 percent and I get what's left after expenses. If I sell a house that's a hundred grand? I get $500 and the company walks away with the other $2,500.

Jack (Dumb Jack) told me that I could "promote" my commission amount once I've earned two million in sales for the company. Given that the only clients I get handed to me are dirt poor or can't land a mortgage? It's been an exercise in frustration, but I'm determined not to give up.

Ivy Smithfield is going to get a better life for herself and her sister, even if she has to climb uphill both ways, I vow. I may not have the experience or the pedigree, but I've got determination.

With that mental pep talk, I feel a little better. I'm going to do this. So I'm still $700K away from getting that pay increase? It's doable. I just need to hustle and hustle hard. I've got this. I do.

"I'll just have to find some new leads," I announce to Farah. "It's a minor setback, but it's not a deal-breaker."

"Whatever," Farah says, giving me side-eye. "You know it's okay to be pissed, right?"

"I'm not pissed," I reply, pulling up local housing forums to scan them for potential clients, just like I do every day. My mama always said "Fake it until you make it," and I'm getting to be a real pro at faking it. Sometimes I even almost believe myself. "Minor setback. I'll just have to work on some other leads."

"Mmhmm." She curls her lip. "Least they put you on the flyer. Dumb Jack told me I was too 'Mexican' looking."

I glance over at her. "I thought you were Persian?"

"I *am*."

I wince. Well, he's called Dumb Jack for a reason. "Ouch. Besides, you know they only put me on the flyer because they had to have a girl on there."

"Oh, I know. Said they didn't want to appear sexist." She puts her fingers in the air and makes a set of quotes. "*Appear.* I mean, they are sexist, they just don't want to look it."

I smile wanly at her. They may be sexist, but they're also the bosses and I can't do much about it. To make things worse, Winky Jack also handles the human resources for the company, so it's not like I can go complain about his buddies. Or himself.

I just need to work harder. Once I've climbed a few rungs in the ladder, I'll make good money and I'll have so many clients I won't be stuck here in the office, twiddling my thumbs. And if at that point I'm still not making good money? I'll at least have enough experience under my belt to go somewhere else . . . or hang my own shingle and get the full three percent commission. It's a nice dream.

It also won't become a reality unless I hustle.

I look over at the picture on the corner of my desk. It's recent, a picture of my little sister Wynonna in her cap and gown at graduation. My arms are around her and our faces are pressed close together. She's so happy, so excited to take on the world. So eager to get out there.

It's for her that I'm doing all this.

So I pull up the forums, put my hands on the keyboard, and go back to work trying to drum up clients online.

It's getting late in the day when I get a call from my sister on my brand-new iPhone. I had to get it because my flip phone and printed maps were making some of the clients look at me funny. Problem is, I can't figure out how the whole "smart" phone works, and so I swipe the wrong buttons and end up missing the call. Farah just snorts and rolls her eyes, like I'm the world's biggest goober.

Maybe I am, but I could never afford a smartphone until now. Actually, I still can't, but I'm forking out extra money so I look legit to my clients. Plus, okay, the mapping application is pretty awesome.

A text comes in a moment later, shaking my phone.

Wynonna: U there, Reba?

Ivy: I am. And remember, I'm Ivy now!!

Wynonna: O god, whatever.

Wynonna: I don't have time for this crap.

Well, she'd better make time. Ivy's my real name now; I had it changed legally. Reba sounded like a redneck cliché, and when my teacher at my Realtor classes suggested that I go by a less "polarizingly Southern" name, I jumped at the chance. I've been Ivy to everyone else for the last two years, but to my sister, I guess I'll always be Reba Lee Smithfield.

Wynonna: I have a flat. Gonna B late getting home.

Ivy: Are you ok?

Wynonna: Rim's bent I think. We got the money for that?

I wince. We don't. We don't even have the money for the insurance for Wynonna's little 1992 Civic, but I'm trying to make it work. I type slowly, since my fingers feel too big and clumsy for the tiny smartphone screen.

Ivy: I'll figure it out. Are you pulled over somewhere safe?

Wynonna: I'm fine. A friend is coming to pick me up, but the car's on the side of the highway. You want me to wait for a tow truck?

Ivy: No, those cost too much. I'll leave work and see if I can change the spare for you. Maybe it's not as bad as we think.

Wynonna: Ok! Just text me when u get there. I'm sorry : (

Ivy: Don't be sorry! The tires were old. We knew they would go soon. I'll handle it.

Wynonna: K! Don't work 2 late! Friend is taking me
2 a used bookstore so I can see if any of my college
texts are there. Maybe I can get them cheap.

Ivy: Smart thinking!! XO

Wynonna: XO to u 2

I put the phone down and resist the urge to bury my head
in my hands. Car repairs—the last thing I can think about
right now. Wynonna needs her car to go to college, and I
need to finish scraping together some money for her tuition.
If it's just a flat tire, we can eat ramen for a week or two and
scrape by. If it's more than that . . . well, I'll cross that
bridge when I get there. I'm just glad my little sister wasn't
hurt.

Of course, this means I really need to get some leads.
Shoot. I might take a clipboard to the mall and pretend to
do a survey, all so I can pass out some cards. It's desperate,
but heck, I *am* desperate at this point, and the Jacks keep
stealing all my good leads. After that, I might stop by the
library and the gym and pin a few cards to corkboards.
Something will pay off eventually, if I just put enough work
into it.

Well, no time like the present to get started.

I gather my things, stuffing my folders and then my laptop into my shoulder bag. No rest for the wicked, and I'm
going to put in a long night tonight trying to drum up leads.
I might even try Facebook ads and Craigslist, if that's what
it takes. All I need to do is sell one house in the next thirty
days and I can pay for Wynonna's tuition. If I get someone
in escrow, I can ask for an advance until payday. I have op-

tions. I just need to get someone in the door. I'm sure I can seal the deal if that happens.

I rush out the back of the office and into the lobby—only to see Winky Jack heading back in. He's got a coffee in hand and his sunglasses on. I smile at him as I pass by.

He stops and points at me. "Ivy!"

I halt, but inwardly I'm torn between snarling at him and just wishing I could race out the door. Instead, I keep a warm smile on my face and try to pretend that someone just stuck gum to the back of his expensive suit. "Hi, Jack, how did the open house go?"

"Fantastic. Got one or two couples that are very interested." One of his cheeks twitches, and I realize he's probably winking at me from behind his sunglasses. Eesh. "It was a great lead. Thanks for sending it in my direction."

But I didn't, I want to snap. *You stole it.* "Of course."

He sips his coffee, ignoring the fact that I was trying to leave. "You said you had some comps, right? Mind emailing me those?"

"Sure." I gesture at the door. It's getting harder to smile by the second, but somehow I manage. "Listen, I have to go—"

At that moment, a man pushes open the glass double doors and walks into the lobby. He's wearing a dirty trucker cap, an equally dirty T-shirt, jeans, and work boots. He's got an enormous, bushy beard covering most of his face and glances around the building, thick brows drawn down as if he disapproves of everything he sees.

The receptionist gives him a blank look, and then her lips twitch with a smirk. She glances over at me and Jack as if to say *can you believe this guy,* then over at the client. "Can I help you, sir?"

He saunters forward with a cocky swagger, stuffing his

hands in his pockets. "Wanted to talk to someone about a house." He's got a thick Texas accent that tells me he's from a small town and not a big city. They drawl more out east and west. I know because it took me thirteen CDs of self-guided voice coaching to try to ditch my own accent.

The receptionist looks over at me and Jack.

Jack takes another sip of his coffee. "Looks like this one's yours, Ivy."

I'm torn. On one hand, I need sales. On the other hand, this guy doesn't look like he has two nickels to rub together. That's why he's "mine." Jack can't be bothered unless it's a million-dollar sale. I smother the stab of resentment I feel. "I do need to go . . ."

But Jack's already turning and walking away. That . . . jerk. Grr. It's not the client's fault for having bad timing, though. It'd be rude for me to take my frustrations out on him. So I look over at the man with the beard and give him a smile, offering my hand. All right then, I said I wanted a sale, and fate is providing. "Hi there. I'm Ivy Smithfield . . ."

And my voice dies off, because he's leaning against the receptionist's counter, dripping red dirt from his hat and shirt, and *devouring me* with his eyes. I've heard that expression before but I've never experienced it. I've never felt like anyone was pulling my clothing from my body with their freaking gaze and eye-fucking me . . .

Until now.

Good . . . goodness. I'm flustered and don't know what to think.

ABOUT THE AUTHOR

New York Times and *USA Today* bestselling author **Jessica Clare** writes under three pen names. As Jessica Clare, she writes contemporary romance. As Jessica Sims, she writes fun, sexy shifter paranormals. Finally, as Jill Myles, she writes a little bit of everything, from sexy, comedic urban fantasy to zombie fairy tales. She lives in Texas with her husband, cats, and too many dust bunnies.

CONNECT ONLINE

jessica-clare.com
facebook.com/AuthorJessicaClare
twitter.com/_JessicaClare

Ready to find
your next great read?

Let us help.

Visit prh.com/nextread

Penguin
Random
House

31901064498910